AND BABY MAKES THREE . . .

July 23, 1987 was D day for Darci Pierce. She'd been putting off her husband, Ray, and family for the nearly fourteen months of her "pregnancy" with one excuse after another. Now, Ray believed there'd be an inducement at the clinic, and there was no backing out. By 5:00 P.M., Darci needed to have a baby.

It was early afternoon as Darci found herself parked outside the local ob/gyn clinic racking her brain for a solution to her dilemma. She thought about stealing a child from a supermarket or a nursery, then driving off, just her and her baby. That's when she noticed an expectant mother dressed in blue maternity pants, a white blouse with polka dots, and white shoes get out of a red Chevy Blazer and hurry into the clinic.

Something inside clicked. "Maybe," she thought, "maybe I could ask her for her baby."

Darci pulled her beatup old Volkswagen bug alongside the woman's car and waited. Over an hour later, she saw her walking back to her Blazer with keys in her hand. As the woman approached, Darci fingered a replica handgun in the door pocket and then got out of the car.

HUSH, LITTLE BABY

JIM CARRIER

PINNACLE BOOKS
WINDSOR PUBLISHING CORP.

PINNACLE BOOKS

are published by

Windsor Publishing Corp.
475 Park Avenue South
New York, NY 10016

ISBN 1-55817-541-5

First printing: March, 1992

Printed in the United States of America

Prologue

The baby had no face.

When Darci Pierce reached into the crib to pick it up, the scream began deep inside, down where she hid her worst nightmare. It erupted from her diaphragm, an anguished, primal cry of a woman in pain, rolling up and out her throat, filling the little bedroom where she slept. Darci bolted upright, soaked in sweat, sobbing.

Ray rolled over and touched her. He held her as she shook. He felt her weight, the heft of a woman heavy with child. He stroked her, trying to calm her. Her breasts were large, her belly hard. He rocked her gently in the bed. In the months they'd been married, he'd come to expect the cries, the screams, the awful nights of his pregnant wife.

Which dream was it? Being chased through the house where she was raised, being shot at? That was the usual one. Darci always screamed when the gun fired. Ray used to think that dream would go away when she moved out of her parents' house. It had not, and now there was another dream.

It was about the baby again, she wept. Darci was overdue. Way overdue. Everyone was waiting: Ray, her parents, all their friends. After two years of

5

trying, false hopes, a failure, the fear of sterility, trying again, tests and delays . . . In the dark of their little bedroom, it dawned on Darci and then on Ray: This was the day, July 16, 1987. By evening they would have their child. The wait would end. Darci's nightmare—a baby with no face—would be over.

As the sun's first pink shafts crept over the Sandia Mountains and down the streets of Albuquerque, another pregnant woman on the same side of town lay awake, worried too. Beneath the covers, Cindy Ray put her hand on her swollen belly, feeling for some sign of life. She was three weeks from her due date, and very large. But the baby was barely moving inside her and Cindy was unusually exhausted.

Cindy's husband, Sam, stirred beside her in the hot, damp bedroom in their little trailer. He slowly came awake and touched her, knowing what was on her mind. His long thin hand slipped into hers, and they lay that way, touching their child, praying that all was well in her womb.

Cindy moved her delicate hand over her baby, stroking it, wanting to talk through the skin. Soon, she knew, it would all be over, but she wasn't sure what that meant. She had called her father and her mother the night before and been unusually sentimental. "I really want you to know I love you," she'd told them.

Cindy stroked her baby again and thought about a prophecy. "Through your children," she had been told years before by an elder in her church, "it will be obvious you are a good mother. Family will be paramount. Your children will bring much admiration. But life will not be easy." She and Sam had talked about it often, even before they married. With a sense of dread they thought it meant they would not grow old together. Cindy had also called her sister the night before. After chatting about the baby, she parted with these words: "I probably won't be able to talk to you again."

In the heat of a New Mexico summer, two young women waited for a baby.

One

The duplex at 5202 Marquette, northeast Albuquerque, was a heat sink in July. The flat roof collected the sun's rays as efficiently as it collected rain from an afternoon thunderstorm. But sun didn't empty the way rain did, pouring out of gutters onto the walk, onto the burned strips of grass. Heat stayed to soak in, radiating through the night and into the day, suffocating the small rooms inside, where Ray and Darci Pierce lived.

The building was a rectangle, lying east and west, made of fake adobe—stucco over concrete block— and painted a pale, runny tan color. There were two apartments, back to back, with a two-car garage on the east end. The doors were painted green. Scrawny shrubs hugged the house and a few juniper lined the alley. The metal-framed windows along the south side, the long side, were also painted green, and they were chipped in the way of rental homes. Other lives could be seen beneath. The windows on the south were like windows to hell during an Albuquerque summer, and slotted blinds did little but slice the sun into parts. The heat came in anyway. When humidity rose, like it did July 16, 1987, the heat pump was worthless. On days like this Darci walked around the apartment with a spray bottle, spritzing her bloated body to cool it.

As apartments go, it wasn't a bad little place. Certainly better than a trailer on some hot lot, and better than a high rise. Ray and Darci were luckier than most young couples assigned to Albuquerque's Kirtland Air Force Base. The neighborhood was a mix of retirees and airmen, a dozen blocks from the base. People came and went and rarely knew their neighbors. A sign in the lawn next door read: Tenant Parking Only.

The duplex was the first house off San Mateo Boulevard, a commercial strip with the look of just hanging on. Quintana Plaza, around the corner, housed a tax service, a sewing center, a binding business and a day care center whose purple and turquoise playground was visible behind a high picket fence that kept the children in. Darci could see the playground when she stepped out her door.

The apartment itself had some character, even if the neighborhood did not. The rooms were fair-sized and the doorways were arched, and in the hallway, on either side of the bathroom door, shelves were built-in for linens and things. As you faced the bath, Darci and Ray slept on the left, in a square room with a south window. To the right was the baby's room — a nursery, with its own little closet full of little outfits on rows of tiny hangers. It faced south, too, and through the venetian blinds Darci could see the narrow yard behind the house with its clothesline on painted T racks, just enough space for a picnic table laid endways, and just enough grass for a mother and her baby to lie in the shade of a neighboring house.

As the first light seeped into her bedroom on this

July morning, Darci lay in uncomfortable silence. She was so heavy; this pregnancy had gone on long enough. She was looking forward to today with dread and anticipation. At 5:00 P.M., she had told Ray, labor would be induced and her pregnancy would end. As she lay in the fog of early-morning waking she could feel Ray against her back. How little he knew about her. While she was thinking about the baby, he probably was thinking about cars. Ray at times seemed not to care about what was going on in her head—or her belly. "Women's stuff," he called it. He'd felt the baby move and knew she couldn't sleep on her back, but he much preferred his model cars with their radio controls.

Ray rolled out and showered. Darci made the bed. As he dressed in his Air Force blues, she made breakfast for him. Food bothered her now, especially in the morning. It had been months since she'd tasted an egg or a pizza. In the tiny kitchen they made their final plans for the day. Ray would pick Darci up shortly after 4:00 P.M., in time to get to the hospital. They'd driven the route a couple of times, just to time it. At 7:40 A.M. he kissed her goodbye and left for the base.

Darci padded to the bath and glanced at herself in the mirror. She stared, not recognizing for a moment the face looking back. Her brown hair was a long tangle. When she and Ray stood before the mirror together the reflection startled her. How she'd changed since they'd met. She was sixty pounds heavier and he was still thin. She used to be such a "turn on," he reminded her. They looked like a younger version of her parents and that scared her, because she was not their child.

Darci Kayleen Pierce had awakened at the age of

eleven days in Portland, Oregon in the home of Ken and Sandra Ricker, with no clue as to who she was. Her biological mother had given her up, at birth, for adoption. Sandra Ricker assured her that she was doubly loved, by two mothers, but Darci never understood how a woman could give up her child. She also remembered the taunts from her older brothers, Craig and Rick: "She's not your real mom," they'd yell whenever they wanted to cut her down. Darci grew up wearing that, like a scarlet A on her heart.

Sandra Ricker was a large, bighearted woman, who kept day-care children in her home and baked cakes to make ends meet. In their working-class neighborhood on Portland's southeast side, there was a great demand for child care, and at times there were as many as eight outside children in the Ricker's modest home, sometimes around the clock. Her baking specialty was wedding cakes, big frosty, fattening delicacies of sugar and spice that kept her kitchen in sweet disarray. From her looks Sandra Ricker ate most of the icing, for she weighed three hundred to four hundred pounds. Darci's father, Ken, ran a forklift at a factory at night, and slept most days. He worked hard, but he was rarely there as a father.

Darci, the family's adopted girl, was treated like a queen. She had a room all to herself where she spent much time alone fantasizing. She pictured herself in a rich family, with a beautiful mom, riding horseback, going to balls, being the fairest of them all. All through school she dreamed of flying, of being an airline stewardess and seeing the world. When she was a junior in high school Darci was named a foreign exchange student to South Africa. She was gone a year, a fantasy year of travel, study, floating through lives of wealthy whites. She'd taken to wearing a Krugerrand on a chain around her neck and developed an accent which she brought home, along with an attitude of superiority. Ray Pierce was one of her friends who stuck with her.

Ray hadn't been her only boyfriend, but he was one of the few who hadn't come on strong for sex. He'd been an Eagle Scout in Seaside, Oregon and was a virgin when they met at a Rotary Club picnic in Portland. He was thin like her father, and, in a way, just as distant. He'd worked in a hobby shop and loved model cars and airplanes. She'd moved in with him in 1985, during her senior year of high school. That fall, while working at G.I. Joes, a sports clothing store, she thought she was pregnant with their child.

It turned out to be a molar pregnancy. It was flushed from her and broke her heart. Darci's mother brought her a Care Bear in the hospital, so she'd have something to take home. The same Care Bears now filled the nursery in the Albuquerque duplex. Her mother had bought every bear picture she could find and the crib was covered with cuddly stuffed bears. Darci pushed the door to the nursery open and looked inside. All was ready: the crib, the changing table, the shelf of books against one wall, bags of diapers, the closet of clothes. You name it, this baby would have it.

Darci thought she was pregnant again when she and Ray got married in December 1986. It was a joyous occasion, in spite of the special maternity wedding dress. Three showers were held and at Christmas dinner Darci turned to a favorite aunt, lifted her blouse and said, "Aunt Donna. Look. I'm getting so big." The women all touched her belly. Counting Ray there were five boys going into the

13

service, and they all gathered at Darci's grandmother's for a good old-fashioned family holiday.

The surprise baby shower Sandra Ricker held for her daughter was one any mother would have been proud of. They decorated the whole house with banners and ribbons, and Sandra baked one of her cakes, with a bottom layer of pink-and-blue clowns on pillars and a second cake on top. She bought a pink ceramic bootie, filled it with icing, and put a little bear on top. About twenty people crowded into the house. Sandra and Ken had bought Darci a cradle, and her grandfather had assembled it. It stood in the living room filled with gifts. Darci wore a new maternity dress and had her hair done. She just glowed as she opened gifts one by one. At one point they played a game in which everyone guessed the circumference of Darci's belly. They wrote their guesses on pieces of paper. Then someone took a tape measure to her middle, and the closest guess won a prize.

On Jan. 15, 1987, Ray reported for basic training at Lakeland Air Force Base near San Antonio. This was followed by technical training at Kresler Air Force Base in Mississippi. While he was gone, Darci moved back with her parents. On April 15, 1987, Ray came home to move Darci and their belongings to New Mexico, his first assignment. It couldn't have come at a worst time. The baby, Darci told him, was due anytime. But on April 26 they took off, with Ray's father along to help. They drove a U-Haul and their 1977 Pontiac Trans Am and pulled the old off-white Volkswagen bug that Darci used, and they arrived in Albuquerque on May 1, 1987 with all their earthly belongings, their two dogs, and the spirit and stress of a young couple starting out. They moved first into temporary billeting on base.

"We spent the day looking at dumps, nice places that were too small and/or fabulous houses that were too expensive," Darci wrote a friend on May 3. "Boy am I bummed out. Ray is unbearable and if his dad wasn't here to get him out of my face, my dogs, the baby and I would probably be on the next flight home."

Three days later they found a house. "It needs some yard work . . . and is only two bedrooms, but what-the-heck it's a place we can call ours!" Darci wrote. "It's got new carpets and fresh paint and is an adobe house. Adobes are very popular here because they stay cooler."

Darci spent her days turning the apartment into a home and filling the nursery with the baby's things: the cradle, the clothes, the stuffed animals and a whole shelf of baby books. On the crib she attached a musical mobile. She also went to the base hospital to see the maternity ward, but they wouldn't show her until May 12, the next scheduled tour. "You get a different doctor every time you go," she wrote home. "Ray is going to be mad at me tonight when I tell him I won't go there. All he has talked about is how I better like it because it's free. There is a really nice hospital right outside the western gate that I'm going to visit tomorrow. I just hope the baby will wait until I find a place I'm happy with."

Alone, without her family and with no new friends, Darci was clearly lonely. Ray came home for lunch nearly every day, and the guys at the office kidded him about his "nooners." When she told him her mucus plug broke their sex stopped but he still enjoyed the break. After work, Ray liked to come home and watch TV in the evening, leaving Darci absorbed with her only companion, the unborn baby. Her mind focused on the upcoming birth. On May 14 she had contractions in the night. They continued for nearly three hours, with Ray dozing beside her and waking occasionally to see if she was all right. At dawn they stopped.

As the pleasant days of May rolled on, Darci reported home endless details of her life. She described the new washer-drier, and the black widow spiders she found living on the porch. She described the Sandia Mountains, comparing them to Mount Hood as smaller but closer to the view from the apartment windows. But she provided little detail about the progress of her pregnancy, and that frustrated Sandra Ricker, who could only write or call. Darci seemed, at times, evasive about the baby, although every conversation focused on it. Ray would usually join in the call but some of the things he said really puzzled Darci's mother.

"Darci must really be getting big," she said one night to Ray.

"Well, no, not really. Not a lot bigger than what she was then."

And when she asked about natural childbirth and the breathing lessons used to help the mother get through the pressure of birth, Ray told her he hadn't gone to class.

"Why not?" Sandra Ricker asked.

"Well, we know how to breathe."

Finally, in mid-May, Darci told her mother that an ultrasound test performed by her new doctor showed the fetus smaller than expected. He had pushed the due date back. On May 29, she complained of the weight of the baby, and how tired she was. The weather was turning hot, and it was almost unbearable in the apartment. In mid-June she reported to her mother that she was beginning to dilate; her cervix was now open four centimeters.

Finally, on Monday night, July 13, Darci's mother heard the good news in a call to Albuquerque.

"Where's this baby?" she asked.

"Mom, labor will be induced on Thursday, the sixteenth, at five P.M."

"Wonderful," said Sandra Ricker. She began calling friends. "Come for dinner Thursday night," she said. "We'll pray and wait for the baby."

The next morning on his way to work along San Mateo Boulevard, Ray watched helplessly as a car in the lane to his right swung across his path in an attempt to turn. The Trans Am smashed into the car's left side, creaming the front end. Ray was not hurt, but the car was totaled for insurance purposes, and that night Ray and Darci began looking for a new one. They checked out an Acura at Montano Acura on Montano Boulevard. But it stickered at fourteen thousand dollars and Ray, an E2 rank, didn't make that much in a year at the base. The sales manager had been real nice.

"Are you employed?" he'd asked Darci.

"No, I'm going to have a baby in a week or two," she said.

"Oh really? I've got a daughter about your age. Are there any relatives in the Albuquerque area that could cosign for you?" He was hoping for a rich old man. The Pierces shook their heads. They had the insurance on the Trans Am for a down payment, and little else. They got up to go.

"Now, you eat right and have a healthy baby," he said. Darci smiled and remembered his name—Rob.

They drove immediately to the used car lot of

17

Richardson Ford, not too far from their apartment. Jerry Fisher, one of the salesman, showed them around, first to a Thunderbird which they asked about and then to something they could afford. They wanted something sporty, but a bit bigger, for they would soon be a family. They didn't like anything on the lot, but Fisher promised to look. That evening he called. He had found a trade-in, a Mustang. On July 15, the day before their hospital date, Darci and Ray met Fisher at Automotive Services, where the Mustang's air-conditioning was being serviced. They couldn't drive the car, but they liked it. With Darci doing most of the haggling they settled on a price, contingent on a credit union loan.

As they departed, Jerry Fisher wondered about the young couple. They were like a lot of young Air Force couples starting out. Naive and car-poor, they kept Albuquerque's car dealers very happy. But there was something odd about Darci. She was heavy, but she'd been able to get in and out of cars with no trouble, and when she first mentioned her pregnancy, it surprised him. If Darci Pierce was pregnant and full term, Fisher thought to himself, she was like no other pregnant woman he'd seen.

Two

It was tough for Cindy Ray to get out of bed. She liked to rise early to beat the heat, but this morning all her energy was gone, as it had been for nearly a month. She had not slept well. She was thirty-six weeks pregnant, three weeks from D day on August 4, 1987, and she was plainly worried. She'd been tired with Luke, her first child, but this baby made her listless, as if the heat and moisture had penetrated the womb. Luke had been an active baby, kicking to get out; Cindy had jogged with him four or five months, and Luke was born running, blonde and blue-eyed, just like his Dad.

This baby was different, and Cindy couldn't decide if it was weather, a defect, or something as simple as iron deficiency—that's what the midwife at the base thought. The baby had barely moved. As she lay in bed, she was glad that Luke wasn't moving this morning, either.

Her exhaustion might have come from the weekend, when she and Sam had endured a long drive to Mesa, Arizona to visit the temple. It was hot crossing the desert, the width of New Mexico, and into Phoenix. The Mormon Temple there was a beautiful retreat, in a grove of tall palm trees, open around-

19

the-clock for prayer. It was their last trip before the baby arrived and they prayed for their growing family. All the way over the baby had laid like a lump inside her. When they were driving back a fanbelt broke and the car overheated. They had to hitchhike to the nearest town. Cindy said a prayer that they'd find someone at the garage on the weekend, and they did. She had that kind of faith. They'd driven back at night and she was exhausted by the time they got home to the trailer.

Sam and Cindy Ray, twenty-five and twenty-three years of age, had moved to Albuquerque with Luke, a Chevrolet S10 Blazer, and a bunch of household gear they'd dragged halfway around the world in service to the Air Force. The trailer they bought when they arrived in town sat by a concrete pad with a single tree in the '66 Trailer Lodge not far from where the famous old highway emerged from a saddle in the Sandia Mountains and entered Albuquerque. Central Avenue, the local name for Route 66, was a seven-lane commercial strip stretching eight miles from the mountains to the Rio Grande River and then out into the desert on the west side of the city. On either side lay sunbelt sprawl. If they looked out their trailer door the mountains seemed close, rising across the highway, but the general impression of their neighborhood was one of noise, day-and-night traffic, cheap adobe motels with rounded doorways and early neon, fast-food drive-ins by the hundreds, and blocks and blocks of mobile home and RV sales lots with names like "Repo Depot" and "Mobile Home City." These distinguished themselves by flapping flags and signs of promise: "Instant Homes" and "No Cash Down"—magic words for Air Force families stationed at Kirtland.

Sam turned over in the bed and opened his eyes. He could lie in bed this morning, having just come off the night shift. It would be a relief to have him home, to handle Luke, to help her with errands. Sam was a great dad to his little boy, and he was looking forward to the new baby. When he worked nights he always got up to go with Cindy to the base obstetrics/gynecological clinic, and he shared her worry about her health.

On Sam's sergeant's pay of sixteen hundred dollars they made payments on the trailer and the cherry red Blazer. They hoped to have them both paid off — their first assets — by the time his enlistment was up in June 1989. They were like so many young families on the base, just starting out, making do. But Cindy saw their lot in life more clearly than Sam did. He left every day for the base and the camaraderie of fellow airmen. Cindy was stuck in the trailer court with a two-year-old and a belly which barely left room for her to walk down the narrow hallway. They tried to go out once a week, but most of their socializing was confined to the church circles. There were picnics and Sunday services. They also drove around Albuquerque, as so many car-happy couples did; they four-wheeled in the mountains; when Cindy was four or five months pregnant they hiked up to the communication tower that topped Sandia Peak.

But for Cindy there were many days of picking up the trailer, cooking for Sam and wiping a young nose, and it frustrated her. That's part of the reason she got into selling Tupperware to other base wives and young mothers stuck at home. The money was important, but so was getting out. She'd dropped out of college in Utah to marry Sam, and she'd put Sam's career first. They'd agreed that after their

21

youngest child was in school, Cindy would return to college. But Cindy was too bright to stay in the stuffy trailer while Sam ran a desk on the air base. She needed personal growth, too, and Tupperware was sort of a compromise. She could get out, meet people, learn sales and have fun. But she had to push herself, because at heart Cindy was shy and reserved. It was hard to meet new people; strangers were not her forté. To talk to a stranger was the toughest thing she could imagine, yet Tupperware was based on who you knew. You'd go to a party, you'd meet new people, the hostess would sign you up, and soon you'd be hosting your own "party," demonstrating the latest plastic miracle, playing games, serving refreshments, telling a joke, making a pitch, and making a little money. She wanted to be more assertive and feel at ease socially, and not be stuck in a trailer all the time, like so many women she knew back home.

Girls played house in Payson, Utah, and they grew up with visions of weddings and kids and husbands who worked while they stayed home. If Ozzie and Harriet had been Mormon they would have lived in Payson and raised their kids there behind a picket fence. As Sam took Cindy in his arms in the Albuquerque dawn she thought to herself, their life as Ozzie and Harriet was beginning.

Cindy's childhood seemed storybook normal: parents who worked, an older sister, Toni, a younger brother, Kip. Payson was two hours south of Salt Lake City along the Wasatch Front, and there were occasional trips to the big city. But mostly life revolved around the small village of fellow Mormons. The girls shared a room filled with stuffed animals named for boys. Cindy's first date was a double date with Toni at the age of fifteen. They had lots of boyfriends and shared them. They had a puppy and a kitty. They did acrobatics on the clothesline in back of the house. They had a treehouse in the Chinese elm. Their parents' house, surrounded by a hedge of trumpet vines, was in a quiet, close-knit middle-class neighborhood, where children were safe in any house, any yard. Cindy took swimming lessons, built clubhouses with neighbor kids, and, when she got older, dragged Main Street and hung out at Payson Place Pizza. She was hell on wheels driving, and wrecked two pickups. She also played in the school band where she met Sam Ray.

Toni had played clarinet but Cindy took up cymbals and dove into the band like everything else she tackled, quietly, conscientiously, concerned about her performance. The marching band in Payson practiced every morning at 6:00 A.M. and spent long hours on the field outside of school. Cindy was never late, and if they raised funds—say, by selling pizza—she helped. She traveled with the band to state competition and they often won. They had a distinctive look: British bagpiper uniforms with kilts, dark green with white braided cords and bugles on the shoulders.

Next to Cindy in the percussion line was a tall, athletic student with sandy hair. Sam Ray was the son of a roofer-contractor. In 1980 he played snare drum and was the percussion section leader. "I was a big senior, she was a little sophomore," Sam often said when describing their meeting. He was seventeen, she fifteen. He was six-foot-four, she was five-foot-three. And what happened to them blossomed before the whole town.

"We kidded them, called them Mutt and Jeff,"

said Jerry Chatwin, the high school band teacher. "To see them together was funny, but there sure was a sparkle there."

Sam had dated Toni before Cindy and was well-known in town, a good-looking boy with a striking physical presence. He kept in shape, helping his Dad in construction. Sam also had a serious, if somewhat self-righteous streak that made him seem princely. More than Cindy, he had a tendency to judge others — for example, his older brother, who Sam thought was "wild" and therefore unhappy. "There's more to life than wild women and wild parties," Sam had told him.

Cindy and Sam courted in the mountains that back Payson on the East. The Nebo loop up Payson Canyon and Santaquin Canyon south of town were favorite spots for kids to drive. Cindy's family had camped there when the girls were little; they had hunted deer with their Dad, and she and Toni had ridden big tree limbs, bouncing up and down on them as if on horses. Later Cindy took a gun training course and a "survival" program in the course of which she spent three days in the mountains, alone with a backpack. She and Sam loved to hike those hills. The year after Sam graduated he taught Cindy the snare drum, but he wanted to cool the relationship. She dated other boys and even called Sam to talk about them. That's something they could always do — talk. They talked a lot about church, their designs on a family, their ideals. They also kissed, but that's about as far as it ever went. Out of conviction, they stayed "clean," as the church demanded of teenagers.

Payson was a community where family values were a creed. But Cindy was driven to them because her

24

own parents, ultimately, had not lived up to her own ideal. Her father, Larry Giles, sometimes worked a double shift in the steel mill, and when he was through he would stop at one of the two bars in Payson. Cindy's mother, Vickie, worked at a state mental hospital and later the same mill. Cindy wanted her mom to be at home like the other moms on her block, and she became upset if Vickie wasn't home when school let out. When Cindy was sixteen Larry and Vickie Giles were divorced, with a devastating effect on the kids, because it was just something Mormons didn't do and because they had to decide who to live with. Cindy, who chose her Dad, became a substitute parent, doting over her brother, especially. She pushed both Toni and Kip to attend church and to study hard. She turned to her grandmother Giles for love and support, who in turn helped mold Cindy's twin lifework of wife and mother, a philosophy that flowed quite naturally from the Mormon Church. Grandma Giles told Cindy that her parents wouldn't have gotten divorced if they had been going to church instead of the bars.

In February 1981 Sam Ray left for a church mission in England, a typical step in the life of serious Mormon men, who become, in effect, missionaries, spreading the word. He knocked on doors and attempted, in a gentle but firm way, to engage young people in a dialogue about their religious beliefs, and to thrust into their hands the Book of Mormon. It was a tough eighteen months because of the doors closed in his face in an Anglican country. "I learned how to love people, whether they hated my guts or not," he said later. But he also developed calluses and never again wanted to show his feelings.

While in England Sam wrote Cindy a few times

and thought of her often, in long, internal dialogues about family and future. Cindy graduated from high school in December 1981 and began attending the Utah Valley Community College in Payson and Brigham Young University in nearby Provo. She wanted a career, she thought, and began a track toward nursing. But then Sam came home in August 1982 and had eyes only for her. The following spring, on April 15, 1983, they got married, and Cindy knew that she had found her home. They were married in the Salt Lake Temple, the most holy of venues for Mormons, where the mirrored walls reflected their vows for "time and all eternity." They were both virgins, which shocked many of Sam's friends in the military. "People still do that?" they joshed him.

On their wedding night Sam cooked dinner: a heaping platter of fried potatoes. Cindy, who had worried about her homemaking skills, quietly told him, "I'll cook tomorrow," and took to domesticity like a duck to water.

Two months later Sam joined the Air Force and left Payson for three months of basic training at Lackland Air Force Base in San Antonio, Texas. Cindy joined him there, flying down with pots and pans to start a home. They didn't even have a car and they lived in a low-rent section near the base. After basic, in December 1983, Sam was assigned to Germany, a pretty scary destination for a couple of kids who'd never strayed far from Payson, Utah. Germany was eight thousand miles away. But they had each other and it was the kind of experience that sealed their union. They saw Europe and created Luke. Cindy cross-stitched and did needlepoint, making Christmas ornaments of stuffed felt. She made their spare house a home. She also took on the chores of finance, saving money, and keeping in touch with both families back home.

Luke was born in 1985, two years after they arrived in Germany. It bothered Cindy to be so far from her mother and sister for advice, but she devoted herself to this "punch-ya-in-the-face" kind of kid. In December 1986 they came home, arriving in time for Christmas. On the East Coast they picked up the Blazer they'd ordered, drove it to see friends and relatives, and then headed West. They had a month in Payson before their new assignment in Albuquerque.

Cindy impressed both families when she arrived. She'd become a woman, a wife. She'd exercised to tighten her belly, and she was nearly back to her high school figure. She also had energy to spare. "After Germany she just blossomed," said Sam's mother, Millie. "She lost weight and looked real beautiful. She had long hair. They say when you're in love you blossom."

Sam had three years remaining on his enlistment when they arrived in Albuquerque in January 1987 and he was promoted from MP to desk sergeant in charge of the law enforcement desk. Shortly after their arrival Cindy became pregnant with their second child.

Three

The morning of July 16 seemed to crawl by for Darci Pierce, and she fell into reverie again. She walked into the nursery and picked up a copy of *Parents* magazine. She ran her hand along the rail of the crib, staring down at the soft, clean sheet. She shuddered at the memory of her nightmare, and reached in to pick up the baby. She turned away to the dressing table, her hand where its head would be, her other hand holding the little body. She laid it on the vinyl top and slowly, gently, removed the pins that held the diaper in place. She looked at where the baby's head would lay, and pretended to clean its bottom. She lifted its legs to place a clean diaper back around its side. "There, there," she said to herself. She could almost hear the baby cry. A few more hours and it all would be over.

As she stood daydreaming one part of her wanted it all to go as planned. Another just wanted to take off. She grabbed a suitcase and threw clothes in it, a few of hers, a few of the baby's. "I'll leave Ray," she said aloud. Ray didn't have a clue as to what was going on in her head. He'd married her when she was pregnant and then brought her here to this desert city where she had no friends and nothing to do

28

but pick up and fold the baby clothes again, and nowhere to go but the mall. That, and the place in her head where she often escaped. As she got closer to her due date, Ray seemed even more withdrawn. Now he was thinking of a second, civilian job to make ends meet. Darci had sold her skis, and put twelve hundred dollars in the bank. But Ray had bought a compact disc player, leaving only four hundred dollars in savings for bills. "I could kill him," Darci wrote a friend back home in Portland. "Now he's found the exact motorcycle he's been wanting for twelve hundred dollars. I told him to sell his (model) helicopter and one of his planes and that would cover it."

Darci threw the bag into her dirty-white Volkswagen, started it, and drove away, not knowing exactly where she was headed. She'd get some money, she said to herself, half of their savings. She'd fill up the car at the air base pumps. She'd take off so Ray wouldn't feel obliged to support her. It was crazy thinking. Passing a mall, she wheeled in and went inside where the air was cool. She paced there, trying to get her head together. She watched other mothers carrying their babies, or wheeling them in strollers. They had babies—why couldn't she? She returned to the car, got in and turned onto Lomas heading West, to a place where babies come from.

For as long as she could remember, Darci Pierce had wanted to be pregnant—and had fantasized herself that way. The pillow beneath the clothes—how young was she then? Six years old? It may have been about the time she learned she was adopted. She loved to play pregnant when Sandra Ricker wasn't watching. Darci's mother had forbidden that game. Darci had daydreamed about giving birth and the

29

"wonderful feeling" of the fetus moving through the birth canal. The infant in her fantasy was always beautiful.

At about that same age Darci Pierce discovered sex. When she was six she showed a boy, who was also six, how to make love. At first they simulated intercourse, but later performed the real thing. They had plenty of opportunity, for they played and slept together regularly — the boy was a cousin. Darci began menstruating at the age of nine, and because she was fully developed with full breasts by the age of ten, she wore her sexuality on her sleeve. It confused and scared her; she didn't know whether to act like a little girl or a young slut. By the time she was ten she was sexually active with teenage boys she did not know. It was as though someone had come in to Darci's youth and stolen the rest of her childhood.

She was getting a "reputation" in school, and by then was having casual sex with men four-to-seven times a week. She never seemed to remember much about these liaisons. She'd make eyes at an older man and the next thing find herself having intercourse. Once she found herself in a hotel sauna with a man and no memory as to how she got there, or anything that was said.

At thirteen she began dating a boy she'd met in church, a relationship that quickly turned sexual, and Darci seemed to slip away from the docks of home and church without an anchor. She got stoned with marijuana after school and tried various drugs — LSD, cocaine, amphetamines. An attractive neighborhood girl, who Darci admired, seduced her into oral sex and then peed on her face, humiliating her.

In her teen years her periods were irregular, which

left her wondering often whether she was pregnant. That happened six or eight times. She never was. But she always thought it a blissful state. "You glow and you're special," she once told a friend. Glamorous stuff, having a baby. A baby would complete her, it seemed to Darci, and bring her the happiness she wanted. When she was thirteen, after a late period, she told a friend she was pregnant and claimed to have had an abortion.

When Darci moved in with Ray and became sexually active with him her period was again late and she complained of abdominal pain. She went to the emergency room at Portland's Adventist Medical Center, where the gynecologist on call, David Sargent, gave her a pregnancy test, which proved negative. He then suspected an ectopic pregnancy, in which the egg begins to grow outside the uterus, usually in the fallopian tube. Before he could operate, the hospital contacted Darci's mother and asked her permission to operate on her seventeen-year-old. Sargent put her under a general anesthetic and performed a laparoscopy, inserting a fiberoptic device into a small incision in her abdomen. On Darci's ovary he found a cyst—a fluid-filled growth that stretches, ruptures and bleeds. He stuck a needle into the cyst to drain it and admitted Darci overnight for observation.

In June 1985, a few months after the discovery of her cyst and a few weeks after graduation from high school, Darci again thought she was pregnant, and read a home pregnancy kit test as positive. Dr. Sargent thought so too, finding her uterus full, about the size that would go with a six-week-old fetus. But in August Darci began bleeding. That's when Sargent discovered the molar pregnancy, which is a fertilized egg in which the placenta grows too rapidly, producing signs of pregnancy, including morning sickness and positive pregnancy tests.

Afterward, Dr. Sargent advised Darci not to get pregnant for a year. But by the middle of 1986 Darci was wearing maternity clothes again. She first told the women at G.I. Joes, and they all laughed. There were at least a dozen other women in the same store having babies, and the local joke was that something was in the drinking water. Darci gained weight, her breasts enlarged and her tummy got hard and round. She was due in September, she said, about the same time as one of her coworkers and friends, Dorothy Spain. But as Dorothy's pregnancy progressed, Darci's was somehow stalled. The due date was pushed back, first to October, then to November. By now she was fifty pounds heavier. She finally told Ray that she was pregnant.

On November 3, 1986, Dorothy Spain gave birth to a daughter. Within days, Darci announced that labor would be induced on November 15. She took maternity leave and asked Ray to pick up the checks. But on November 15 Darci called her friend Dorothy with the horrible story that the baby had died in her womb. The women cried and cried on the telephone. The next day Darci received flowers of condolence from the staff of G.I. Joes. That evening, Darci drove to her mother's house in tears, came in the kitchen, and told her about the lie. Sandra cried.

Darci promised she'd never lie again. A month later she married Ray, and the following spring they moved to Albuquerque. Shortly after arriving Darci took her medical records to the ob/gyn clinic at the old base hospital.

"I'm Mrs. Pierce. I'm pregnant and I'd like to get

into your OB clinic," she told Diane McDonald Gray, the technician on duty. Gray took her file and looked through it. She noted the molar pregnancy from 1985 and showed the file to a doctor to determine whether Darci should be assigned a midwife or a physician. But the file lacked any maternity record; there were no positive pregnancy tests. Despite Darci's obvious condition, Gray returned Darci's record and told her she couldn't get in.

That week Darci's mother made a quiet call to Darci's old physician, Dr. Sargent, in Portland as part of a surprise. She wanted to travel to New Mexico, arriving about the time of her birth. The doctor's receptionist was reluctant to give out confidential patient information, but she did say that Darci was not being treated for a pregnancy. In fact, she said on February 27, 1987, a pregnancy test administered to Darci was negative. Sandra Ricker made a frantic call to Albuquerque. Darci only laughed.

"Mom, you know I'm pregnant."

"Yes," said her mother, "I know you are."

Darci swung the Volkswagen bug into the University of New Mexico Hospital and went inside through the big, automated, glass doors. Past three steel elevators she faced a directory: Chapel to the right. Nursery, third floor. Admitting to the left. She walked down the hall. The clock in admitting said four P.M. — an hour before her scheduled inducement. Darci pushed the big wood door. The room was small, filled with chairs of purple vinyl. Two pay phones hung on the left. The back and side walls held abstract paintings. Just on the right was a high

33

desk of purple Formica, imposing to patients and daunting to the clerks who had to peer over it. It was easier, gentler, to stand in front of the desk. When Darci walked in three women were talking there and she eyed one, a young, thin woman in a stylish dress.

"May I help you?" said Kelly Jean Lyden.

"Can we talk some place?" Darci said.

"Sure." Lyden, a business student, had just begun her night shift and the room was empty. As she motioned to a chair Lyden took stock of Darci: she was heavy, about her height, with a soft, pleasant voice. She was dressed in a maternity smock.

When they were seated, Darci began bluntly. "I can't conceive a child. I'm not pregnant. But my husband thinks I am."

Taken aback, Lyden just listened.

Darci explained that she had found a surrogate mother to have a child but she did not want her husband to know it wasn't his child, and she did not want the child to know that it was adopted. "You see," Darci said, "spilling out her life story, "I was adopted. I know how it feels." But, Darci said, a problem had developed. The surrogate was supposed to be induced today but the procedure had been postponed at the last minute. Darci's husband would be arriving in an hour, expecting to see "his" child.

"I'm sorry," said Darci. "Everything is going wrong. My plans aren't working. I'm going to have to tell my husband." She looked in Lyden's eyes. "I want to protect him. I'm sorry I lied to him. I'll tell him everything tonight at home. But he's coming here, in an hour. He'll be so angry and humiliated."

Lyden wanted to help her. Darci paused, looked directly at Lyden. "Would you tell my husband that the doctor has postponed my inducement?"

Lyden thought quickly. She believed this woman, for some reason, and she didn't think it her place to give bad news to her husband.

"Yes," she said, nodding. Darci became business-like.

"We'll be back at five P.M., in an hour. Let me give you my name so you'll know who I am when we come in."

"What is it?"

"Darci Pierce. Mrs. Pierce."

Kelly Jean Lyden went about her business for the next hour, nervously awaiting Darci's return. Right at five, the door opened and Ray and Darci Pierce walked through, carrying a suitcase. They wore outfits that matched. Lyden was alone.

"I'm Mrs. Pierce. I'm here to have my labor induced," Darci said in a clear, firm voice.

Lyden, nervous, with a visible shake in her hands, replied in a tight, high voice.

"Mrs. Pierce, the doctor has been trying to reach you. He's been called away. The inducement has been postponed a week."

Darci and Ray looked surprised. They looked at each other, turned and left.

That night at home Darci called her mother.

"Don't worry Mom. I don't have the baby yet."

Sandra Ricker was surrounded by expectant friends who'd come to pray and cheer. "How come?" she said, nearly in tears. Darci explained about the clerk, the doctor and the delay of the family dream one more time. In her little home in Portland, Sandra Ricker wept. As the gathering of friends drifted off, empty, no one apparently stopped to think how long Darci Pierce had been wearing maternity clothes. If they had, they would have counted fourteen months.

Four

It was a miserable day to be pregnant.

Hot and humid, even at dawn, when clammy skin stuck to sheets in wrinkled wads of irritation. The kind of day for bad temper and sick desire, when fat people cursed their fate and even skinny people sweated.

Muggy was a dry joke in Albuquerque, except during the "monsoon." Until July, humid meant a little haze that turned light pink when the sun rose. It hung like a veil on the western flanks of Sandia Peak, the aged, ridged uplift which gave the city character and twelve minutes of shade after sunrise each morning. Until July, the clear desert nights cooled this city of peach-pit adobe built from the mud of the Rio Grande.

July brought rain, adobe's nightmare. Rain took back the river's child, turned it back to liquid languor and washed it home. Afternoon thunderstorms cracked the mountains. Before and after, great white wet dumplings floated in a blue soup sky. As a result, the air over Albuquerque turned wet enough to hold the heat through the night and anyone with just a swamp cooler slept in dank disarray. That's how dawn arrived on Thursday, July 23, 1987.

Cindy Ray rose at 5:00, an hour before the sun,

and felt tired again. It was 67 degrees outside, headed for 97. She knew, on some visceral level, that it would not be a pleasant day. What luck, she said to herself as she pushed out of bed, to be pregnant and due in an Albuquerque monsoon.

Sam was up now. While he showered, Cindy fixed his breakfast. While he ate, she fixed his lunch. He was on the day shift today, and she was left with a list of errands as long as Sam's arm: a midwife checkup and many Tupperware deliveries. Cindy's Tupperware parties were held once a week in and around the base. Each Thursday was pickup day, the day when she delivered her orders. She would pick up the order in the Blazer and drive around, knocking on doors. Cindy was not looking forward to it, with no help from Sam, and Luke in tow.

Sam rose to leave. He would ride his bike to work, two miles to the law enforcement center. He would be at his post before 7:00 A.M., before the traffic, and work until 3:00 P.M. By then Cindy would be just across the street at the ob/gyn clinic. She stood up to say goodbye and they kissed. Not just a quick peck, but a little ritual they had. A pause for love. Just for a second they'd hold hands and look at each other.

Sam looked sharp in his crisp, blue uniform. On his head was a blue beret, a hat that set an Air Force cop off from an airman, even at a distance. Sam wore the beret with pride, along with a stiff countenance and a gun.

Cindy was not fat, even with the baby. Her gain was all baby, with most of the weight right in the abdomen. Her legs hadn't swelled. Her face was normal. She was thin, actually, except in her belly.

Then Sam was gone, into traffic and a morning

38

that would soon turn miserable. Cindy cleaned up the trailer, got her things together, and pulled on blue maternity pants and a white blouse with polka dots. She woke Luke, who was sweaty in his crib, and dressed him lightly.

If love was the measure, Luke Ray was a spoiled child. A wanted child, too, by a mother who saw her role not strictly as nurturer but as part of a spiritual calling. To Cindy Ray, Mormon families were large and forever and Luke was just her first child. She and Sam wanted to raise four, at least, and then judge their feelings about an even larger family.

They had planned Luke. Cindy carried him in Germany and wrapped love around him, before and after his birth. She was careful with him in her womb; she ate right and exercised, even jogging until she cramped. After his birth, her life became the little boy. Germany at the time was filled with terrorist threats against the United States, so Cindy stayed in. She had few friends anyway. She taught Luke to talk at nine months, and the alphabet by the time he was twenty months. By the age of two years, he could sing Mormon songs; Luke and Cindy surprised Sam one Monday night—family home evening in their church—by standing before his father and singing:

> I am a child of God
> And he has sent me here,
> Has given me an earthly home
> with parents kind and dear.
> Lead me, guide me, walk beside me
> that I must do to live
> with him someday.

This boy was growing up Mormon. So as frustrated as Cindy got at home, it was Luke's unending delight and growth that kept her sane. Cindy lifted Luke and stepped outside into the balmy air. She buckled him into his seat in the Blazer and took off. She usually took Luke everywhere, Tupperware parties being the one exception. That's when Sam would keep him. Cindy liked to take Luke on her deliveries, and to the ob/gyn clinic, as well, to get him used to the idea of a little sister or brother. Sam would have been there today if his shift had not changed. To make things easier, she decided to drop Luke with a church friend before her checkup. She waited for traffic to pause, turned across Central and headed away from the sunrise toward the Tupperware warehouse. As she began her work, the heat of the city began to build. By noon it would be 93 degrees with cumulonimbus clouds rising in the mountains—a sure sign of lightning and thunder later in the afternoon.

The heat, the traffic, the trailer living—it was all such an alien world to Cindy Ray. But she had internalized, from her grandmother and from the teachings of the Mormon church, the tenet that her husband came above anything, and children second only to that. As her bishop, Brian Harwood, would say, "Only if you are a successful spouse can you be as successful as we desire—the ideal." As a result, Cindy's hope for her family was almost naively high. "Cindy saw the challenges in her parents' marriage and wanted to improve on that. She always saw a greater commitment from those in church. Her parents were good but did not give a lot of time to the kids. She wanted to change that. Rather than just take her children to church or activity (as her parents did) she wanted to participate." She also believed that no mother could have an outside career and give her husband and children the attention they deserved. In other words, at an early age, Cindy became a mainstream Mormon on the holiest path: devotion to husband, devotion to children, a selfless woman who put her family first. "All the things Cindy had hoped for found expression in her marriage," said Bishop Harwood.

"You are Eve," she was told as she and Sam married in the temple. There was no greater calling for a Mormon woman. Through her, man would multiply and husband the earth. It was the woman's sacred role. Sam was Adam, who held for Cindy the keys to all the kingdoms of God. In their wedding ceremony, Cindy pledged her vows in endowments, sacred covenants she made with God. Forever after she would be reminded of these covenants by the silk undergarments she received after the ceremony. She wore them almost always — even while making love — and removed them only to bathe. They protected her from evil, from harm and moral decay. Shortly after the Rays were married the church moved away from the uncomfortable one-piece undergarments for women. Cindy now wore two pieces, a pantaloon that came to above her knee and a camisole. They were the outward manifestation of her devotion. Even in the heat of a New Mexico summer, she and Sam wore the underwear beneath their street clothes.

Except today. Because of her appointment with the midwife, Cindy had put them in her purse. She would don them after her exam.

By noon, even without the garments, Cindy was hot and frustrated and stopped to call Sam.

"There's a problem with the order. I must have made a mistake. I have to go back after my checkup."

41

The room where Sam worked was abuzz with the goings on of a big air base—radios, police calls, security questions. It took some effort to concentrate on his wife, but Sam listened. She didn't even have time for lunch.

"I love you sweetheart," she said to him.

"I love you, too," Sam Ray said to his wife.

At about 1:00 P.M. Cindy Ray drove to Jackie Bloomfield's. Baby sitters were at a premium around a base full of young parents. When Cindy had trouble finding one, Sam had suggested Jackie, one of Cindy's two "visiting teachers," as the church called them. Two men and two women were assigned to each family. They visited the home each month to make sure they had enough food and clothing and emotional support. Jackie Bloomfield had boys of her own and she readily agreed to help Cindy out. She lived in a trailer in a mobile home park about a mile outside the base's Eubank gate. Cindy told Jackie she hoped to be through her errands by 3:00 P.M., to pick up Luke and meet Sam.

Cindy drove back on the base, turned onto Gibson and pulled to the back parking lot of the old base hospital. USAF Ambulatory Health Center, said the big blue letters on the long, tan building. At one time it had been the base hospital, self-contained and full-service, but little by little the medical work had been contracted out to other hospitals and clinics. Just a month earlier, on June 19, the last of the babies was delivered here. Air Force wives now delivered at the University of New Mexico Hospital, two miles north and west, on Lomas Boulevard. But the ob/gyn clinic, the midwife service and the pharmacy remained in the old building. The entrance was on the south side, through the door to the pharmacy.

The parking lot was blazing hot. Cindy chose a parking slot near the door and hurried in. The clinic was down the main hall, the last door on the left. It was cool inside and the receptionist greeted her by name. Cindy felt among friends here, a place where she could express her worries about the baby and share her pride in her pregnancy.

Cindy took a seat next to Elizabeth Herman, the wife of a Public Health Service dentist, who was pregnant with her third child and was a Tupperware colleague. They were in the same selling unit, and had sat next to each other at Monday rallies. They fell quickly into an animated talk about babies. Elizabeth was due just after Cindy.

"Listen, I'm going to a New Mom's meeting after my checkup," Elizabeth said. "It's at three thirty. Are you going?"

Cindy didn't think so. "I don't know if I'll have time."

The meeting would explain government insurance and hand out the paper. It would be their last chance before their deliveries at UNM. "You really need to go," said Elizabeth. "It's just next door, at Que Pasa, the recreation center."

"Well, I'll try to meet you there," said Cindy.

"I'll save you a seat," said Elizabeth.

At 1:30 P.M. a medical technician pulled Cindy's record and escorted her to an examining room. Staff Sergeant Angela Morgan took a urine sample, Cindy's weight and blood pressure, and marked it on a chart. Then Sister Rosemary Homrich, Cindy's midwife, came in.

Homrich was a Dominican sister, a strong woman of medium height who carried on her face the motherly look of a teacher. An RN for thirty years, she

43

saw patients nearly nonstop at the clinic; they were scheduled every fifteen minutes. She also worked at the University of New Mexico Hospital and was on call two nights a week for labor and delivery.

Sister Rosemary first saw Cindy on February 23, shortly after Cindy and Sam were transferred to Kirtland. She gave Cindy her initial physical and had seen her four times since. Glancing at her chart, Sister Rosemary saw that Cindy had gained thirty-two pounds. The last entry also mentioned a dip in her iron count.

"How are you feeling?" she asked.

"Tired."

Homrich listened for fetal heart tones. She measured Cindy's girth and found the baby's head. She noted that Cindy was thirty-seven-and-a-half weeks pregnant and was due August 4 or 5. Everything seemed normal. But Cindy was clearly worried because of the baby's lack of movement during the last week. Sister Rosemary ordered a nonstress fetal monitor test, and Sergeant Morgan took Cindy to the room across the hall. The midwife excused herself to see another patient and Cindy lay on the cool vinyl and watched as Morgan placed the metal transducer on her belly. Wires led to a machine which traced the baby's heartbeat. Across the top of the transducer Morgan laid a soft, white, elastic belt, which wrapped clear around Cindy and held the transducer to the uterus. The two women bantered as Morgan set the machine.

"I can't wait for the baby to get here," Cindy said. "How much longer?"

"August fourth! I'm really tired. I just want to get this over with, go home and rest."

The baby's heartbeat began to scratch on a paper

tape, but it was flat.

"What did you have for lunch?" Morgan asked.

"Nothing, really," Cindy said. "I was running like crazy."

"Cindy, you need to eat more. You need to gain strength. Your baby needs it. You need it." Morgan, a good-natured black woman, was gently insistent. "You aren't eating enough."

She tore a strip of the tracing and showed it to Sister Rosemary. The baby appeared sleepy for lack of food. She asked Morgan to give Cindy something to drink, to stimulate the fetus. Normally that would mean orange juice, a quick sugar fix, but the clinic's refrigerator had been moved in the transfer of the delivery room to UNM. Morgan bought a Coke instead and handed it to Cindy. She drank it, though she never drank Coke because of a church rule. No caffeine. She didn't say anything, until Morgan remembered.

"Oh god," she blushed.

"Forget it."

As they waited for the soda pop to circulate Elizabeth Herman stuck her head in the room and saw Cindy strapped to the machine.

"Are you okay? Are you going into labor?"

"No, I'm okay. They're just checking the baby."

"Don't forget the meeting. See you there."

"Okay."

Within minutes the sugar had moved to the baby and its heart picked up. The new tracing looked better and Cindy could read the improvement in Morgan's eyes. She smiled, then glanced at her watch. She had been on the monitor forty-five minutes and would be more than the hour she promised the babysitter.

"You know, I'm really getting late," she told

45

Homrich. "I'm supposed to be at a babysitter to pick up my two-year-old. Will you call my husband and have him pick up the baby?" She gave her the number. By the time Sam had done that, Cindy would be through and the three of them could finish the Tupperware order and go home.

Sister Rosemary called Sam. His day had gotten worse, but it would soon be over. The baby looked okay, she told him, but they wanted Cindy to be comfortable and were keeping her on the monitor awhile. Hanging up, she checked the test again, said goodbye to Cindy, and headed home. She was on call that night at UNM.

A few minutes later a clinic doctor approved the test results and Cindy hurried to dress. Morgan folded the white monitor belt and handed it to her with instructions to wash it before next week's appointment. She also chided her again about eating right. Cindy tucked the belt into her purse, a brown-and-straw bag she'd won for selling Tupperware. Inside were her keys on a ring with a heart-shaped "Cindy" name tag, a present from her father. A tiny Tupperware lid was attached to the ring as well. Stuffed in the purse, too, were the silk undergarments. Traditional Mormons would have called her vulnerable without them, but because of her hurry she did not stop to put them on.

Reassured about the baby, Cindy found her keys, made a new appointment at the desk and stepped out into the heat. Things were okay after all. As she walked toward the Blazer, she didn't notice at first the dirty-white Volkswagen parked in the next slot, close to her door, or the heavyset woman who emerged just as Cindy reached out with her keys.

Five

"Come hell or high water, we're not coming home without a baby, Mom."

The voice shook Darci Pierce. Was it hers? Her mother had called at 11:00 P.M. to bug her about the baby again.

"How come you haven't called?" she said. She was a little whiny, a little pushy. It had been six days since Darci's inducement had been "delayed."

"Darci goes in tomorrow," Ray said on the phone. "At five o'clock. Come hell or high water . . ."

"We'll be expecting to hear from you this time, you know," said Sandra Ricker.

Her mother's voice rang in her ears as Darci Pierce opened her eyes. She padded to the kitchen, an L beyond the living room where Ray was eating. She was not hungry and was rather constipated. Ray was talking about the car again.

"Just one day," he was saying. Just one day he wanted their Mustang not to be a family car. He wasn't a father yet, not until 5:00 P.M. He wanted to drive it past the gate and have someone notice. Darci wanted to install the baby seat. They'd argued about it the night before when the car was delivered and they took it for a test drive. Jerry Fisher, the sales-

47

man, rode with them, the block north on Wyoming from Richardson Ford and east on Interstate 40. Ray had accelerated, listening for problems. The car handled nicely. They went three miles toward the mountains, to Tramway Boulevard, then turned around and came back. Just before they pulled into the car lot Darci asked Ray to drive on, toward Montano Acura, seven miles away and clear across town. It didn't make sense to Fisher, or to Ray.

"It's neat driving around there," Darci said.

"No, let's just drive it in," said Ray. They signed the final papers and took the Mustang home. That's when the arguing began. Darci hauled out the baby seat and tried to install it. It wouldn't fit, and she got mad.

"Relax," Ray had said. He took the seat, got it in, and then took it out. Darci threw a tantrum.

"You don't care about the baby," she cried.

Maybe it was a little macho, he admitted, but just once he wanted to drive it before it was a family car. Call it a final fling. He put the baby seat in the garage and they took a spin, driving east to Montano, and north into a new development, to let Darci test drive. The neighborhood north of Montano Acura was a perfect place for it, with new streets and no houses or traffic.

Ray stood up to leave. It was 7:20 A.M. He'd be home for lunch, as usual, and today he'd try to leave work early, to drive her to the hospital, in the Mustang. Ray leaned to kiss her and stepped outside. It was cooler than in the house, but not by much, and not for long.

Now it was D day for Darci. After all those years of wanting a baby, dreaming a baby, she'd have one. But alone in the duplex, Darci felt like falling off the

48

face of the earth. She'd been putting this off for months, with one story after another. She'd narrowly escaped the week before; the clerk had saved her hide. Now there was no backing out. On July 23, 1987 at 5:00 P.M. Darci needed a baby "come hell or high water." She looked at her watch. It was 11:00 A.M.

When Ray arrived home at 11:20 A.M. he was full of news that he could leave early from work and be home in plenty of time to take her to the hospital. They talked again about the car seat and about a stroller Darci wanted to buy.

"We've got to hurry up and find a stroller," she told him, but they agreed that their savings couldn't stand the hit now. No, said Ray, let's put it off. "We really don't need to stroll around a newborn. We don't need it for a couple of months."

Darci tried to open to him. She told him of her fears — having a baby was a big step. "I'm not sure I'm ready to be a mother," she said.

Ray soothed her. It was just cold feet, he said, perfectly natural. He left for work, promising to return at 3:30 or 4:00.

Darci got dressed. She pulled on a striped house-dress, tentlike in its proportions. She took her bank card and drove the Volkswagen onto the base. Off Gibson she gassed up, then drove to where Ray worked, the technical branch, where equipment spec-ifications were checked. Darci parked there awhile, just staring at the new Mustang and the building.

"I'll leave," she said to herself. Leave Ray, take the baby and run. She began to sweat in the heat. She began to think of her mother. Not Sandra Ricker. Her real mother, the one who gave her away. That was the root of Darci's vague discontent, a haunting

49

she'd felt since she was six. It had happened on an autumn night in 1967 when friends of the Rickers hosted a pots and pans party, like a Tupperware party without the plastic. They had refreshments, the host received a gift, and a traveling salesman made a pitch for pots and pans. From those parties friends booked new parties at their own homes. The salesman got drunk toward the end of the evening, and began carrying on about his daughter, who was fifteen, unwed and pregnant. She didn't want the baby, he slurred, nor did she want to put it into an adoption agency. She wanted it to go into a home right away. The hosts called the Rickers.

"We just wanted a baby," Sandra said later. It made no difference what sex it was. They paid a lawyer a fee, plus $125 in travel expenses for the teenager, and waited. On Friday, October 13, 1967, a girl was born.

When the girl was eleven days old, the adoption was approved and she came into the Ricker home. They named her Darci Kayleen. She was doted over, spoiled. In the extended family there were several adopted children and every effort was made not to treat them differently. But from the moment Darci learned she was adopted she was bothered by it.

In her freshman year of high school, Darci actively sought the identity of her biological mother. While taking a summer school course, she went to the courthouse but found the file closed to her until she was twenty-one. At that time, Sandra had promised, she would tell Darci what she wanted to know and Darci could put out feelers for her mother. "You are very fortunate," Sandra told her. "She could have had an abortion. She was fifteen, she couldn't keep you, and she wanted her child in a home with a

50

father and mother."

Darci couldn't buy it. Darci called her mother's decision to give her up "the ultimate rejection." It was the beginning of a lifelong hurt, and it fed her fantasies: growing up in a better house with a beautiful mother. She even told a schoolmate once that her real mother had approached her while playing outside and told Darci she wanted her back. Darci talked about it all one Friday at school. Her schoolmate believed her. "She hated the fact that she was adopted. It meant that her real mother didn't want her; nobody should have to go through that." The following Monday, the schoolmate asked if her mother had come. Darci said, "I don't know what you're talking about. You must be imagining things."

Darci's hurt meant she never fully bonded with Sandra Ricker, and they played out a love-hate relationship all of her life. Darci felt smarter, prettier. She was athletic and Sandra was fat. "Is that fat cow your mother?" a boy asked her once. Darci had decked him. But the weight that bothered Sandra Ricker all her life also bothered Darci. After Sandra's weight caused her to fall down the stairs several times, Darci moved her room to the second floor, which they decorated in dark blue with red and white stripes across the ceiling and wall. She began spending endless hours there alone. It was about this time that she started hearing voices, a man's voice, speaking gibberish to her. One word she remembered: "Kemojo." The man would call her name, usually just before she fell asleep. She learned to silence it by changing her position in bed. But bedtime began to terrify her. She kept a knife under her pillow and a rifle under the bed. Her dad would

51

find it and take it back, again and again.

She disconnected a buzzer her mother used to call her, and she began a sick fantasy of sneaking up on her mother with the gun—and killing her! She'd stand with the unloaded .22 and pull the trigger as if Sandra Ricker were entering the room. Sometimes she'd load the gun and stand facing the door.

From where she sat in the Volkswagen, Darci could see the base hospital. She decided to go in. She walked to the ob/gyn clinic, lingering, fingering a brochure on prenatal care and courses for new moms. How she wanted to be enrolled. The urge welled up from deep inside. She took one of the brochures and began to walk out. One office door caught her attention. A notice was posted: a meeting for new moms' insurance was scheduled later in the day.

At about one o'clock, Darci went back to the car, started it, and pulled out onto Gibson, headed for the base gate. She glanced north, toward the parking lot used by patients in the ob/gyn clinic, and noticed a red Chevy Blazer and a pregnant woman, short and pretty, with dark hair, just getting out. The woman hurried inside the door. Darci turned into the lot and pulled alongside the Blazer. She turned the Volkswagen off and sat, waiting. "Maybe," she thought, "I can talk to her. Maybe I could ask her for her baby." Her mind was baked and her reasoning blurred. The sun beat down and Darci sat in the hot VW sweating. She had been given away by a young woman nineteen years before; why couldn't it happen again? She waited for the woman to come out. Darci just wanted to talk to her.

An hour went by. Darci got out, walked to the clinic door and turned around. She paced back and forth in the hot sun. Rivulets of sweat ran down her back beneath the dress. She went back and sat in the car and fingered the replica gun in the door pocket. A woman with two children two cars away watched her; they were hot, too, and went inside to cool off.

Darci watched the door. Her hopes rose with each swing. Twenty pregnant women came and went, but not the woman she wanted. Maybe she worked there and wouldn't be out until 4:30. Waiting—that seemed to be the story of her pregnancy. But time had now run out. She thought about leaving again. Getting on the interstate, driving to Santa Fe, driving off forever, her and the baby. She thought about stealing one from a supermarket or a nursery. Where was this woman?

As the temperature in the parking lot reached 100 degrees, the clinic door opened and Darci saw her. She was dressed in blue maternity pants, a white blouse with polka dots, and white shoes. From a straw purse, she put on a pair of blue-tint sunglasses against the glare. She headed for the Blazer with keys in her hand. As the woman approached, Darci got out of the car.

Ray Pierce got permission to leave his desk at 3:00 P.M. Everybody in the office knew he was about to pop for cigars, and they joked with him as he left. The men in the office, Sergeant Williams, Sergeant Rivers, Colonel Schmella, they all knew Darci. She usually stopped in once a week after her clinic appointment across the street. They'd teased her about her due date delays, and she had laughed with them. They wished Ray luck and he drove away in the Mustang, turning on the air-conditioning.

53

As he turned onto Marquette, somehow it didn't surprise him to find the Volkswagen gone. The dogs were in the house but Darci wasn't. There was no note. Ray had an idea where she'd gone—off to the mall again. That's where she'd gone last week, psyching herself up for labor, going through that old thing of "Gee, do I want to stick around and have this baby for him, or do I just want to go somewhere else and hide for the rest of my life?"

He didn't know what was going through Darci's mind, exactly. He guessed it was normal for a pregnant woman. He didn't think she'd leave him. Darci could play him like a fiddle, when she wanted to. No, Ray didn't worry too much about his wife, until he noticed how late it was getting. At 5:00 P.M., he made a call, and right in the middle the operator broke in. It was an emergency.

At 3:30 P.M., Theron Hartshorn, a stocking supervisor at Modern Wall in Albuquerque left work and headed for the house he was building in the Monzano Mountains. He drove east on Interstate 40 for fifteen miles and exited at Tijeras, a small village in the saddle between the taller Sandias to the north and the gentler Monzanos on the south. He turned right at the exit, drove through town and headed south on State Highway 14, which climbed in gentle curves into the Cibola National Forest. It was a beautiful drive if you weren't in a hurry. The road had been carved from a rugged landscape of sandstone outcrops, eroded gullies and a thin topsoil that supported a forest of scrub oak and juniper trees.

Hartshorn had built his house out here for the remoteness, on a dirt road surrounded by U.S. Forest

54

Service woods and meadows. There were power and phone lines, but few neighbors. The closest one had a windmill that spun above the trees. It was rugged country, not for the city dweller, and Hartshorn drove a pickup truck, a 1976 brown-and-beige Silverado, to get in and out. It took him about thirty minutes to drive home. Although it had rained earlier, it was sunny and bright by the time he got into the woods.

Five miles south of Tijeras he turned left onto Forest Service Road 242, which ran along the north bank of a deep-cut stream. Seven tenths of a mile in, at a break in the fence, he turned left across a cattle guard onto Forest Service Road 252, a one-lane dirt road. His house was one half mile up this road.

A quarter mile in, he came on a dirty-white Volkswagen, stopped in the middle of the road, facing him, with both doors open. It sat beside a clump of trees on the left, a tall juniper backed by scrub oak in full leaf. Behind the trees the ground dropped off into a gully, still wet from the thunderstorm runoff. Hartshorn saw no one around, so he got out to close the Volkswagen doors. There was room enough to get by on the driver's side. As he approached the car, a woman suddenly appeared from the bushes on his left. She was brushing at her dress. His first thought was that she had been raped.

"Everything's okay," she said. "My friend and I need to be left alone."

"Okay," said Hartshorn. "I need to shut your door."

"My friend and I need to be alone," she repeated. She was husky, with long brown hair and wearing a whitish dress. She was extremely nervous.

"Okay," he said again. "I need to shut the door

55

to get around."

"Okay," she said. "My friend and I need to be alone."

Hartshorn closed the driver's door, walked back to his truck and began to drive by on the shoulder. As he passed, he looked left beyond the clump and saw someone—he thought a woman—lying on the ground in the tall grass, about twenty-five feet from the road. The woman he'd talked to was back, kneeling and crawling towards her. The woman on the ground wasn't moving. Hmmmm, he thought, crazy as it seemed, it sure looked like two women playing around in the bushes.

At the law enforcement desk, Sam Ray finished his paperwork between 3:15 P.M. and 3:30 P.M. and walked across Gibson, across the lot to the old base hospital. He was glad to see the red Blazer sitting where Cindy had parked it. She must still be inside. In the seat were Luke's stuff and Tupperware boxes, and Cindy's purse was gone. Sam put his black leather gunbelt on the seat along with a bag containing police forms. He knew if he crossed paths with Cindy she would not leave with his stuff in the seat. He went inside.

"Is Cindy Ray still here?" he asked at the desk.

"Yes," said a clerk. "She's right around the corner."

Sam walked into the examining room, stuck his head in and found another woman hooked to the fetal monitor. Her husband was there, too, and it embarrassed Sam. He withdrew and went back to the desk.

"What happened? She's not there."

56

"She just left. You just missed her."

There must be another way, he thought. He hurried outside, but he could see from the doorway that Cindy wasn't there. He went back inside and walked the long hall, checking each office. No Cindy. He asked the clerks to check the bathrooms. No Cindy. Sam looked around the hospital for forty minutes, inside and out, increasingly perplexed. This wasn't like her. She was always where she said she would be. He checked his watch, then hopped in the truck to get Luke. The babysitter's house was just outside the base gate and he could be back quickly.

At Jackie Bloomfield's Luke had wet his pants and was dressed only in his underpants, so Sam perched him on his arm and went back to find Cindy. Carrying Luke he searched the hospital again. He went back to the law enforcement desk, hoping their paths had crossed.

"Hey, have you seen my wife?" They had not.

He drove all over the base, back and forth to Jackie's again. It was very hot and he was perspiring, as much out of frustration as exertion. He just couldn't imagine where she could be.

Six

There was a high-tech look to Montano Acura, a concrete and glass emporium of cars on Montano Boulevard, half a mile west of Interstate 25 on Albuquerque's northern side. It sits in a retail warehouse area with companies like Price Club and Office Club surrounded by huge parking lots that seem full seven days a week. The lot at Montano Acura is full, too, with new Japanese cars, each bearing fluorescent green tags on which are written miniature sales pitches, like "'87." The cars gleam from the regular washes they are given to rid them of New Mexico dust.

The building is made of poured concrete with vertical stripes. Two red stripes run horizontally high on the walls, and a steel-colored frontispiece held up by steel-colored pillars wraps the building on two sides. The name of the dealership is spelled out in big red letters on the east side of the frontispiece, the side facing the interstate. Below the name is the showroom, floor-to-ceiling glass containing a few bright cars and a dozen bright salesmen who watch with eager interest anyone who drives in.

When the dirty Volkswagen bug pulled in and stopped by the door, it was not hard to miss. Mike

McKellar, the salesman who bounced out in the heat to greet the driver, returned in seconds, visibly shaken.

"Rob," he said to Robert Mohr, the new car sales manager whose office was by the door, "There's a lady having a baby in the parking lot. She's asking for you. I'm going to call the ambulance."

"Hold on," Mohr said. "Is she asking for the new car sales manager or me personally?"

"She's asking for you by name, Rob."

Mohr, sharply dressed in a blue, wool, and silk suit, stepped outside and sized up the car, an off-white 1978 Super Beetle with oversized tires. On the right front side, dirt and grass were rammed around the hubcap. The right rear fender and taillight, made of fiberglass, were shattered. Mohr bent by the driver's door.

"How are you doing?" he asked.

She was clutching a newborn to her chest, wrapped in blue and white cloth that was blood-stained and wet. Her hair was plastered down with sweat, and she was dressed only in a slip soaked through with perspiration.

"I just had a baby," she said.

"What? Where?"

"On the side of the road. Nobody would help me."

"Why did you come here?"

"I didn't know where else to come. I want to make sure my baby's okay."

Mohr looked closer at the infant. It was bloody and stained with fluid, with fluid in its mouth and a waxy substance on its skin. It seemed sluggish, but it was sleeping peacefully. The smell in the car was powerful. Mohr squatted by the car. It was about 4:30 P.M.

"What did you use to cut the cord?"

"I bit it," she said.

"Is it a boy or a girl?"

"A girl. Amanda Michelle." The woman smiled a little.

She'd remembered Mohr as someone who might help, she said. Mohr looked at her again—the pregnant woman who'd looked at an Integra with her husband nine days before! He didn't remember her name.

"I was driving to Santa Fe to go shopping. But I changed my mind. I had a contraction and lost control of the car a little bit. I was hurrying to get back to Albuquerque when my water broke. Then I had a contraction so bad I lost control and went off the side of the road." Her words tumbled out. She had discarded her underwear, had the baby, wrapped it in her dress and driven away.

"Where did this happen?" Mohr asked.

"Between here and Santa Fe."

"How did you get grass and weeds in the hubcaps?"

"There was high grass I went through. Nobody would help me. I had the baby myself. People were driving by and nobody would stop." She was angry and Mohr felt indignant, too.

"Do you want me to call your husband?"

"No," she began, then, "yeah, call and tell him what's going on. I want to have the baby checked." Mohr asked her for the telephone number but she couldn't remember it. Mohr suddenly realized he had it on his desk. He started to rise.

"Don't leave me alone. I want someone to talk to."

Mohr motioned for John Drexler, one of the salesman standing in a knot on the sidewalk. Drexler was

Mohr's best friend and had recently witnessed the birth of his own child. Drexler knelt with Mohr. They checked the baby. She was quiet. Drexler ran his fingernail along her foot and on her palms for a reaction. The baby appeared slightly blue but seemed to be breathing fine. "Anybody got a blanket?" he hollered. Someone brought a pile of car polishing cloths which they piled around her.

Inside, Mohr checked his sales log for July 14 and found the name: Ray and Darci Pierce, 5202 Marquette. The telephone was listed. When he dialed it was busy. Half a minute later he dialed again. Still busy. Mohr called the operator and asked her to break in.

"Ray Pierce? This is Rob Mohr of Montano Acura. Darci's here at my dealership and she's had a baby, a baby girl."

"What's she doing there?" Ray asked. It seemed to Mohr an odd first question.

"I really don't know. I'm going to send her to the hospital in an ambulance. Why don't you go there and greet her? The ambulance hasn't arrived. Don't be in a big hurry and have an accident."

Out in the heat, still sitting in the Volkswagen, Darci was rambling on to Drexler. She and Ray were having problems, she said. She was running away to Santa Fe but had come back to Albuquerque because she only had four dollars and no luggage. On the way back, between Algodones and Albuquerque, she'd gone into labor. Drexler praised her for handling it all by herself.

Darci opened the Volkswagen door but remained seated on the ratty fake-sheepskin seat cover. The car's interior was red and worn. Drexler could see that Darci was barefoot and that her slip and thighs

61

were bloodstained. She told him about the planned inducement at 5:00 P.M. She was three weeks overdue, she said. She was afraid Ray would be upset with the damage to the fender.

Her story, at times, was disjointed. Details were missing or vague. But Drexler thought it natural, given the event. Darci then asked him to take a gun from the back seat and put it in the map pocket of the driver's door. She carried the gun because of a recent jail breakout of convicts. Drexler picked the gun up. It was solid black with a clip in the handle. It looked real but had no weight.

"Don't worry," Darci said. "It's a toy." She was still holding the baby tight to her bosom. When the paramedics arrived she had to be coaxed to let them take the baby. Darci got out of the car but appeared faint, and they laid her on the ground, giving her oxygen. She kept pushing the mask away to ask how the baby was, to ask Drexler for her wallet, and then to ask him to go with her to the University of New Mexico Hospital, where military dependents could be treated at no charge.

At about 4:30 P.M., Darci was placed in the ambulance with the baby in her arms. Drexler sat in front with the driver. As they drove away, Mohr rejoined the sales force in the showroom and began retelling the story. They all were proud of having played a minor role in a drama of childbirth. "The irony of somebody with nowhere to turn coming to a car dealership — for someone she trusts — when most people distrust and hate car dealers with a passion," Mohr said later. "It was great. If you can't trust your car salesman, who can you trust?" The buzz in the showroom lasted for the rest of the evening.

Before he went home, Mohr wanted to move the

Volkswagen. It looked like hell by the door. But when he glanced at the wet seat and his suit he said, "I'll move it tomorrow." He rolled up the window, locked the doors and took the keys inside for the night. He didn't notice on the passenger door what looked like "Help" scratched in the paint.

At Kirtland Air Force Base, Sam Ray was searching his mind, trying to think like a detective, to figure where his wife could be. He returned to the hospital and asked the women to check bathrooms again. Then someone remembered the insurance briefing at the recreation center.

"Great," he thought. "She's over there. I'll go pick her up and we'll all go home." At Que Pasa, Sam ran into a fellow airman who knew Cindy and was there with his wife. They had not seen her. At Sam's request, the wife checked the bathrooms.

Sam had known Cindy for eight years and never known her to be irresponsible. She had, in fact, called him at work so as not to put Jackie out. That was nearly two hours before. Cindy was very organized and kept to a schedule. "She wasn't the kind of person who would jump in a car with anybody and go for a joy ride."

Darci Pierce, holding a baby and wearing a Motherhood brand slip, arrived at the emergency room of the University of New Mexico Hospital at 4:45 P.M. on July 23, 1987. As the ambulance stopped, John Drexler helped get the stretcher out. He walked beside Darci as she was wheeled in. Ray Pierce was waiting, an expectant, relieved young father. Darci was holding the baby to her breast, and despite the mud and blood and sweat-soaked dress, Ray thought she looked happy, the happiest he'd ever seen her.

She handed the baby to him and cried. "I'm sorry. I was going to leave you but I couldn't."

Darci was checked for vital signs at 5:15 P.M. and Labor and Delivery was notified of a woman who had given birth outside the hospital. Dr. Susan Graham, the third-year resident physician, who had just begun her evening call, ordered the standard procedures: an examination in a delivery room to check for possible tears or a placenta still in place. "Send her up," were the instructions.

At 5:40 P.M., still holding the baby, Darci was wheeled into an elevator for a ride to the third floor. Ray and John Drexler walked with her. Janet Nalda-Lyons, a nurse on duty, directed the entourage through an electric door to Delivery Room 3, a twenty-by-twenty sterile surgical suite of tile and gleaming stainless steel used for the delivery of babies. They lifted Darci onto a delivery table, the ambulance crew left, and Ray and Drexler retreated down the hallway to talk. Mindful of trouble at the Pierce home, Drexler tried to assure Ray that children were joys. He talked about his own two daughters, and what fun Ray and Darci would have with their new one.

Dr. Graham asked a physician intern, Dr. Leigh Hoppe, to check Darci. Nurse Nalda-Lyons went in with her. Less than ten minutes later Nalda-Lyons returned to the nurse's station to report that when they began putting Darci's feet in stirrups she refused to be examined. She got angry, in fact. Dr. Hoppe asked Dr. Graham to come in and talk to her.

Darci was agitated when Dr. Graham walked in,

64

which struck the resident as unusual. Pregnant women usually become very calm as soon as the baby is out. She also noticed some odd details about Darci. She had the fullness of a postpartum body, and mud and blood-tinged stain on both legs up the mid-thigh. But there was no fresh blood on her buttocks or perineum. Her white slip had blood-tinged amniotic fluid all over the front, but there was no fresh bleeding or dark blood from the perineum, and no blood from the pubic bone to midthigh. On the other hand, her abdomen bulged from her pubis to her belly button and she looked like a woman who had just delivered—or a woman about 20 weeks pregnant.

"Mrs. Pierce, I'll have to examine you," she said. Dr. Graham was a forceful woman, tall and red-haired.

"No," said Darci. "I don't want anybody to put their fingers up there."

Dr. Graham told her of possible complications: internal bleeding, infection, a piece of the placenta left inside, cervical laceration. "It's really important that we have a look."

"No," she repeated. "I want the baby examined."

Dr. Graham reached over to touch Darci's tummy, to check that the uterus had become firm and clamped down. Darci rolled over, but not before the doctor noted its softness. That could mean the uterus was still quite boggy—which didn't make sense without blood on the perineum—or that there was no enlarged uterus. Dr. Graham didn't press the issue, but she had never seen a woman so agitated after delivery.

"Fine, when you're ready to be examined let me

know. In the meantime, we'll move you somewhere else."

At 6:00 P.M., Darci was wheeled out of Delivery and into Labor Room 2, a quiet room of mauve blinds and purple-flowered wallpaper. There was a private bath and through the blinds an east view of the mountains. In the hallway Dr. Graham turned to Ray who was wearing blue scrubs, and asked him to speak to his wife and explain the importance of the exam. Ray was upset about Darci's attitude and went inside to talk to her.

"Honey, be reasonable. It won't do either of you, you or the baby, any good if you are sick or dead. You could be bleeding internally. They have to find out now, so they can straighten it out." But Darci refused.

In the hallway, Dr. Graham was telling her attending physician about the strange behavior of Darci Pierce and of the baby that arrived with its umbilical cord unclamped. John Slocumb, a good-looking man with a salt-and-pepper beard, listened quietly, then stepped in to see Darci, and reiterate why an examination was needed. Ray stood by and listened. As Slocumb talked, Darci was trying to nurse the baby. She'd calmed down and looked very happy. Ray noticed around her neck the gold chain she always wore, but it was broken and dangling. The Krugerrand was missing. She didn't need another reason to get upset, so as she fussed with the baby, he slipped the chain off her neck and put it in his pocket.

Slocumb felt strange vibrations in the room. Darci's behavior with the baby seemed forced, acted, and aimed more at Ray than the baby. She cooed, but it didn't seem real. The baby would try to suck

66

and pop off. There was no real feeling between mother and daughter, it seemed to Slocumb. Ray, strangely, stood off in the corner, not really part of the scene.

Darci resisted Slocumb, too. She did not want to be admitted to the hospital, she said. She only wanted the baby checked. Perhaps at a later time she would allow herself to be examined. Slocumb left to perform an operation on a floor below. Ray then placed a call for Darci to Carol Raymond, one of Darci's friends in Portland.

"I've just delivered a baby girl, alongside the road," said Darci. The two women talked excitedly. Ray took the phone and asked Carol to convince Darci to be examined. Darci told Carol she wanted to sign a waiver to leave the hospital.

"Let us go now and I promise I'll go see a doctor tomorrow or Monday, whenever we can get it," she said.

"No, Darci," said Ray. "You're staying."

Seven

At 6:30 P.M., Sam Ray's police mind began to suspect the worst about Cindy's disappearance. That was the burden of a cop. He thought back to the places they'd lived since their marriage: San Antonio, in a rough section near the base; and Bitburg, Germany, at the height of European terrorism. Sam had been a gate guard in Germany, then a cop breaking up family and bar fights. It was depressing work. Then he was assigned to narcotics, even more depressing. When terrorism got bad he worked twelve-hour shifts carrying an M-16. He was often called out in the middle of the night and worried about Cindy. He could see the way men looked at her. She was cute and athletic. The base was a small town. There were more men than women. And there were men he didn't trust. He'd investigate them one day and the next see them at a snack shop, buying something from Cindy who clerked part-time.

Sam couldn't erase rape from his mind. He'd talked to Cindy about it, about what to do, what to avoid. If overpowered, with no options, go along peaceably. If confronted with a weapon, go along, try to gain the assailant's confidence, look for an advantage, a letting down of their guard, then head toward people.

At 6:30 P.M., still carrying Luke, Sam Ray went to the desk where he worked and faced the sergeant who had relieved him three hours earlier.

"Look, I need to file a report here. Cindy is not . . . she is nowhere to be found."

The sergeant told him to go home and wait for a call. As Sam Ray drove off the base, he was nagged by one question: Why would someone abduct a pregnant woman?

At 7:00 P.M., Nalda-Lyons took Amanda Michelle from Darci and gave her to a nurse from the nursery. The baby still was covered with vernix and patches of blood and mucus. The nurse weighed her, cleaned and dried her, trimmed her umbilical cord and wrapped her in a fresh blanket. She brought Amanda back to Darci.

At 8:00 P.M., Sister Rosemary Homrich, the midwife, arrived at the hospital where three of her patients were in labor. On Labor and Delivery, a nurse told her in a whisper, "There's something strange here. Someone came in and claims that she had a baby, and it isn't hers." The patient was catty-corner across the hall. Shortly afterward, Sam Ray called Sister Rosemary.

"Cindy's not home," he said. "Was she sent to the hospital for any reason?"

"No," said the sister.

"Have you seen her?"

"No, I'm sorry." With three patients in labor, Sister Rosemary went about her business and never mentioned Sam's call to anyone.

Downstairs in admitting, meanwhile, clerks were catching up with the news of the baby's arrival. An emergency room clerk called admitting to log in the baby born outside the hospital. The baby already was in the nursery, she said. The admitting clerk, Kelly Lyden, jotted down some data, then turned to type the baby's name into the hospital computer. "Pierce baby," she typed. Because no one knew the baby's actual time of birth, Lyden logged it as the time of hospital arrival, sometime between 4:30 and 5:00 P.M. She chose the middle ground, 4:45 P.M. — 15 minutes before Darci Pierce's scheduled labor induction.

As Lyden typed the information, something nagged her about the name. As she made out the little card for the baby, it clicked. She felt a chill — the week-old scene flashed in her mind. Mrs. Pierce, the surrogate mother and the husband who didn't know. Lyden had to calm herself before speaking to a colleague.

"There's no way that this is legally a Pierce child," she said. Her coworker called Labor and Delivery.

"This sounds like a real stupid question," she began. "Does Mrs. Pierce look like she had a baby?"

"There's no way that this woman had a baby," came the reply.

"Then this baby came from a surrogate mother," said the admitting clerk.

"Where's mommy?" Luke asked as Sam Ray put him to bed. The boy hadn't left his father's arms in five hours, since his mother had disappeared. Now, in the loneliness of his bed, he asked for her.

70

"Mommy's lost," Sam said, choking at the words. "You can't have Mommy tonight. But you can have Daddy." They hugged and kissed and Luke lay down.

Out in the living room of the trailer, Sam picked up the phone again. He called Jackie Bloomfield. "What was Cindy wearing?" She told him, a polka dot blouse and blue pants. Soon the word spread through the Mormon community. Sam's LDS home teacher called, asking if he could help. A half hour later the ward bishop knocked on the door. He was there to spend the night with Sam. Sam tried to send him away. "If you think you're man enough to make me leave, you can try," he said. Together they went over Cindy's day again.

"She either couldn't come home or didn't want to," Sam said. But they hadn't argued. The baby was okay. Maybe she was depressed and took off. The bishop called other men in the church and they checked every possibility they could think of, the airlines, the bus depot, car rental desks. Everywhere they called they asked, "Have you seen a nine-month pregnant woman heading for Utah?" They called every hospital in town. "Is Cindy Ray there, in labor?"

With dread, Sam called home. He felt responsible. That was his role in their marriage, to provide and shelter. Cindy had always looked up to him—physically and spiritually. Neither family had heard from her.

At 10:00 P.M. Dr. Slocumb reappeared on Labor and Delivery and was told about Darci Pierce's encounter with the clerk a week before. He entered the labor room, asked Ray to leave, and confronted

71

Darci with the suspicion that the baby was not hers.

"You'll have to prove to me that you're the mother," he said.

"You're right," Darci said. "I'm not the mother."

Twenty minutes later, Dr. Slocumb emerged from the room with news that Darci had agreed to be examined. The baby was in fact a surrogate, she told him. She had paid ten thousand dollars for her. The mother was a woman Darci met outside an abortion clinic in Portland, Oregon. She had dissuaded her from an abortion, offering instead to buy the baby. The woman had delivered the baby in Santa Fe with the help of a midwife, and Darci had gone to pick her up there. The midwife had splashed blood and amniotic fluid on Darci to make it look real. She couldn't remember the midwife's name.

Slocumb thought Darci was protecting the midwife from prosecution. Her story was vague in places but convincing. He believed it more than the original roadside story. She'd agreed to be examined on the condition that Ray not be told the results. She didn't want him to know the baby was not his.

With Dr. Slocumb watching, Dr. Graham began the exam. As Darci lay on the table her abdomen looked round between the belly button and pubic bone, exactly the look of a twenty-week pregnant woman or someone who had just given birth. But when she pressed on the bulge there was nothing there. It was soft and depressible and not tender. No fundus was palpable.

In the pelvic exam, there was no blood on the perineum and no blood in the vaginal vault. The cervix was nulliparous—it had never given birth—and the os was closed. The uterus was small, firm and nontender. In short, Darci was not pregnant and had not given birth, although she had taken on the cursory signs of a woman who had just given birth. Her blood pressure was slightly elevated on her arrival, the abdomen was enlarged and her nipples were slightly darkened.

Darci told the doctors that she had pretended to be pregnant for nine months and had moved her stomach muscles so that her family could feel the baby move. She had attended Lamaze classes with a friend, and had kept a suitcase ready for her "delivery." But she was infertile, she said. The surrogate mother had been arranged months before and the midwife had called just that morning. Dr. Slocumb knew several midwives in Santa Fe and tried to pin down where the delivery might have taken place. Darci was too vague about the location and about her own treatment for infertility.

At about 10:45 P.M. Darci asked to see the baby again and Nalda-Lyon agreed to wheel her down to the nursery. Ray, who had been waiting alone in the staff lounge all this time, walked along, through the huge doors with the glass top and steel bottom, through the postpartum area, to Newborn Nursery A. They stood at the basinette, commenting on who Amanda looked like. Darci saw a little of Ray in her nose. Ray thought she looked like Darci. Darci apologized to him for her earlier snit. "I'm sorry Ray, for the argument, for the way I acted. You were right about the exam." They stood in the sterile room and warmed at the sight of life just beginning. The baby's head was perfectly formed, round and soft. What neither of them knew was that the roundness was a clue to the truths that lay hidden behind Darci's story.

At the nurse's station, meanwhile, a frantic effort

73

was underway to call midwives in Santa Fe. What midwife would leave an umbilical cord unclamped? Drs. Slocumb and Graham couldn't decide what to do with Darci. He wanted her admitted to gynecology, with a visit by a psychiatrist. She wanted Darci admitted to the mental health center. "We have no idea where the baby came from," said Dr. Graham. The hospital's social worker, who had been called in to talk to Darci, had concluded, "You have a pathological liar here." They agreed to notify Child Protective Services in the morning, admit Darci, and not release her or the baby. They would try to solve the mystery in the morning. Slocumb went home.

At 11 o'clock, the shift changed on Labor and Delivery, bringing on duty Elisabeth Koehler, the charge nurse. A tall, willowy woman with a wild streak of cold steel, she was dressed in hospital blues. She was briefed, first, about the woman in Labor Room 2 with the unbelievable story. Nalda-Lyons introduced Koehler to Darci and Ray. The two women had something in common, said the departing nurse. They had both been to Africa. Darci had been an exchange student, and Koehler had traveled there twice in the last year. Ray mentioned the missing Krugerrand, and Darci asked Koehler to call the Albuquerque Ambulance to see if they had found it. It wasn't the monetary value, she said, but the sentiment. She also wanted to find her dress.

There was only one other patient on the floor at the time, so Koehler assigned her to the second nurse. Koehler took Darci's case. She began with vital signs. Temperature 37.7 degrees, heartbeat 112. Blood pressure 138 over 86. Darci was calm, relaxed and happy over the baby. She was hooked to an IV. Darci asked Koehler when she would be transferred to a regular hospital room, or to postpartum. Koehler told her not for at least another hour.

Sometime after 11:00 P.M. Sam Ray called Sister Rosemary at the hospital again. "I'm really, really worried. Cindy hasn't come home. Are you sure she isn't there?"

"I'm sure, Sam," she said. "Has she ever done this before, you know, gone someplace and not told you?"

"Absolutely not. I picked up the baby, the baby is sleeping, the baby is fine, but I haven't heard anything from Cindy. I called out the security police basewide and city police to look for her."

"I really don't know what else to do," said Sister Rosemary. "But I'll tell the doctors and see if they have any suggestions."

About midnight, she did mention it to Graham and the news reverberated from one end of the hall to the other. "One of my patients is missing," she said. "Cindy Ray had been in for a nonstress test, the test had been reactive, and she'd left the base ob/gyn clinic around 3:00 P.M. Cindy was thirty-seven weeks pregnant."

A sickening dawning came over the floor. In a group sitting around the lounge, Nurse Trish Upton turned to Dr. Graham and said, "Susan, I think you better call the police." At midnight on July 23, 1987, Dr. Graham dialed them. She also paged the pediatrician on call and asked him to reexamine Amanda Michelle with these questions in mind: How old was the baby? With no molding or overriding of sutures—a perfectly round head—how was it born? Could this baby have come through a birth canal as Darci had claimed, or was she delivered abdominally?

Sister Rosemary called Sam Ray and asked him Cindy's blood type, a question he thought odd at the time. Dr. Graham then asked the hospital security to post a guard on Labor and Delivery, to keep Darci and the baby in custody until police arrived. Two guards arrived within fifteen minutes. Down the hall the three wooden doors to the nurseries were secured. Amanda Michelle Pierce — or whoever she was — was locked inside.

Eight

In the minutes after midnight, on Friday July 24, news of the newborn began to awaken Albuquerque's law enforcement apparatus. At 12:30 A.M. the police department operations desk called Kirtland's law enforcement desk to inform them that a newborn infant and a female who claimed to be the mother had arrived at UNM hospital and that the woman's story smelled. Sergeant J. Scott Wilson of the Albuquerque Police Department was dispatched to the hospital to investigate this "suspicious situation."

At 1:00 A.M. Ray and Darci asked to see the baby in the nursery again, so Koehler accompanied them. They again said how much Amanda looked like them and both beamed. At 1:25 A.M. Darci went back to her room and encouraged Ray to go home and get some sleep. He drove west on Lomas and north on Interstate 25, to Montano Acura, to check on the Volkswagen. It was parked in the eerie light of night security lamps, and Ray stood there with a security guard and checked it out. He saw the broken fender, the grass and dirt stuffed in the wheel wells. Then he went home to feed the dogs, let them out and sleep, unaware of the commotion beginning at the hospital over his new baby.

The pediatrician reported that the baby had not been born through a birth canal. In the nursery, Dr. Slocumb, who had been called in, looked at the dress that the baby had been wrapped in. Cedar twigs were stuck to it. Darci's Motherhood-brand slip had amniotic fluid stains but no blood stains. Darci's second story was a lie, too.

At 1:23 A.M., Sergeant Wilson arrived and talked to Slocumb and Graham. He was told that Darci Pierce had arrived with a baby, covered with blood, but that she had not delivered a baby or even been pregnant. Wilson radioed dispatch to send a squad car to search the Volkswagen. Then he filed a report: "Due to the fact that writer could not determine where the baby Pierce . . . had come from, and that writer learned that a pregnant female was reported missing from Kirtland Air Force Base, writer notified violent crimes detectives." The "suspicious situation" had become a possible violent crime. Slocumb and Graham were now worried about the missing mother.

"One of our patients is missing," Slocumb told Darci. "We're quite concerned. We want to know if you, in any way, took this baby from somebody else."

Darci looked him in the eye. "No."

They asked for more details of her surrogate. Darci answered calmly, patiently, propped up on her bed.

While living in Oregon, she said, she had found a woman named Sherry Martin outside an abortion clinic and had talked her into keeping her baby. Darci said she paid Sherry Martin ten thousand dollars for the baby. Shortly after arriving in Albuquerque in May, Darci had arranged for a midwife in

78

Santa Fe, paying her two thousand dollars. Mrs. Martin had come to Santa Fe two months ago and the midwife had called Darci periodically to report on her condition. Yesterday, the midwife had called and said Mrs. Martin was in labor. Darci drove to Santa Fe. The midwife's yard had no sidewalk and was muddy. She walked through the mud to get to the house and when she walked in, the midwife handed her the baby wrapped in a towel. She unwrapped the baby and Darci took off her dress for a wrapping. The midwife then poured a bucket of blood from the delivery onto Darci to make it look like she had delivered the baby herself. Darci then drove back to Albuquerque but had an accident en route, skidding off the highway and hitting the right rear against an embankment. She had stopped at the Acura dealer because she wanted it to appear to her husband that this was her baby.

During the entire story, Darci remained calm, unconcerned with the skeptical questions being posed to her. Slocumb and Graham then took a break, and Dr. George Leiby, a psychiatric resident, and Nurse Koehler, took a turn with her. She again went into great detail about how she had obtained the baby. They talked for nearly an hour, and she remained steadfast about the surrogate. At 2:30 A.M. Leiby left the room and Darci asked for an update on the baby. Koehler checked and reported everything fine in the nursery.

Darci told Koehler of her attempts to get pregnant, the molar pregnancy, the D&C, the loss she felt. Ray didn't want her to get pregnant, she said, but she wanted a baby. She felt infertile, and because she was adopted, wanted a baby that looked like her. "I was adopted when I was eleven days old," she said. "And every year, on my birthday, or eleven days later, I always think about a little yellow outfit I had on when I was adopted." Darci said she was really uncomfortable not knowing who her parents were or why they had given her up. Koehler said she understood; her own sister had been adopted and shared some of the same feelings. Darci opened up even more to the nurse, telling her about her family, the dad she liked, the brother she didn't.

She also detailed her pseudopregnancy: she had gained thirty-eight pounds in the nine months, and her uterus had grown. The areola of her breasts darkened and enlarged, she had morning sickness, and she couldn't eat pizza the entire time. She claimed she even made her blood pressure drop the day she was supposed to be in labor because she knew a pregnant woman's blood pressure changed then.

"A woman can fake a pregnancy," she said. "You know how powerful the mind can be."

"Everything you tell me is very convincing," Koehler said. "The only problem with this story is that the baby never came out of your uterus."

"I know it didn't come out of my uterus, but it's mine. I paid ten thousand dollars for it."

Koehler also couldn't believe that any midwife in New Mexico would go to such extremes for two thousand dollars. "I find that hard to believe," she said.

"Maybe it wasn't a certified midwife. I never saw any credentials." Darci had an answer for everything.

"Darci, you know, things just are getting a little bit confusing around here. There's a missing woman in Albuquerque who is term, and we don't know where she is. We don't know where the baby is, either. And frankly, it's not looking too good as far as the surrogate mother story goes."

Darci said she knew nothing of a missing woman. She also didn't know that police were hovering outside her room. All questions were put to her by nurses or doctors.

At 3:00 A.M. Ray Pierce was awakened at home by a nurse who told him the baby was anemic and that he needed to come down right away. While he was en route, Slocumb, Leiby and Koehler went back to Darci's room. They were angry, and growing frantic. A woman was missing, perhaps dead or bleeding to death. They wanted police to begin checking roads in the mountains but they were getting little response from the patrolmen at the hospital. "I had to do something to find where that mother was," recalled Slocumb. "She could be close to death." He confronted Darci again.

"Do you know Cindy Ray from Kirtland?"

"I've never heard of her," she said. She was calm. "I don't know anything about her. I'm sorry she's missing."

"Do you know any pregnant women in town?"

"Oh, two or three that I've met at the laundromat or somewhere. I've got no friends who are pregnant."

"There might be a mother out there dying, and we need to know where she is," Slocumb pressed.

Darci did not respond.

At 3:30 A.M., Slocumb, Graham, Leiby and two or three policemen met with Ray Pierce in a small conference room near the entrance to Labor and Delivery. As he sat at the table, he was told that the baby was not his and that his wife had, in fact, not delivered her. Ray was crushed.

"No. I don't believe it." His face fell, and everyone

81

watching knew he couldn't have been acting.

Ray was told about the missing pregnant woman and their concern for her. He then was told Darci's story and asked if he knew of any way she could have raised ten thousand dollars to buy a baby. She had claimed it came from a trust fund.

Ray knew of no trust fund and no way she could have earned that amount of money. Once, he said, in a fight, she told him she could earn all the money she ever needed as a prostitute. If she had ten thousand dollars, her husband said to the gathering, that must have been the source.

"Do you keep any weapons at home?"

"Yes," said Ray, and told them about the .22-caliber Ruger they'd acquired because there were "too many crazy people in Albuquerque." They kept it in his underwear drawer, and the clip for it in another drawer.

"Do you know where the gun is?"

"As far as I know, it's at home, unless Darci has done something crazy."

"Was Darci squeamish in any way, at the sight of blood?"

"No." When she was an exchange student in South Africa, she had some kind of experience in orthopedic surgery, he remembered. She had also dressed deer with her father.

By the time the questions were over, Ray Pierce was empty. He'd thought he was a father. He thought his wife had been pregnant. She had lied to him for ten months. He felt guilty. Maybe if he hadn't been so busy, and had gone with Darci to the doctor's, all this wouldn't have happened. If he had spent more time with her, maybe he would have known this wasn't his baby. He thought back to

Portland and the stillborn story that Darci told. He asked about the missing woman. He was so shaken he asked the psychiatrist to stay with him.

At 3:50 A.M., Kirtland's law enforcement desk put the puzzle of the two military dependents together and contacted the Office of Special Investigations. Twenty-five minutes later, at 4:15 A.M., the first OSI officer, Steve Coppinger, arrived at the hospital and talked to Sergeant Wilson.

At 5:00 A.M. the telephone rang at the home of Detective Tom Craig of the Albuquerque Police Department Violent Crimes Bureau. He had just crawled into bed after an all-night homicide chase, a shooting at Gerard and Central in which a motorcycle rider was shot off his bike. The rider had gotten into a shouting match with a passing car and they'd dragged along Central, heading West, shouting drunken obscenities at each other. At the corner of Gerard, a passenger in the car reached an arm out the window, pointed a gun over the top of the car and fired. The motorcyclist caught the bullet square in the head and sprawled dead on the boulevard.

The wake-up call was from Sergeant Archie Lueras, asking Craig to head for UNM, Labor and Delivery. All they knew was that a woman had arrived with a newborn baby, and that a pregnant woman from the air base was missing. Hospital personnel suspected a connection. Craig crawled out, dressed and headed for the hospital. He arrived at 6:15 A.M., met Lueras and OSI agents Coppinger and Mike Thyssen. Coppinger briefed Craig on the disappearance of Cindy Lynn Ray and noted that Darci Pierce was the wife of an airman, as well.

In her room, meanwhile, Darci was repeating her story for Slocumb, Graham and Koehler. But they

83

had decided by this time to use whatever means they could, including deception, to find Cindy Ray. "The feeling changed from one of loving support to exactly what Darci was doing to us—a front with other intentions," said Slocumb. "In a sense we agreed to lie to her, and tell her we were her friend." Because Darci did not relate well to either Slocumb or the visibly angry Graham, Koehler was chosen to befriend her, to gain her confidence in whatever way she could, for the sake of the missing mother.

From 5:40 A.M. to 6:45 A.M. Darci rested, dozing on and off. She asked Koehler if she'd be able to go home in the morning.

"Not in the next two hours," Koehler said. "We're still concerned about who the baby's mom is, and where the baby's mom is."

Darci said she wanted to be home before noon because Ray was coming in at noon and she didn't want him to know anything about the surrogate. Ray's parents also were coming later in the day, she said, and she'd like to be there, even without the baby. She'd tell them the baby was anemic and had to stay in the hospital for the weekend. Ray would take his parents sightseeing around New Mexico and then she'd be willing to talk to anyone or go anywhere for an interview about the surrogate.

At 6:45 A.M., Ray Pierce was questioned again, this time by Detective Craig, OSI agent Coppinger and Dr. Slocumb. They set up a tape recorder and began with the obvious questions about Darci's pregnancy.

"Did she look pregnant?" asked Craig.

"Yes, as a matter of fact, I'd say she still does look pregnant," said Ray.

"It's true," injected Slocumb. "She's been able to

change her body such that even our nurses felt that she was twenty weeks pregnant when she came in."

"Well, we're concerned about a mother out there some place," said Craig.

"I am too," said Ray. "I didn't know she'd do this. I don't know how far she'd go. And that's what scares me so much."

He told them about lunch at home and told them about the cars. "I wish I had known this was coming up. I wouldn't have bought [the Mustang]. It's obvious we are going to need the money now."

"Had she been seeing a doctor or anything at the base?"

"I was under the impression she was. She told me last night that she hadn't been."

"You never went with her any place?"

"No. Obviously, I should have. I just, I was just under the impression or something that women can handle it on their own. And I couldn't see taking an afternoon off just to take her to the hospital, the doctor."

"Did you ever know her to have any type of depression or unusual behavior?" asked Lueras.

"Shortly after we met, she mentioned that at one point she had seriously considered suicide. I remember the odd feeling it gave me, like, wow, what kind of person is this? I thought I knew this person better than that. And then before I left for basic, when she was on maternity leave, she came up to her mom and I one day, all upset because everybody at work was expecting her to have had the baby then. And she was going on about how she fabricated this and she didn't want us to tell anybody and on and on."

"She fabricated what?" Craig asked.

"She told them that she was pregnant earlier. They

expected her to be due in, say, September. And at this point we believed she was only, say, three or four months pregnant. That was our knowledge—our families'. And the deadline came up for her to tell them at work. They were wondering where the baby was, and there's no baby."

"Haven't you kind of been wondering yourself?"

"Yes sir, big time. See, when we left home to move here, which was in May there was a question in everybody's mind whether she should even attempt to make the trip. It was a seventeen-hundred-mile trip and I didn't want to get half way here and her go into labor. So we had her check with her doctor . . . I was going to make sure that she checked with him. I don't know what I did, but one way or the other I believed that the doctor said it was okay. Now I'm expecting the baby in the middle of May, and it didn't come. So now it's overdue, and she goes to a doctor—so I believe—and she says, according to an ultrasound, it's not that far along. So that was plausible . . . she hasn't been regular since we lost our last baby a year and a half ago. Then last week it was going to be induced, and we got there and she had apparently told the girl down in admitting to tell me that the doctor had to cancel . . . I knew there was something odd because she had kind of a terrified look on her face. So I, everybody, believed that we were going in to have the baby. We got ourselves into the car and all that garbage and we came down and the girl at the desk told us the doctor cancelled . . . So here we are."

"What happened a year and a half ago?"

"She was actually pregnant and she got what's called hydatidiform, which is a cancer on the placenta, and it killed the baby in about the sixth

86

month. And she aborted. Well, it was tough for all of us. Apparently, it was tougher for her than any of us ever realized."

"Who are your close friends?" Coppinger asked.

"Well, my parents are supposed to be here today or tomorrow. They were in Minnesota visiting relatives and they're stopping back here to see our dream kid."

Fearing the worst for Cindy Ray, the cops then began asking Ray about Darci's ability to kill. Did Darci have any medical training that he was aware of? What about her hunting experience?

"She's got a lot of hunting experience. She knows how to handle a rifle real well. Or, at least so I understand. I've never seen her do it."

"Have you ever seen Darci push anybody or be aggressive physically with anyone?"

"No."

Craig asked Ray, "Have you got any questions?" He paused a long time.

"You guys gotten any leads on the disappearance of that woman, or where the baby is from?"

"Not yet," said Craig.

"I'll do what I can," said Ray. "I'll try to help you out as much as I can because we've got to find out who that baby belongs to."

Nine

Friday, July 24 dawned just as warm and muggy as the previous day. It was 71 degrees at 6:49 A.M. and in his trailer, in a bed he had not slept alone in for four years, Sam Ray woke fitfully. At 7:00 A.M. a fellow cop from the base came to keep him company, relieving the bishop. Luke was sleeping, unaware that his mother had not come home and would not be there to dress him.

Sam called Cindy's Tupperware manager to ask again the questions that nagged him, to fill the silence. "Where is she? Is she suffering? Was it something I did?" He couldn't get the fear of rape out of his head. During his conversation with the manager Sam learned the news of a woman at the hospital with a baby that wasn't hers. Suddenly it dawned on him, a sickening, fateful realization of what might have happened, the reason Cindy was missing.

"They wanted the baby," he thought.

By now the news hounds of Albuquerque were beginning to pick up scents of the story. There was activity at the hospital, involving a baby. At the very least, a woman coming to a car dealer with a baby was news. Sources at the police department began their usual leaks. The first inquiries were coming as

88

Dr. Slocumb and nurse Koehler went into Darci's room, removed the IV from her arm and told her they were taking her down the hall to talk to some people.

At 7:30 A.M., seated in a wheelchair, Darci Pierce was rolled into the 3-East conference room. Five or six men were there, including Craig and Coppinger, by now the lead detectives on the case. She was wheeled to a table where Craig had set up a tape recorder. He advised her of her rights.

"We know the baby is not your baby. So we suspect that a crime has been committed. I want you to understand that you have the right to remain silent . . ." He read the Miranda card and asked her to initial it.

"Am I being arrested for something here?" she said.

"We're investigating a situation," he repeated. "You have a baby that doesn't belong to you. We want to talk to you about it and get it straightened out . . ."

Darci pointed to the tape recorder. "Can we do something off the record first, before I do any of this?" Craig snapped the recorder off and Darci asked what the law was in New Mexico regarding purchasing babies from surrogate mothers. Craig replied that he could not advise her on those matters. The recorder was turned back on as she signed the form. Craig wasted no time.

"I guess my first question, then, Darci, would be where did the baby come from?"

"A girl named Sherry Martin."

"Where can we find Sherry Martin?"

"At this point I don't know."

"Where did you meet Sherry Martin?"

"In Portland." There was a pause. "Do you want to know exacts? Okay, at the Lovejoy Abortion Clinic, Twenty-fifth and Lovejoy."

"What were you doing yesterday afternoon? Let's start at noontime."

"Getting in my car and driving toward Santa Fe."

"What were you going to do in Santa Fe?"

"I was going to pick up my baby."

"How did you arrange to take custody of this baby?"

"It was, uh, arrived by agreement between she and I."

"Was there money discussed?"

"No comment."

"Alright, I understand that you were supposed to pay her ten thousand dollars, is that right? For this baby?"

"No comment."

"Where would you have gotten ten thousand dollars?"

"No comment."

"Okay, so at noon yesterday you were driving to Santa Fe, right? What happened from there?"

"I went to Santa Fe . . . I believe it was a midwife's house. I took the baby from her."

"Were you there for the delivery?"

"No, I was not."

"How did you get blood all over you?"

"She did it . . . put the blood on my clothing and stuff."

"Why?"

"Because we had to stage some form of a scene to make it look as though they were actually mine."

Darci admitted she was not pregnant but told Ray she was, "because I wanted to have a baby . . . He

90

thinks I had a baby yesterday. As far as he knows I have carried that baby for the past nine months, I gave birth to that baby, and that child is his, biologically and any other way." She said she had brought the baby to the hospital "to complete the scenario. What kind of concerned parents could deliver their child by themselves and not go to a hospital and have the baby checked? I had to establish with people here that the baby was indeed mine and that it had been indeed born, you know. I stopped at the Acura dealership because there's a salesman out there . . . he was very personable. He wished us well with the birth of our baby. So I pulled in there to get some help, to be brought here."

"What time did you leave Santa Fe?"

"I left Santa Fe about, gosh, I don't wear a watch. I don't keep track of time, but I would say around four, maybe before."

Craig thought to himself: Darci was a good liar. It was more than an hour's drive from Santa Fe to Albuquerque, and she had arrived at the car dealer's before 4:30. She also said she had flown Sherry Martin from Portland, Oregon to Santa Fe; Craig knew that all major airlines flew to Albuquerque, not Santa Fe. She also claimed not to know the midwife's name, or the address, or even the directions. "I didn't write them down. I went from remembering them and . . . I could not repeat them exact now."

Darci was looking at Craig directly, intently, and the hairs of his neck were rising. This was a demonic liar, he thought. When he spoke, his voice had a hard edge.

"I'll tell you what. None of this makes sense, okay? As far as we're concerned, none of this makes any sense. As far as this baby is concerned. Do you

91

know a lady by the name of Cindy Ray?"

"I do not."

"Cindy Ray is missing and she was due to have a baby. Do you know where Cindy Ray is?"

"I do not." Darci was looking Craig in the eye.

"Is this Cindy Ray's baby?"

"No."

Craig paused a moment while others asked questions, then he started again, his tone unbelieving.

"How did you pay for plane tickets from Portland, Oregon to Albuquerque for this woman on an airman's salary? Where did you get your money? What airline did you use? How did you pay for it? Darci had some answer for everything.

"Describe Sherry Martin to me."

"She looks a lot like me as far as coloring. She also had dark hair. She was thin, athletic looking. I only saw her once when I first met with her."

"How long did you talk to her?"

"Hmmm, I don't know exactly, but after I finished talking with her I had lunch with a good friend of mine, so we completed talking at 12:30."

"You made all these arrangements by 12:30 one day in one meeting?"

"Pretty much all of it."

Craig couldn't believe Darci's chutzpah. The name Charles Manson rose in his mind. Darci went on to explain her accident "scene" on Interstate 25. "I pulled off and I allowed the car to slide so that the back end hit part of the embankment. I let it fishtail. There was nobody on the road. It was getting toward evening." All the cops knew that Interstate 25 from Albuquerque to Santa Fe was extremely heavy with traffic at that time of day. Coppinger asked her about the mud and dirt on her clothing.

92

"Whatever was on the dress, [the midwife] put it on there. The whole scene was supposed to be as though I had delivered the baby at the side of the car. It's hard to get blood on your dress if some dirt doesn't stick to it, if you're delivering at the side of the car. She understood that that's what it needed to look like. I was too busy enjoying this baby to pay mind to really what she was doing."

"I don't believe you one little bit," Coppinger snapped. "We have a pregnant woman that's missing and you're coming up with a story that has all these holes in it and we're concerned. I've got some concerns for your hands. There's something under your fingernails there. The story of wrecking a car and then it not being wrecked . . . your story's not very good."

"We're all real concerned," Craig interrupted. "We're worried about this other gal. We need to find her and we think you know where she is."

"I don't," said Darci, facing him. "I don't know who she is or where she is or what has happened with her. I don't know."

"Your story is never going to hold water, okay?" snarled Craig. "Never. It is so punched full of holes that it's just, it's silly. Everybody in this room has seen through your story already. We all know what happened. We just don't know where this gal is." There was a pause. "You do know where she is."

"I don't know," said Darci. "I do not know who she is or where she is."

There was quiet in the room as the cops considered strategy. Sergeant Lueras asked again about the accident. Coppinger about the gold necklace. Craig about Sherry Martin. They got nowhere.

"We've been sitting here listening to so much crap

93

now for the last thirty minutes and in the meantime there's a gal out there that's missing and you're not helping us at all," said Craig. "You've lied to us ever since you've sat down here. You've been lying to your husband for years now. When are you going to start telling the truth so we can get this straightened out?"

Darci looked him in the eye. "I've not been lying to my husband for years now and I have not been lying to you."

"Everything that you have told us here is the truth? Is that what you are saying?"

"Yes."

"Yeah, and you expect us to believe it?"

Coppinger began a softer approach. "We understand . . ." And then the tape ran out. The interview went on in the same frustrating vain. Craig, his eyes bloodshot, his temper short from lack of sleep, grilled Darci. Coppinger tried to soothe her, patting her hand. It was the beginning of a good cop-bad cop set up.

"You could see she was lying," said Craig. "It got kinda spooky. You couldn't sit in there and know what we knew. All you had to do was put two and two together." Several times Craig turned and raised an eyebrow at Archie Lueras. He was thinking, "God she's cold."

At about 9:30 A.M. they took a break. By now the news media was crawling all over the hospital. The administration dragged Craig away to talk. They wanted to know whether Darci was a patient of theirs, or a prisoner of his.

94

Ten

Darci was wheeled to a smaller lounge across the hall from the interrogation room, and she sat there with Koehler and Dr. Graham, who maintained an exterior calm while fretting about the missing Cindy Ray. It was now midmorning following her disappearance, and their medical minds raced at the possibilities. She could still be alive, but bleeding to death.

Darci seemed more anxious and puzzled and began asking about the baby. Koehler thought she might be on the verge of breaking and thought of a way to soften her.

"Do you want me to get the baby for you?" Darci said yes. Koehler went to the nursery, carried the baby to Darci and gently laid it in her arms.

"What a beautiful baby," Darci said. She stroked its head, talking softly. "This baby makes me feel like someone for the first time in my life." She mentioned, again, that her own mother had left her when she was eleven days old and that it hurt her deeply.

"I'm afraid the same thing will happen to this baby," Koehler said. "How do you think the mother of this baby would feel right now?"

Darci didn't answer. She stroked the baby girl's head. Koehler's intuition told her to turn up the psychological heat.

"Darci, we can't just keep the baby in the nursery forever wondering who the mother is. She'll probably go up for adoption if we can't find out." She paused. "Do you think something might have happened to the mother of this baby?" There was another pause. She could see Darci shifting, weakening. When she began to speak it was in a different, less defiant tone.

"I know it's not my baby," she said. "I know I probably will never get to keep it." Darci grew visibly upset, and a distant look came into her eye.

"There's something there," she said. "But I can't bring it up."

"What is it?"

"I know it's there, but I can't bring it up."

Dr. Teresita McCarty, a resident psychiatrist who had slipped into the room, asked Darci, "Have you ever forgotten anything before?"

"Yes," she said. Once, in sixth grade, when she was twelve, she was grading papers for her favorite teacher. Two girls were taunting her through the window of the door. And then the glass was broken. "They said I did it, but I don't remember."

Dr. McCarty puzzled over her answer. Darci continued to caress the baby.

"Do you have any idea where this baby's mother could be?" Koehler pressed.

"Maybe something terrible has happened. Maybe I did something terrible. But I can't bring it up."

"The mother of this baby is out there somewhere and needs help," said Koehler.

Inside Darci's head, pictures started flooding in, terrible, terrible things about driving in the woods and the baby and another person.

"I'm afraid I'll lose Ray," she said suddenly. "I'm afraid they'll handcuff me and take me to jail. I don't want to lie to my husband."

"You've been lying to him for months," said Koehler.

Darci suddenly handed the baby back and asked Koehler to return her to the nursery. After she departed, Darci looked at Dr. Graham and apologized for "not being nice" when she first arrived at the hospital. Koehler reappeared.

"Where is the baby's mother?" she said.

"Well, maybe there's something there, but I can't bring it up."

"Do you think you could live with whatever it is that you can't bring up?"

A tear ran down Darci's cheek. Then another.

"Maybe I've done something terrible."

She asked to speak to the policeman in the beige pants. She asked Koehler and Graham to leave the small room. They went into the hall and asked for Steve Coppinger. Darci wanted to see him alone. Coppinger was in another room on the phone to his office when his pager went off. The message: contact Agent Thyssen in the hall. It was 10:15 A.M. Coppinger went into the room with Darci. He wanted another female present because of Air Force rules, but Darci wouldn't talk that way. Darci told him, no notes, no tape recorder. Coppinger asked Koehler and Graham to stand right outside the door.

"Darci had obviously been crying and she began

97

to tell me that things were starting to come back to her."

"Terrible, terrible things are starting to come back to me about a woman," Darci said, pausing. "I had been out to the base." That was a direct contradiction to her earlier statement. "Yes I was out at the base. I went to the hospital and talked to a woman. She got in the car. The gun wasn't real. It was just a toy. It wasn't a real gun."

Darci was crying, her story disjointed. "And then I was in the car and we were driving. Oh God, what I've done. I could see the Monzano fenceline." She was crying hard now. Sobbing. "What have I done? What will happen to me? Oh God, Oh God, Steve, I killed her. What's going to happen to me? What will my family think? What's Ray going to think? The gun wasn't real."

"OK, Darci, I understand. The gun wasn't real. Go on." Coppinger's thoughts raced ahead. He knew that time was running out for Cindy Ray, if she were alive at all. Dr. Slocumb had said that was unlikely, but possible. Coppinger tried to calm her. He got her some apple juice and she took a sip.

"Will you take me to where the woman is?"

Darci nodded yes. Coppinger wanted to bolt from the room.

"Are you going to tell the others?" she asked.

Coppinger said something noncommittal.

"You won't make me stay there if I take you there, will you?"

Coppinger agreed, but it was important to find Cindy Ray. Fifteen minutes after he entered the room, he raced out.

"Go back in. She's confessed," he said to Koehler.

He turned to Craig. "Can you get your car?" He alerted the base. Koehler and Graham entered the room where Darci was sitting in the wheelchair crying. She turned to the nurse who had befriended her through the night and said through tears, "Elisabeth, I killed her. My mother is going to hate me. My mother is going to hate me."

Craig still thought there was hope of finding Cindy Ray alive, but not much. He was worried that some animal might have found her body; it had also rained the night before, making evidence-gathering tougher. He wanted to race to the scene. "Let's get out of here," he said to Koehler. "Come with us." She helped Darci into a robe, and the two cops and Koehler pushed her wheelchair to the front entrance, through the electric door, to the curb where they got into Craig's beige, 1983 two-door Monte Carlo, an unmarked detective car. Darci was put in the front right seat. Koehler sat in the back, behind her, and Coppinger sat behind Craig. It was 10:47 A.M.

As they wheeled away from the hospital and west on Lomas, Craig turned the police radio down, held the microphone close and tried to whisper, "We're headed out to the mountains."

Sgt. Lueras came back: "Do you need help? We can send units. We can get you a helicopter."

"No!" Craig said. "Cool it! She's taking us out to look for the victim." Craig turned north on Interstate 25 and east on Interstate 40 as Darci directed. As he sped east, Craig could see in his rearview mirror three or four Albuquerque police cars and two or three Air Force OSI units falling into place.

A few blocks away, along Central Avenue, another

99

caravan was forming at the '66 Trailer Lodge. Sam Ray had just received a call. "Your commander is on her way to your home." Sam knew why commanders went to houses. When Major Sherry Webb arrived she was in her dress uniform, a dark blue shirt and wool jacket, and she was accompanied by a first sergeant and the Mormon chaplain. Sam knew what they were about to say.

A woman had abducted Cindy for the baby, they began. The woman was in the process of taking authorities to a body. There was a good possibility it was Cindy's body. The police were en route into the mountains now. Sam listened, holding Luke in his lap. Sam's new baby was in custody, the commander said. She wanted to take him there. The bishop drove Sam, following the escort. They arrived at the UNM hospital and Sam was taken to the third floor nursery. The pediatrician handed Sam his baby.

She was tiny, six pounds, eight ounces. Luke had been eight pounds one ounce. Luke had been two weeks overdue. This girl was two under. She was wrapped in a pale green bunting. She was a healthy pink, with a small bandaid on her head.

The police caravan led by Craig was approaching the eastern edge of Albuquerque and the radio traffic was bothering him. He thought it might distract Darci, so he reached to turn it off.

"Oh, that's okay," Darci said. She held a white washcloth to wipe her tears, but appeared clear-minded and able to answer questions.

"Is this the road you were on?"

"Yes, but I got on at an upcoming entrance."

Darci began describing the previous day and the ride with Cindy. "She was talking to me. She rolled the window down and was calmer."

If was hot in Craig's car; Koehler thirsted for an iced tea. They drove on and on. Craig assumed the spot was on the edge of town and kept asking Darci at each exit, "This one?"

"No, keep going. I'll tell you. Just keep going."

They drove past the Carnuel exit. Darci seemed to know where she was going. She was trying to pronounce the exit she wanted—Tijeras—and Craig said, "That's clear up here."

"How did you get Cindy Ray to go with you?" Koehler asked from the back seat.

"I have a model gun that looks real. It shoots blanks. It's not a deadly weapon," Darci said. "That's what I used. Oh, please don't let her be dead." She began crying again. Koehler patted her hand. Darci calmed and was quiet. Just then she saw the exit sign. "Tijeras. I couldn't remember before. Get off here."

Down the exit ramp Craig faced a fork in the road. A right turn went through Tijeras; a left turn back under the interstate to head back west. "Do we go left or right?"

"I wanted to go left here and take her back to town but I didn't," said Darci. "I turned right." There was a pause. "Is this the point where I'm supposed to say I'm not going to say anything until I get my attorney? Is this the point where I'm supposed to be quiet?"

State Highway 14 went through the little village but began to climb fairly rapidly into the foothills. There were many turnoffs, Forest Service roads, exits to a concrete plant. Craig was worried that Darci wouldn't recognize the turnoff and pestered her. "Is this it?"

"No, it's on up here. I killed her. God, I hope she's not dead." On one curve Darci pointed to a rock embankment. "That's where the car went off the side of the road and dented the back. It didn't really happen coming back from Santa Fe. I know where I'm going. The turn is a left turn onto a dirt road." Craig slowed down at the next exit left. "Here?" Craig noticed that Darci averted her eyes from the road. That's why he kept asking, fearful that she was leading half the Albuquerque Police Department on a wild goose chase. After all, she had lied through her teeth just an hour earlier.

"Nope," she said. "It's on up here. I'll tell you when we get to it."

"How was the baby born, vaginally or by C-section?" Koehler asked.

"I took the baby."

Five miles down South 14, where the road rises into a sweeping right curve, Darci suddenly pointed and said, "It's coming up right up here." A minute later she pointed left. "This is it."

The small Forest Service sign said Juan Tomas, and Craig, surprised at Darci's sureness, swung the Monte Carlo onto the dirt road which ran along a creek. The caravan of cars behind did the same. As he turned, Darci's mood changed abruptly. She started to cry hard and raise her voice.

"I know she's dead. Don't let her be dead."

"Is she down this road?"

"Yes," she sobbed. At the next turnoff she started to point then said, no, it was farther on.

She calmed a bit.

"Will we come right up to the body?"

"Yes." Darci was approaching hysteria now. Craig was afraid he would drive over the scene and he tried to ask casually, "Is it far? What are we looking for?"

"It's up here, and we have to turn."

At a break in the fence line Darci said, "Turn here." The car bumped left across a cattle guard and Darci came unglued, nearly screaming.

"Don't worry, calm down. It's going to be all right," said Koehler. They were driving slowly through a scrub woodland where it would have been easy to conceal a body. The narrow dirt road, with two tracks and grass in the middle, ran directly north in a straight line, alongside a creek on the left, which had carved a shallow gully. Water sat in shallow pools. The grass along the banks was high and dry. On the right side of the road the trees came close to brushing the car. A quarter mile from the cattle guard a big clump of juniper and scrub oak grew close to the road on the left. As the car drew alongside, Darci thrust her arm in front of Craig's face and screamed:

"There she is!" Craig looked over and the hair stood up on his neck. The weeds were high behind the clump and he didn't see anything at first. Darci was screaming incoherently. From his seat in back, Coppinger could see what appeared to be a body behind the clump of trees.

"I know she's dead," Darci screamed. "I don't want to be here. Get me out of here."

Now Craig could see something in the grass. His first thought was "secure the scene." He looked in the mirror and swore. Coming close behind were

103

three police cars and two OSI cars. Craig wanted to back out but couldn't. He pulled over, fifty feet beyond the clumps and the other cars pulled up. He jumped out to stop them, but they came to a stop in the middle of the crime scene.

A small path led to the body, around the clump. Craig led the way with OSI agents Roy Flint and Coppinger right behind. They found Cindy Ray lying nearly spread-eagled and facing south, her blouse pulled up and her slacks pulled down. She was obviously dead, her skin pale and cold. They checked for vital signs and found none.

In the car, Darci was screaming. Elisabeth Koehler, alone in the car with her, was helpless and upset at being left there.

"I killed her. My Krugerrand is there."

"Do you want them to bring it to you?"

"I'm a disgusting person. I killed her." Darci kept screaming. Coppinger could hear his name in the commotion. "Steve, I don't want to be here. Get me out of here." All the while, Darci was gently holding Koehler's hand.

"Eli, kill me," she said. "Please kill me. I'm sorry I put you through this. I'm sorry you had to be involved. Get me out of here. Steve!"

Craig, meanwhile, was running through crime checkpoints, among them the question of jurisdiction. The body was somewhere in a federal forest, and the participants were both dependents of Air Force employees. It might be a federal case, but Craig couldn't think with Darci screaming. He went to the car, turned it around, pulled past the body and parked it. He asked Darci if she would allow police to search her Volkswagen, which was still

104

parked at Montano Acura. She agreed and signed a form. Coppinger then put Darci in an OSI car and with Special Agent Flint drove her away. It was about 11:30 A.M. The crime lab in Albuquerque's police department was notified.

Craig, by now bleary-eyed but juiced by the discovery, thought the FBI might take over, so he drove down the road to a phone and called the FBI office. Within a halfhour federal agents had arrived along with the crime scene experts. They decided there in the woods that it should be a joint investigation, handled under New Mexico law.

As the lab technicians began working, the true heinousness of the crime began to seep in. It had rained during the night and a lot of blood had washed away from Cindy. A technician bent over her and began making notes. One of the first things he noticed was a set of keys. It held a heart-shaped handle with "Cindy" inscribed by a rainbow. The keys were lying next to Cindy's cold hand, and something about them made him say to himself, loudly enough for Craig to hear, "No, that can't be."

Back at the UNM hospital, Sam Ray continued to hold his baby. But his commander interrupted.

"Sam, they found Cindy."

So, he said to himself. That's what was coming. If she hadn't thought more about the baby's life than hers, she would have survived. She placed her baby's life before hers. It was an even tradeoff. Cindy Ray gave her life so the baby could live.

He looked at the baby again. She would be called Amelia Monik, the name Cindy wanted, for a woman in Payson who used to baby-sit her. He'd call her Millie for short, after her grandmother. As he stood there, holding his baby, gazing at her face, Sam realized that Amelia Monik looked just like her mother.

Eleven

In the course of eighteen hours the murder case involving Cindy Lynn Ray and Darci Kayleen Pierce had unraveled. The baby was with its father, the body had been found and Darci had confessed. The "whodunit" was over. But the investigation was really just beginning.

"It wasn't a matter of solving the case, but putting the case together to show she planned it, how she picked out a victim and so forth," said Detective Craig.

Nobody knew anything about Darci Pierce, except what little her husband had provided in the middle of the night, in shock and dismay over losing his baby and his wife. The details of Darci's life were missing. In the coming hours and weeks, police, lawyers, psychiatrists, and reporters would lay her life bare. Her innermost secrets, fantasies, and obsessions would be made public. The dragnet that would collect the bits and pieces of one life would sweep into it the lives of many others, too, exposing their secrets and their failures. In the end, it was Darci's story, the story of one young woman with a terrible need for a baby.

As Coppinger and Flint left the murder scene, Darci's mood changed dramatically. Back on South Highway 14, she pointed to the place where she'd gone off the road. Coppinger could see skid marks and a knocked-down tree. Flint stopped the car and flagged an Albuquerque police car coming up the road. He pointed out the spot to the driver. Darci stopped crying and began talking about subjects that seemed totally irrelevant. She noticed on Coppinger's hand a Krugerrand ring and started talking about the one she wore and lost, the one given to her by a family she had stayed with in South Africa. She talked about the families there, and their wealth. She said they called mother and father Ma and Pa. She translated words from Afrikaans. She even discussed details of airline tickets to Africa. Her manner was irritatingly cool and chatty, rambling on and on. She never mentioned the crime, and she held Coppinger's hand as she talked.

The agents drove onto the base to their office. Inside, Darci made a list of items she wanted Ray to bring her, including clothes, skin cream, and a photo album from her South African trip. Coppinger couldn't believe it. He called medical technicians to check an infection on her foot, and he offered her soft drinks and food. She declined the food. "She was acting very calm and relaxed. She was walking around the office and looking at the plaques and talking about South Africa," Coppinger said later. The agents set up a tape recorder for another interview. It was one o'clock when they sat down at a table with Staff Sergeant Cindy Uglow from the 1606 Security Police Squadron.

"Okay," Coppinger began. "Just don't even worry about the tape recorder . . . Anytime you want to stop, you say so, okay?"

"How many times are you going to go over this with me?" Darci asked.

"We're going to go over it once. We're gonna let you tell the story." He repeated her rights. She wanted to know the punishment for homicide and Flint assured her she was only suspected of a crime.

"Yeah," said Coppinger. "You're guilty of nothing, you're guilty of drinking a Sprite, that's what you're guilty of."

Coppinger began a slow and easy interview, and found Darci almost jocular at times.

"Who else lives with you?" he asked.

"Two black widows."

"Do you tolerate black widows?"

"No, we burn them."

"I don't either."

Coppinger asked about her work in Portland and her pregnancies, the first in 1985. "Before you and Ray got married, you had a very traumatic event in your life, that's correct?"

"I was getting ready to graduate from high school and Ray and I had just moved in together. It was May, June. I was just sick all the time. You expect that in a pregnancy but it was twenty-four hours a day. So I contacted my doctor . . . he recognized it as a danger signal. My doctor wasn't available at the time and I had to take his colleague who was really rough and gruff. And I went alone. Ray was working that day. And the ultrasound came in and I was sitting on the table, and the doctor said, 'Well, I think you're losing the baby,' and walked out. I was quite hysterical and one of the nurses came in and calmed me down and sent me for a blood workup."

Darci explained the hormone tests to Coppinger and the semimonthly monitoring she underwent until September. "And all the time they were telling me that it might be okay, but it might not be okay, but I just kept living with the hope, you know." On September 11, 1985, she said, an ultrasound showed a "high hydatiform," a pregnancy that had developed into cancer, and she was admitted immediately for a dilatation and curettage, commonly called a D&C, in which her womb was scraped of the fetal tissue. After the first D&C she kept hemorrhaging and had to undergo a second. Darci was seventeen at the time.

In the days following, she said, she went on a trip with Ray and his folks and was hassled by Ray's mother about sleeping in separate bedrooms, at a time when she needed Ray. "They made it really, really hard."

Darci said she had no problems for a while but began bleeding again. "My doctor . . . thought that it was probably endometriosis because it was awful pain during intercourse. He told me he was real sure it was endometriosis . . ."

"And how well were you handling that?"

"Not well. Endometriosis—your chances are like nil to get pregnant. The doctor says the best way to cure endometriosis is to get pregnant but Catch 22 because you really can't. There's too much scar tissue."

"How was Ray handling this?" Coppinger asked. "Do you feel like he was being supportive and your friend, or do you feel like there was some pressures?"

"I never told him that it was endometriosis. I just let him know that I was not feeling well. I was kind of obvious sometimes, you know, I'd be screaming in pain. So I didn't share a lot of that with him because he's never really shared in any of those women-type things that happen. They're just kinda women problems."

"Does that upset you a little bit?"

"I think he could have been a little more supportive at the time but it doesn't affect me if that's his attitude, 'cause if I were a man I certainly wouldn't want anything to do with women stuff, either."

Darci then told the agents of getting high on the barbiturate prescribed by her doctor after the D&C. "I felt great." When the prescription ran out, she went crazy, screaming at Ray to get more pills. "And then I guess that when I finally hit bottom . . . I cried and cried and cried." She tried counseling through Catholic Family Services but gave up. In the following months, into 1986, Darci said she tried to get pregnant again.

"I put a lot of pressure on myself. I felt like any woman can carry a baby to term and have one. Why can't I? What is it that I'm so deficient that I can't do this? So I was trying so hard to do it, so that I could prove to myself that I was capable of doing this basic function. And also there was such a void there, such an emptiness, such a longing, 'cause I've always loved children so much."

Darci said she cut off her friends and then Ray left for basic training. She moved back in with her mother, but the relationship was strained. "So I really wasn't that happy."

"And the one person that you really trusted and

111

depended upon wasn't there—Ray?"

"Right . . . We need to back up a little bit, though. The reason that Ray married me in December is because he thought I was carrying his baby . . . because I don't think he would have married me at that time if he hadn't thought that." During the summer prior to their marriage, she said, she really thought she was pregnant, but she had heavy periods— "and it was all over. But I started letting everybody know that I was pregnant. I guess I wanted to be so badly. And when the period came I couldn't tell everybody that I wasn't, you know. It was so important."

Darci told Coppinger she felt pressured by friends and her parents. They'd ask, "Do you want a boy or a girl?" and "When are you guys getting married?"

"My mom came over and had a knock-down drag out kind of thing with Ray, and I think that's when he decided to say 'okay we're getting married.' But then I was too far in to say, 'wait a minute guys, it's not . . .' "

At her workplace, a fast-food joint, losing the first pregnancy to cancer was "like you're a leper victim or something, people just don't want to be around you." She quit that job. At G.I. Joes, pregnancy was rampant. "One would just start a pregnancy and one would end a pregnancy and one was in the middle. All those babies around you all the time. And that kinda made it hard, because there were these women and some of them weren't married and some of them weren't sure if they were gonna keep their kids. Here they were able to make a decision like that when I didn't have a choice."

By January 1987, she said, she was in too deep.

"My family and Ray's family had baby showers for me just before he left, and we got everything that we needed for the baby except a crib and a changing table."

"Okay," said Coppinger, "two weeks ago Ray is expecting this baby and the pressure is really being turned up."

"I think I was losing touch. I was getting really desperate trying to figure out what I was gonna do, how I was gonna find someone to give me their baby now. I was just gonna leave one day, and just not come back. Ray doesn't know this but I had my one bag in the car and was heading out. But . . . I couldn't leave him. I would rather face him than to walk out. But now I look back and God I wished I had walked out."

Coppinger led her back to her relationship with her parents. She described her mother as supportive to the point of intrusion. "When I moved away from my house I basically told my parents to go to hell. I was sixteen and that was that. None of my family had anything to do with me for a very long time after that. They didn't want me around. I went so far as to crash my older brother's wedding . . . I just showed up."

"Did you feel you really wanted to have a strong family and you weren't getting it?"

"Yeah, I did. For a long time I walked around with a chip on my shoulder because of the fact that I'm adopted. I don't think I can take all the blame myself for the way I feel about being adopted because my oldest brother, whenever we had fights or anything he would always say to me, 'I don't have to take that from you because you're not my real sister.'

113

My whole family has always treated me very special. I've always had everything that I've wanted because I'm the youngest. I'm the only girl, I'm adopted. I had all the cards as far as getting everything I wanted, but I don't know if I should have gotten everything I wanted all the time because it made me feel even that much more of an outsider and it put a lot of distance between my brothers and myself, my youngest brother, particularly."

Coppinger asked Darci about the trip to the hospital the week before the murder, for the scheduled "inducement."

"I had fabricated the pregnancy to the point where people were [thinking] 'she's overdue. Why aren't the doctors doing something?' At first I'd chalk it up to typical military doctors—don't know anything. You know fifty percent of the malpractice claims are ob/gyn related. So, I'm going on with this thing. My mother kept calling and kept calling and kept calling and saying, 'Where's this baby?' So I said I'm supposed to be induced on Friday. And Friday I almost left. That's the day when I had the bags packed and I was ready to leave and then I decided I'm gonna level with Ray on this whole thing and I'm gonna tell him the truth. But then I couldn't do that because if I told him then everybody else had to find out. Somehow I had to buy some more time, so I went into the admissions desk." Darci explained how she got the clerk to lie to Ray. "So that bought me more time to try to figure out what I was going to do or get up my nerve to say something."

With another deadline looming, she said, "I had to figure out something to do before five o'clock didn't I? I went to the gas station to put gas in the

114

car 'cause I was going to leave again. I was just calling it all quits and let everybody figure out where I had gone . . . I think they wanted the baby more than wanting to talk about what my situation actually was.

"I went to the parking lot that is in front of the hospital. I hadn't been in the hospital since right after we got here, and I walked through it and I saw all the new carpeting and stuff and I thought it looked really neat and I picked up a brochure in there — it's in the Volkswagen still — about prenatal diagnostics care and courses for it. I think it was almost one o'clock and I was getting ready to drive off and I realized that the ob/gyn clinic was around the other side. I went back out to my car and was driving like I was gonna go out the Gibson gate and, uh, a woman caught my eye and she was very pregnant and she had just climbed out of a red Blazer and I decided that I was gonna wait for her to come back out and I was gonna talk to her and try to get her to give me her baby.

"I waited and I waited and I waited and I started thinking, oh gosh, maybe she works there. She pulled in right at one o'clock. I think it was three o'clock before she came out of there. I was gonna drive away and she came out. I parked right next to her car and I got out of my car — the passenger side, her driver's side, 'cause she was getting in, and I asked her to get in the car with me, that I needed someone to talk to, that I had some problems right now, I didn't know anybody, I just needed to talk. And she looked startled and I told her, 'please, I just need somebody to talk to. I'm not going to hurt you.'

"So she got in the car with me and I said 'why don't we go back to my place and we can sit over a couple glasses of iced tea and we can talk?' I think even to talk to somebody would have been real nice. Well, I drove down San Mateo and turned left on Marquette and saw that Ray's car was in the driveway, so I did a U real quick and got back on San Mateo . . . I thought it would be real nice just to drive around and talk to her. I asked if her husband was in the military and she said yes. I never got around to actually telling her what my problem was. I don't remember the conversation between us. I do remember that she rolled down the window and just relaxed, sat back. We were just talking . . . and I was just driving, and I just drove."

Darci said she never knew Cindy Ray's name, but she described her accurately, except for the color of her blouse, which Darci remembered as black-and-white striped.

Darci told Coppinger she had one of Ray's replica guns that fires caps. She kept it in the Volkswagen for security. "I took the gun out of the [door] pocket . . . and set it on my lap."

"Did she see it?"

"She saw it but it didn't involve her," Darci said. "She didn't look at it. I just told her again I wasn't gonna hurt her, you know, and she, she trusted me."

"How would you classify your state of mind at this point?"

"Hysterical. I don't recall anything that was said between us . . . I only remember snatches of the road that we were taking." At the Tijeras exit, she said, she considered turning around and leveling with everyone. But she didn't. "She was still talking and she was real relaxed and she was talking about the thunder and she always liked the lightning even though it scares her. And she and her husband always came out here four-wheel driving. I asked her, 'Do you think the bug would get stuck if we took any of them?' And she said probably not. And then I didn't feel like driving anymore. I just wanted to stop and talk. So I stopped the car 'cause there was a bunch of trees that overhung and we could be outside but be under the branches of the tree and not get wet. We got out of the car and we walked up the length of the trees and back and just kind of stood around."

"Had you talked to her about this baby situation at this time?"

"I asked her all about her baby, when it was due . . . I was just coming to the point of asking her to give me her child and I decided no, I wanted to go home . . . forget the whole thing and go home . . . and we were getting back in the car and then . . . that's, that's, I don't know from the car until I was driving real fast down the road and I had the baby in my arms and I, I don't know what happened from the time we were getting in the car. I don't know it."

Twelve

Coppinger knew he was near pay dirt, if he could only get Darci to confess the details of the murder. For the next hour, he dragged Darci back to the scene she hated to remember.

"Did you have a fight?"

"No, no. We were getting back in the car." There was a long pause. "I think, I think I hit her in the head or something."

"Did she fight or did she pass out?"

"She, she . . . started scratching me and . . . she fell out." There were long pauses between her words. "It's not there, I . . . we . . ."

"Did you hit her again?"

"No . . . We were on the ground, but I didn't hit her again."

"Did she stop moving?"

"No, I don't think so."

"Did you hit her with a rock? Maybe she stopped moving?"

"Maybe, I don't remember."

"You knew you had to have a baby. How were you going to get it? By cesarean or something like that?"

Darci paused. "I don't remember how the baby came. The baby was just there, so I took it."

"Did you have some way to cut the cord?"

"I bit it . . . I held onto it so it wouldn't bleed. And I pulled off my dress and wrapped the baby in my dress and put the baby against my chest because my slip was real low to keep the baby warm, and I got in the car and I was driving really fast, really fast. There's a big hole in the road, and I hit that hole, and I thought I lost the car in it."

"Was it raining?"

"Raining, yeah, raining a lot, and I rolled up the window so the baby would stay warm and I had the baby clutched against me. I was driving with one hand and I don't remember how I shifted. I think I took my hand off the wheel . . . there was a big curve and I knew that I needed to slow down and I lifted my left foot to go for the brake but I hit the clutch and the car started sliding and I was going backwards on the road and then I hit the side of the mountain thing." The jolt moved her seat, so she put the baby in the passenger seat with its sheepskin cover and readjusted the driver's seat to reach the pedals. "I shut the door and I started the car and it started right up and I pulled out onto the highway . . .

"And then I started thinking: I can't just show up someplace with this baby in my arms and not have some kind of story. So I drove to I-25 and I knew that if I pulled in at the Acura dealership . . . that I could tell him that I had been leaving and decided to come back and deliver the baby and that I needed an ambulance 'cause we needed to get to the hospital. That ambulance pulled up and they wanted to take the baby, and I didn't want to let the baby go. I finally did 'cause it was for the good of the baby and they needed to make sure the baby was being warmed. I remember they were going to take her in another ambulance and I wouldn't let them. I wanted to be with her."

"What happened at the hospital?"

"We went in and my husband was inside and they gave the baby to him and he was real proud because here was our baby and everything was okay, you know. I had been leaving him and decided to come back and had the baby on the road and it was okay. I was all right. He understood it all because I had told him before that it would probably be better if I just left. He knew that I had been thinking about that, honestly, going to disappear off the face of the earth and not tell anybody . . . everybody would assume that I had the baby and I was just off on my own."

Darci retold her hospital stories. "I wouldn't let them examine me for obvious reasons, 'cause it was very obvious that I didn't have the baby . . . I knew they had taken my blood and I figured that they had taken blood from the baby and I hadn't thought about blood types not matching. And at that point it hit me that that was a very obvious thing to determine whether a child was yours or not." That's when Darci made up the black market surrogate story. "The doctor told me that he wouldn't yield to sign any birth certificates . . . I offered him money. I asked him not to take it wrong, but I asked him how much it would cost for him to sign a birth certificate. He shook his head at me and said no. I told him about the endometriosis and the fact that I'm not ovulating and that I've been trying to get pregnant and that this was a conceivable way that I could feel getting the child that I always wanted . . . Obviously I had not delivered a baby [but] I was believing the story. And nothing else was in my mind . . . What I was saying is actually what happened . . . it's what I believed, it really is.

"And then they brought the baby in, and they let me hold her. All of a sudden I got the feeling that I had done something so bad." Darci began crying. "And things started flooding back about driving in the woods and about a baby and you had told me about a woman who was pregnant and she was missing. And I started thinking about who was this person that I was seeing in these, these images that I was getting, while I was holding the baby. And then, I started realizing that, my God, maybe it was the same person and maybe I had done something really terrible . . . so then I asked for you . . . because of all the investigators . . . you seemed to be the one that wasn't getting so excited. The other guy that was with you, had blue eyes — they're really bloodshot — he was shaking over this whole thing and he was playing this game with me of 'come on, you can tell me, I'm on your side.' But yet the tone of his voice and the actions were, 'come on wench, spill it, tell us the story and just get it over with, we want to get out of here.' And I had the feeling that if I said one thing, if I even said, my God, I'm having these feelings, that they were just gonna slap on the cuffs and haul me off. So I asked for you . . . And then all of it started coming back . . . and we went out in there . . ." Darci began sobbing, ". . . and we found her."

Coppinger called Darci courageous and brave for telling her story, and she began to cry again.

"I don't remember doing any of this, though, really, I mean it's, it's like a nightmare that you have at night, and you wake up from and the boogie man's not coming through your windows and there's no burglars walking around in your house. And I'm expecting to wake up any minute here, you know. It's like, 'somebody slap me or something' because it's still not there. I can sit here and say that this is what's happened, but I didn't do this, I mean I didn't. You know?"

Coppinger again moved Darci back to the crime scene, to the moment after Cindy Ray began scratching her.

"And then you fell out of the car, is that right?"

"I think I fell over . . . 'cause she was scratching me, she had ahold of me."

"Like your hair, you mean?"

"Yeah."

"Okay, you both fell out on the passenger side. You hit the gravel there. Would you describe that as big gravel or small gravel?"

"Sore gravel."

Coppinger laughed. "Did she stop moving after she fell out? How did you get down there in the tree area?"

"I don't know what happened there."

"When you hit her, was there any chance at all that the [gun] could have been in your hand?"

"It might have been . . . I can't say yes."

"And then she ended up, you and her, ended up down below in the trees, in the tall grass, is that right?"

"Yeah, and somebody came along."

"In a car?"

"In a truck . . . he yelled, 'Is it okay if I shut your door?'"

"At this point, somehow the baby was just there, is that right?"

"The baby was born, yeah. The baby was there. So I took it."

"Did she say something like 'my baby's coming' and you had to use a knife or something and do a cesarean? Did you help her, or did she say, 'cut me' or 'help me' or what happened? Can you remember? You must remember. Try real hard. You had to help her with the baby. Did you have a razor blade or a knife?"

"No I didn't have anything. I, I didn't have anything."

"You had to get the baby out somehow. There had to be a way."

Darci paused. "I don't remember how the baby was born. The baby was there and I bit the cord and I, I cleaned its mouth and I breathed into its mouth a couple of times and the baby started fussing, and so I was running to the car and trying to get the baby to the hospital."

"When you were biting the cord and stuff, was the mother moving? Had she stopped moving at this point?"

"I don't remember if she was moving."

"Was she talking to you?"

"No."

"Was she screaming?"

"No."

"You're fairly sure of that? Was there any, you know, like a scalpel, or anything that you used to help get the baby out?"

123

"No, I didn't have anything. I, I had nothing on me."

"Did she ask you to help her, or did she say 'the baby's coming, you've got to help me?'"

"No, uh, she wasn't, she wasn't talking to me."

"Okay. Alright. Do you think she was unconscious at this point?"

Darci paused.

"I don't know. She wasn't talking to me. I . . . I don't know."

"You're not sure? Calm down. Relax for a minute. Do you want something to drink?"

Ray Pierce arrived at the OSI office just as his wife's confession ended. They were given a few moments alone.

"I'm sorry, I'm sorry," Darci cried, hugging him. "I don't remember doing it. I didn't recognize the place but I took them right to it. I've never been there, but I took them to it." She was more upset than Ray had ever seen.

"It may have been your body out there, but it wasn't your mind," he said. "The woman I fell in love with isn't capable of doing this."

Darci gave Ray her purse and jewelry and told him, loudly enough to be heard by the OSI agents, "They found my Krugerrand under the body." The statement was carefully noted by the detectives because Cindy Ray's body had not been moved, and no Krugerrand had been found yet.

Detective Craig and FBI Agent J.G. Hughes arrived and took custody of Darci and drove her to the police lab where hair and blood samples were taken, her fingernails scraped and detailed photographs shot. Two forensic doctors, Karen Griest and Ellen Clark, examined Darci for marks and injuries. In a written report filed with police, and later testimony, Dr. Griest said she found several small bruises and red abrasions on Darci. On the back of her left upper arm, she spotted three small bruises and two faint red lines, as if someone had scraped her skin. Similar scrapes were seen on her neck, near the left clavicle, her right shoulder, and left knee. Pinpoint abrasions were found on her left elbow and the right lower leg. There were no scratches on her hands, and Dr. Griest described the abrasions as minor.

That same afternoon, Drs. Griest and Clark went to the newborn unit at the University of New Mexico Hospital to examine Amelia Monik Ray. They reported a six-pound, eight-ounce baby girl, a newborn without head molding or evidence of vaginal delivery. The umbilical cord had been trimmed and clamped. There were small injuries, including two very small red-brown abrasions on the baby's right thigh, a rough discoloration on the inside of the lower right leg and scraped skin on the inside of the right thigh. On the left thigh were six pinpoint red-brown abrasions. There were no bruises on her head, face or arms, and nothing to indicate that the baby had been forcibly pulled or tugged. As Dr. Griest examined the girl, Amelia defecated, "meconium-stained fecal material," she noted in her report. "The actions of the baby are normal and external examination shows the baby to be completely normal."

Arrangements were then made to draw two milliliters of blood for typing. What Darci had guessed in her talk with Dr. Slocumb—what convinced her to change her story and allow herself to be examined — had, in fact, not been done.

All through Friday afternoon, July 24, the technicians of Albuquerque's criminalistics lab worked at the crime site in the Monzano Mountains. They photographed the scene from every angle, they collected copious notes and looked for every piece of physical evidence and every clue they could find. Nothing escaped their vision, including the weather: clear, warm, a slight breeze, with rain clouds nearby. They even noted the National Weather Service conditions for the hour of Cindy's death: sunny skies, visibility fifty miles, temperature 97 degrees, wind from the south at six miles an hour, humidity 14 percent, with thunderhead clouds to the north, east and south, and rain and lightning to the east.

Cindy Ray was found lying on her back in tall grass on the west side of the juniper and oak stand. Her light-colored clothing was partially visible through the weeds, if you knew where to look, but she could not be seen through the trees. She was no more than twenty-five feet through the clump, from the road.

The technicians found tire tracks on the dirt road similar to those of the Volkswagen. Shoe prints similar to Cindy's shoes were found along the road by the trees. A pair of sunglasses, tinted blue and belonging to Cindy, were there by the road. Above the glasses, hanging in the tree as if thrown there, was the white elastic belt used by Sergeant Angela Morgan at the base clinic to hold the fetal heart monitor to Cindy's abdomen. There were hairs imbedded in

126

the fabric. The lab technicians suspected that the belt had been used to strangle Cindy.

Cindy was on her back with her face turned slightly to the right. She was fully clothed, with beige Hush Puppies lace shoes, white socks, light blue denim pants, "Room for Two" green panties, a J.C. Penney brassiere, and a white blouse with dark dots.

Her thighs were spread wide and the pants pulled down to the crotch. The left leg was bent inward at the knee. The blouse was pulled up above her breasts, exposing her bra. Her arms were at her sides, with her left arm straight down. Both hands were clenched, except for a left index finger. A hair was found in her right hand. Near her right hand, a set of keys was found. The key chain held a heart-shaped name tag which read "Cindy." The ring also included a tiny Tupperware lid. The keys were blood-stained, and skin and body tissue were stuck to the key blades.

By Cindy's left arm was her straw purse with brown, copper and ivory stripes, a purse she had won for Tupperware sales. It was lying open and was bloodstained. The purse contained a checkbook, a comb, coupons, a watch with no band, a calculator, cosmetics, fourteen cents in a small coin purse, a New Mexico driver's license, a Visa card, a First Interstate bank card, an Air Force ID, a social security card, a Church of Jesus Christ of Latter Day Saints Temple "recommended" card, a Circle K video card, miscellaneous papers, and a medical appointment slip dated July 23 at 1315 hours for the base OB clinic. Hanging out of the purse were one pair of expectant mother white silk pantaloons, size 32, and one white silk camisole—the sacred undergarments of the Mormon Church normally worn for protection by Cindy. They were stained with blood.

The only apparent source of blood was the large gaping wound in her stomach. It showed numerous tearing and gouging marks, both vertically and horizontally across the abdomen. The baby's umbilical cord was hanging out of the wound. There was blood on her right hand, and her shoes. Rain had washed some of the blood away.

Because of scrapes on her face and torso and dirt, and mud and weeds on her clothing, the technicians guessed that Cindy had been dragged over the damp soil. It also appeared she had been dragged by her arms at one point, and by her feet at another. There were drag marks on her pants and weeds in her cuffs. The bra had scuff marks and there were mud stains on the front and back of the blouse. Mud was wedged into the shoes.

After noting all this, the lab technicians turned Cindy onto her side. Lying underneath her, at approximately the center of her back, was a gold Krugerrand coin.

Cindy Ray's body was encased in a white plastic body bag and carried to Albuquerque, where she was laid on an examining table at the office of the Medical Investigator. Dr. Ross Zumwalt, the assistant chief medical investigator for New Mexico, performed the autopsy.

He described her as 129 pounds, five-foot-four, and twenty-three years old. Submitted with the body was her key ring with seven metal keys, including two ignition keys with rubber-coated heads. One of them had abundant fat tissue and hairs dried to the lock portion.

Looking first at her face, Dr. Zumwalt noted her forehead, eyelids, and upper face dotted with tiny petechia, pinpoint hemorrhages that come from being strangled. There were three impact hemorrhages on her head and a contusion on her jaw. Around her neck was the mark of a ligature, less than half an inch wide. On the back of her neck were four small abrasions, and near her sternum was the mark of a thumbnail. There were bruises on both shoulders and signs of a struggle on her arms.

In her lower abdomen, in exactly the right spot for a cesarean section, was a gaping, irregular wound, one and a half inches wide and five inches long. The edges were torn and pieces of abdominal muscle were protruding. A thirteen-inch length of umbilical cord stuck out with teeth marks that matched Darci's. The uterus was visible in the depths of the wound, it too, cut in an irregular way. On either side of the wound, extending for three inches, were scratches in the skin. When the Blazer ignition key was laid on these scratches, the sharp ridges matched almost perfectly.

Dr. Zumwalt testified later that although the skin is very elastic and fibrous a sharp key could puncture the taut, stretched skin over a pregnant uterus and then be drawn along in a half-cut, half-tear. The underlying muscles and fat appeared to have been first cut with the key and then pulled apart with fingers. It would have been a bloody act. At the same time, because of the thin uterine wall, care would have been required not to punch through and injure the infant, whose head lay close to the skin.

In a hospital he said, physicians use a transverse incision that is slightly larger than the wound in Cindy, cut just above the pubic bone because the muscles are thinner and fiberous, and can be separated. The patient then can have another child. A hospital cesarean normally takes five to seven minutes as the baby is pushed and pulled through the hole by its neck. Often, two people perform the delivery and even then, head and neck injuries are common. The key-cutting procedure probably took ten to fifteen minutes but there were no signs that Amelia Monik was deprived of oxygen because blood was still flowing when the wound was made. In other words, Cindy Ray was alive during the cesarean.

Dr. Zumwalt concluded that Cindy was strangled, possibly with the fetal monitor belt, and then bled to death through the cesarean wound. He speculated that her struggle with her killer was short and that she probably died within several minutes after being cut.

Thirteen

By Friday afternoon, July 24, the news media in Albuquerque had a good whiff of this unbelievable story, a sensational tale even told straight. As Detective Craig and FBI agent Gene Hughes drove Darci to the Bernalillo County Detention Center, the news story came on the radio. Craig caught Hughes' eye in the rearview mirror and Gene raised his eyebrow in a wince.

"Oh, I don't mind hearing it," Darci said pleasantly. In the mirror, Gene raised another eyebrow.

Dashing into the courthouse past news cameras, Craig put his jacket over Darci's head to avoid possible identification problems with witnesses. At 6:40 P.M. Darci was booked on an open charge of murder, and booking photographs were taken. She was wearing blue thongs on her bare feet, short sweatsuit pants and a baggy blue blouse with teddy bears all over it. She looked like an overweight child.

The next morning the *Albuquerque Journal* ran the story on page one with a subdued, one-column headline: Deadly Abduction Stuns Officials. "I thought I'd seen everything but apparently not until now," it quoted District Attorney Steve Schiff. The

131

story included the fact that Cindy had been "sliced open" and Darci's confession that she "took the baby." Trying to fashion some meaning of it, the paper quoted Ray Pierce: "I can't comment at all. There's nothing I can say."

At a news conference, Lieutenant Roger Anderson of the Albuquerque police said it appeared that the baby was taken "by means of a crude cesarean-type operation." The newspaper didn't print it, but reporters learned that the tool probably was a car key.

Friends of Cindy and Sam Ray were quoted, too. "Obviously, he's relieved that the baby is fine," said Earl Greer. Sam's unit on the base, the 1606 Security Police Squadron, set up a Cindy Ray donation fund. The news had begun to spread across the country, touching people in a particularly threatening way. Mormon friends gathered at the Rays' trailer. With a network second to none for responding, the church wasn't leaving Sam alone.

In Payson, Utah, Cindy's father, Larry Giles, made plans to fly to Albuquerque. Ray Pierce's parents, en route from Minnesota to Albuquerque to see the baby, called Ray from Trinidad, Colorado and learned the news on Saturday. They came on anyway, with dread in their hearts. In Portland, Oregon, Darci's parents were beside themselves with the turn of events. Helpless and stunned, they, too, got on a plane for Albuquerque.

"I've known Darci for over a year," the manager of the model shop where Ray worked told the *Portland Oregonian*. "I can't imagine her doing anything like what's been described." At the Church of Christ near the Ricker home, the Reverend David Brink read the story with a sick feeling—and some guilt. Perhaps,

132

he said, he had seen the warning signs, years before, and hadn't done enough to steer Darci straight.

On Friday night, July 24, 1987, at the Bernalillo County Detention Center in the third-floor women's section, Darci Pierce was locked in a pale, nine-by-seven cell with a long skinny window in a heavy door, and dressed in the standard blue jumpsuit prison garb. But she was no ordinary prisoner. There was real fear among the jailers that the woman accused of this heinous crime was some kind of crazed animal. They isolated her, restricted her movements and watched with a wary eye. Darci was a puzzle, as everyone who came in contact with her realized.

"Resident is nineteen-year-old caucasian female. Presents well-dressed and groomed. Alert, cooperative and friendly. Activity and speech normal. Good eye contact. Average intelligence," therapist Charlene Chavez wrote in her first report at the jail. "Thought processes are intact. Resident has no history of psychiatric problems, or treatment. No history of alcohol or drug abuse. Never had legal problems. Never been to jail before. Denies history of audiovisual hallucinations. Reports normal childhood. Reports being straight A student in school. Many activities in school."

Darci gave Chavez a brief pregnancy history, one that exaggerated her sense of loss: "They have lost two babies. Since last miscarriage (December 1985) reports very irregular menstrual cycle, sometimes 3-4 months apart or sometimes twice per month. Describes but does not admit to depression. Loss of interest in friends and social activity. Loss of interest

133

in hobbies and sport activities. Frequently 'plays couch potato' watching TV all day. Reports blackout during alleged crime . . . no suicidal indication, past or present. Resident is upset and frightened about being in jail. Tearful and nervous. Afraid of being harmed."

Under the section labeled "tentative impression," Chavez wrote: "Resident is very stressed and anxious about charges and incarceration. Will monitor resident due to obvious unpredictable behavior. Resident has been placed on protective custody due to charges." She recommended counseling observation checks every fifteen minutes.

That night at 11:00 P.M. Chavez spoke with Darci again and reported her "feeling more comfortable . . . Asked many questions regarding jail policy and legal process. Appears to be coping adequately at present. Discussed coping strategies and relaxation."

On Saturday, July 25, 1987, the news media began going crazy with the story. A local gynecologist was quoted as saying that a crude cesarean was impossible—and it was a legitimate doubt in the medical community. Craig and Hughes drove to Darci's apartment and asked Ray if she had any medical books of any kind. He pulled out *Family Medical Guide* by the American Medical Association and another one by the editors of *Better Homes and Gardens*. Craig looked at the books; they were both new, bought for the coming family. "There were no dog-eared corners or any other signs of use," he noted.

At 2:00 P.M. the pair drove again to the crime scene to find someone with a white pickup truck.

134

They drove past the clump of trees and knocked on the doors of five residences along Forest Service Road 252. John and Donna Bundock said they'd come home at 8:30 P.M. on the night of the murder and did not see anything. A house guest, John Watson, had gone jogging along the road, but he was out. Tom Hund, another neighbor, had come home at 5:00 P.M. and seen nothing unusual. At the home of Theron Hartshorn, the cops left a card. Craig then went home to sleep and Hughes sent a teletype to Portland, asking the local FBI to help find clues to the demon in Darci.

In the jail, meanwhile, Darci received a note from another inmate saying she would be killed. It panicked her. She asked a guard why other women might hurt her. The guard explained that it was the nature of the crime. "Oh," Darci said. The guard noted in a report that Darci seemed to understand what was going on but showed no emotion. Another guard helped Darci breathe deeply and settle down, while she rambled on with stories from her childhood, a behavior "inappropriate to this setting and situation," the guard wrote.

Darci also mentioned that her parents were flying in for the weekend; Craig and Hughes lost no time in interviewing them. Ken and Sandra Ricker were friendly and helpful as they sat in Darci's apartment and talked about her pregnancy history and possible motives. Sandra, a huge woman given to wearing house dresses, told Craig she was convinced that Darci was pregnant, but that Darci would never let her go with her to the doctor for prenatal visits. As the cops sat in the small living room, Ray Pierce brought out another book, *The Complete Book of*

Baby Care with a whole section on cesarean deliveries.

On Sunday afternoon, Theron Hartshorn called and said he might have information on the case. He had driven past a white Volkswagen and spoken with a girl on July 23, he said. After reading about the case in the paper he had called. He was shown a photo array with a picture of Darci but he couldn't pick her out. He was distraught that he had not been more curious. "I might have been able to save her life," he told Craig.

Craig and Hughes also went to visit Jane Hillman, a woman who had been at the airbase hospital on July 23 about 1:30 P.M. She had seen a woman waiting in a Volkswagen and had wondered why she was sitting in the heat. Mrs. Hillman and her children went inside the building to wait in air-conditioning. She, too, looked at photos of suspects but could not identify Darci Pierce.

On Monday, July 27, Darci Pierce made her first appearance in Magistrate Court in the basement of the county courthouse. Her family, with nothing but a blue collar income, had asked that a public defender be appointed, and agreed to a ten thousand dollar reimbursement contract. The case automatically fell into the lap of John Bogren, a slouching, ex-Chicago street kid from a Catholic neighborhood. He was used to defending weird cases, but this was beyond anything he had handled. "What would it take to gut another woman?" he asked as he read the case in the papers. Bogren asked Tom Jameson, a friend and fellow public defender, to join him on the case. Jameson, a thin, tentative man, met Darci moments before the bond hearing, in a small cubicle without a door, just long enough to get some basic information.

"I remember going over and meeting her there, and being struck that she just looked like a frightened nineteen-year-old who was very cooperative and very friendly and looked very normal. She was dressed in a blue prison jumpsuit. Her hair was tied back. She was scared and disoriented. I'm not sure she'd slept for a while." They talked briefly, and Jameson discussed the legal process. "I found an attractive, pleasant, articulate woman who'd been accused of doing something really, really bizarre."

One of Jameson's first duties on behalf of his new client was to deal with jail paranoia. Just before Darci left for the arraignment, for example, guards had removed all her personal items and bedding, afraid, apparently that she might harm herself. "They didn't know what they were dealing with. They kept her isolated, in a segregated side. Usually you have contact with other prisoners there but she had received threats and the jailers were worried. They were treating her somewhat like an animal. They didn't know what they were dealing with. They took every single thing away from her, and kept her on a twenty-four-hour suicide watch. They didn't want to give her a blanket, clothing. They didn't want her to have underwear, they didn't want her to have a toothbrush, toothpaste—anything. They wanted, basically, to keep her in an empty room. It was a constant fight, throughout the entire case, to let her have anything. We had to fight about letting her brush her teeth. We had to fight about letting her

137

comb her hair. We had to fight about letting her read a book. They wouldn't let her have books. They wouldn't let her have a pencil. They wouldn't let her have paper. And any concession we would get would be through tremendous wrangling with the bureaucracy over there. I guess they thought she would eat a book and kill herself. It was somewhat irrational. But they treated her very, very harshly, both because they didn't know who they were dealing with, and they were scared, and because she had committed a particularly unpopular crime. It was very talked about and on everyone's mind. They would let her out of the cell long enough to take a shower. She was kept in a small room twenty-four hours a day. Occasionally they would let her stay outside for maybe half an hour a day, but she spent twenty-three and a half hours in isolation."

The jailer mentality mirrored that of the city: divided between deep sympathy and hatred. Darci was an animal and what she did was disgusting. "Don't ask me to feel sorry for somebody who did this," was a typical reaction among women in Albuquerque. That reaction may have been heightened by the picture news photographers were able to snap of Darci as she was led to her arraignment. Her long brown hair was loose, and hid her face in a wild tangle of locks.

Harry Zimmerman, an assistant district attorney, handled the initial appearance for the state. He told the judge that Darci had used a gun or a replica to abduct Cindy Ray, and asked that she be arraigned on an open charge of murder and kidnapping. State District Judge James O'Toole ordered Darci held on $500,000 bond for a preliminary hearing August 6.

Zimmerman said he expected the case to go to the grand jury before then. Zimmerman also said Darci had acted alone and that Ray was not implicated.

Ray and Darci's parents watched silently from a crowded room separated from their Darci by one-way glass. When the arraignment was over, Greta Thomas, an assistant DA, approached them, apparently thinking they were Cindy's parents. "We're going to do everything we can to get a conviction, and we're going for the death penalty." Stunned, the families members nodded politely.

Late that night, in her jail cell, without a blanket, Darci broke down and cried while retelling parts of the murder to a counselor. They talked about the death penalty and Darci said she saw herself "being injected with lethal chemicals." When asked about the possibility of long-term incarceration, she mentioned body building. She also talked about the nursery at home, and her belief, still, that "the baby is there sometimes."

The July 26-27 papers carried the recollections of Robert Mohr, the new car sales manager of Montano Acura, who by now was bummed out by the turn of events. "Mrs. Pierce was very pregnant as far as I could see. They said they were expecting a baby in the next week or so, and they said they'd make a decision on buying a car after the baby was born." Mohr said he felt pretty good about the event until he came to work on Friday morning and found the Volkswagen cordoned off and guarded by police.

Lost in the news was the quiet flight to Utah of Sam Ray and his family. As Darci was arraigned, he was officially granted custody of Amelia Monik, and he left the nightmare of Albuquerque with Cindy's body and the four-day-old baby. As he left, Mormon friends and base public relations personnel spoke for him: "An unfortunate chain of events has left two little children motherless and a husband longing for his wife. We feel sympathy for women who cannot have children of their own," said a statement read by Kirtland spokesman George Pearce.

Reporters had jumped to the same motivating conclusions. Death Suspect . . . Obsessed With Babies, rang the headline in the *Portland Oregonian* on July 28. Quoting the Pierce's former landlady, Velma Stockton, the paper reported, "She had an obsession with motherhood, and that's the worst thing I could say about her. They were very nice people, just the loveliest couple. They were excellent tenants. He was a steady worker." The Pierces had lived in her duplex from May 7, 1985 until January 1986, when Ray began boot camp. "She had a miscarriage when she lived there, or that's what she told me. She told me the fetus starved to death because her body didn't support it with nourishments." Mrs. Stockton also revealed that Darci's sister-in-law, Mary Ricker, who moved into a neighboring apartment after the miscarriage, was upset with Darci. After Mary gave birth Darci tried to "take over the baby . . . Mary told me that Darci tried to take full possession of it. She even wanted to nurse it. There was bad blood between them." Mrs. Stockton also was under the impression that Darci was pregnant when she moved away from Albuquerque. "I know she really put on a lot of weight, but it was fat. Even her legs were heavy."

The *Oregonian* had marshaled a brief sketch of Darci's life: she had graduated in 1985 from LaSalle High School, a Catholic school in Milwaukie, a suburb of Portland. Schoolmates called Darci "just kind of quiet" with few friends, a girl who stuck to herself. She had worked as a cashier at the Arctic Circle hamburger stand on 8111 S.E. Foster Road, and later quit to take a job in the sports department of G.I. Joes in the Eastport Plaza. "She was a good employee and well-liked by everybody here," said Kelli Walker, Assistant Store Manager. Darci had been pregnant and had a miscarriage while working there, Walker recalled.

Along with the reporters, both the prosecution and defense teams were madly collecting data. The race, basically, was between one side trying to prove that Darci had stalked her victim and killed her, and the other contention that Darci was mentally ill.

"We were looking for anything to give us an indication of what was going on in Darci's head," said Craig. The prosecution needed evidence of premeditation—intent—before a first-degree murder charge would fly. Craig and Hughes tracked down the car dealers who'd seen Darci the week before the murder. Her visit to Montano Acura seemed part of a setup. They found John Drexler and recorded his story of moving the replica gun to the Volkswagen door. It looked as if Darci set out to kidnap Cindy Ray.

The defense team, meanwhile, was just confused. They assumed that the murder was deliberate but didn't know what to do. "It struck us right off that there was going to be some kind of psychological defense, some kind of insanity defense because it was such a crazy act," said Jameson. "But we didn't know what we were looking for." They wanted a psychiatrist to examine Darci soon, to preserve whatever mental state she was in. Mental states, they knew, could shift over time. But getting help was not easy. "Early on I took the task of trying to find some experts," said Jameson. "I called different doctors. Our initial feelings were we needed somebody who was a gynecological or obstetric expert to go and examine her, because we thought perhaps there was a different hormonal issue or body chemistry issue. We also knew we were going to need some kind of psychiatrist, too, but initially we felt we were going to need a gynecologist who would explain to us the phenomenon of making your body appear to be having a child when you're not pregnant. We thought there was much more to the phenomenon of false pregnancy."

Jameson didn't get much help from the local doctors. They'd say, "Well, we heard about it and we're not interested. We just don't handle things like that."

"It was horrific. It was disgusting," Jameson said. "To most doctors, especially obstetricians, it was appalling the thought of somebody performing a lay cesarean section with a car key. It turns out to be somewhat amazing to a lot of these doctors. I met a lot of doctors who still find it almost impossible to believe she could have done the job she did with no injury to the child."

Jameson, Bogren and social worker Bill Chambreau sat down with the Pierces and Rickers. They asked about upbringing, family, people who knew her. "This wasn't a missing evidence case in the classical sense," said Jameson. "The missing evidence here was psychological evidence." They wanted some indication of mental illness throughout Darci's life.

That evening, less than a week after the murder, Darci's parents visited her in a tearful reunion in the jail. On her return to the cell, Darci was attacked by another inmate. She was uninjured but shaken. In talking with a psychiatric aide late that night Darci asked that the door be locked behind her. She didn't want to leave again. She also began reading the Bible. The next day, Darci was diagnosed by a psychiatric aide as "compulsive and unpredictable" and a possible suicide risk. She was given a blanket, but was placed on continuous suicide supervision.

Fourteen

Bill and Millie Ray's house looked as if it had been added onto over the years, working from a basic square. A bedroom added here, a family room there, a car porch beside the kitchen. If you walked through the kitchen door on July 30, 1987, you had to step around the table, so small was the room. The family room was off to the right and the living room and dining room were to the left, up a step into what looked like the original small bungalow.

A big family was raised well in this house: eight children, two boys, and six girls. There were eleven grandchildren. Amelia Monik made it an even dozen. At the time of Cindy Ray's funeral, two of the kids still lived at home. That was where Amelia would live, too, for a while.

"I still find it hard to believe such a cruel, wicked thing could happen to Cindy," said Millie Ray. "I'm not crazy about Darci getting the electric chair. I just don't want her to go free. I can't see Cindy being resentful, though. She was a sweet, kind person. I never remember her saying anything bad about anybody. I know everybody says nice things about people who die, but she was a sweet girl. Amelia, when they brought her home, was such a tiny little thing. When my husband brought her off the plane I asked him to uncover her, and it just made your heart break. It's miraculous that Sam got her back. Her hard time is going to come later, when it finally all has to be explained to her. There's really nothing we can do but give her lots of love. That's what her mother would have given her."

In front of the Ray house the road ran north and south, a two-lane country road, with a crown. Up the hill to the south was an upscale neighborhood. Down a long slow slope to the north, the street dead-ended at the town cemetery. The street that ran perpendicular, along the cemetery front, was the street that Cindy Ray had lived on when she was a girl. Cindy and Sam had worn grooves in the blacktop at that intersection, courting. On July 30, 1987, they met there again to say goodbye.

Sam was dressed in his Air Force uniform with a military beret. Cindy was dressed in her silk undergarments and her white temple dress, a floor-length gown with long sleeves and a high neck. She wore white hose, white shoes and a pleated pinafore with a green satin apron, embroidered with leaves, symbolic of the fig leaf worn by Eve. Around her waist she wore a white voile sash. On her head was a bonnet with a veil tied under her chin. The veil was up and the family could see her face in the casket.

Sam, four years into his six-year hitch, by now had decided to seek an early release from the Air Force and return to Utah. He had been offered a humanitarian honorable discharge, or reassignment. He planned to transfer to inactive duty with an Air National Guard unit to attend Brigham Young University in Provo. The military paid to ship Cindy's

145

body home, and for her funeral expenses. It also moved the trailer to Utah and set it up in a trailer court not far from the cemetery. On the trailer's walls hung needlepoint that Cindy had sewn. There also were boxes of stuff she had left: a list of songs she had taught Luke, an album scrapbook with her parents' wedding certificate, her birth certificate, a whisp of blonde hair, a whisp of darker hair, and pages for each school grade, beginning with first grade. There were notes on a talk she did in church on prophet Joseph Smith, T-ball certificates, valentines from long ago, and pictures of their family on vacation. Honor cords from graduation, a napkin from their wedding reception, pictures of old boyfriends, a Volksmarch medal.

"I don't have any hard feelings for Darci," Sam Ray said, looking through the box. "I feel sorry for her. One of my best friends couldn't have babies. It's a hard thing. I was surprised that one woman could overcome Cindy. I realized how fragile a pregnant woman was. The Cindy that wasn't pregnant would have got out and run. But Cindy was small, exhausted and eight and a half months pregnant. She could see what was happening. I have no doubt she prayed her mind out that if she couldn't survive it, the baby would be okay. And Cindy had that kind of faith to make it happen. I picture Cindy dying and seeing Darci driving off with that baby, praying her heart out that she would find us. It's really a miracle that within twenty-four hours, I had my baby in my arms and we knew what had happened.

"I want the kids to know who their mommy was. What kind of person she was, how she lived her life. The most prominent thing was she loved other people with all her heart. I imagine she felt sorry for Darci. Cindy was selfless. She cared more about her little boy, about me, about the baby in her womb, than herself. All Darci cared about was herself. The hardest part isn't for me. The hardest part is watching those kids go through the pain. To see that little boy hug me and cry and to see that little girl grow up without her mom. I think when that little girl's a teenager she will be a constant reminder of what I've lost.

"I was a cop. I'd watched people die. It was all this big facade. My life's crumbled around me, but I can deal with it. I cry plenty in private. I feel like I've been carried by a loving, heavenly father. You know how a little kid is hugged and kissed and held?" Sam received thousands of letters and about four thousand dollars for the kids. He planned to attend college and leave the kids with his mother. At night, Luke would sleep in the trailer.

Down at Cindy's house, Larry Giles had his daughter's picture on the wall in the living room. "She kept a record, a journal, a life journal. She never got to finish it. I figure she gave her life for the baby." Larry quit drinking when she died. "It was either one way or the other—to the bottom of the bottle or . . . I didn't need any more trouble than I already got." Larry also received a letter after the murder from a woman at Clovis Air Force Base: "I can picture Cindy in my mind, the Sundays I'd see her holding Luke and rocking him and playing with him (so patient, so loving!). Never once did I see Cindy lose her temper or get angry. She had such a great love for her family."

147

More than one hundred fifty people gathered at the 9th Ward Chapel of the Church of Jesus Christ of Latter-day Saints for a service for Cindy. Fifteen minutes before, the bishop met with Sam and Cindy's relatives for a family prayer. The veil on her face was lowered, and the casket closed. An organ played as she was wheeled into the wardhouse. After an opening prayer, friends spoke of Cindy.

Margene Wilson, a neighbor who watched Cindy grow up with her daughter, read a long testimony:

"The Giles family moved to our neighborhood when Cindy was three years old. We were delighted when we found out there were two little girls, Toni and Cindy and baby boy Kipper. Those three little girls became very good friends right from the first and you seldom saw one without the other, right up until the time they graduated from high school and moved away from home . . . There were a lot of slumber parties. Many a time I found three girls all asleep in one bed. I'll never forget the time Cindy was about thirteen or fourteen and she asked me if she could have a surprise birthday party for Toni. She said I didn't need to worry about anything. Maybe I remember this so vividly because I am so disorganized, but I could not believe how a young girl could put something over so smoothly and have it so well planned. She had the decorations planned, and had all the games written out. She had all the food prepared, and even a diagram of where everyone was sleeping. Afterwards she cleaned up. No wonder I loved her and felt like she was almost one of mine.

"Cindy was very agile . . . and learned very early

148

to do flips. Occasionally she'd miss and come down on her head . . . she always had a bump on her forehead—they called them Cindy's horns. She took first place her senior year in high school region in parallel bars and vaulting. She was a real competitor. I'll never forget the year the girls played Payson City League T ball and won the championship. I can still see that glint in her eye when she got up to bat. They won, mostly because of Cindy's play and her leadership ability."

Mrs. Wilson went on about Cindy's good grades in school, her work in the church, and her devotion to the work ethic—house cleaning and packing cherries in a plant. She remembered how Cindy and Sam had met in the Payson band. "There were many girls who had a big crush on Sam, but the one who stole his heart was Cindy. He gave her his senior ring when she was a sophomore as part of a promise ring. She didn't dare tell her parents for about two weeks. Finally she got enough nerve to show it to her parents, who immediately made her give it back to him because she was too young. Her mother told me this was the most upset Cindy had ever been with her.

"When Cindy was a senior in high school and in the Young Women's Association, her teacher Duana Memmott asked all the girls to write a letter to themselves saying what they would be like in five years. I would like to read the letter Cindy wrote to herself. It was dated October 1982, when Cindy was 18:

"Within five years I will be married (in the Temple, of course) and will have started my own family. I will have gone to school to hopefully have graduated to be someone in a medical profession. In five years I will be a little more mature and hopefully I will be a little more patient. I will have read the Book of Mormon and will have a stronger testimony of Jesus Christ. I will be striving to help my eternal mate and I to be one. Right now there is so much I want to accomplish and so little time to do it in. I hope I can accomplish all that the Lord wants me to."

Mrs. Wilson then concluded her eulogy:

"Cindy was a beautiful, well-rounded woman in every respect, spiritual, physical, and intellectual. She loved life, her husband and her heavenly Father and I can think of no one more prepared to go back to her Heavenly Father. She lived as good a life as possible and I am sure she is a special daughter of the Lord. I pray that the Lord will bless and comfort the family . . . I pray that the sad tragic circumstances of her death will be softened in their hearts and they will be able to remember the way Cindy has touched their lives and the love she gave them. I pray that her family will not dwell on the tragic circumstances of her death but instead be able to teach and tell her children of the example she set for them and for all of us."

After the church service, the funeral moved to the cemetery for the dedication of the grave. Sam stood there holding Luke over his chest. Although he wasn't scheduled to speak, he chose to address the congregation as the funeral came to an end.

"A lot of people see the tragedy and it is very tragic and not so nice. But there was one joyous sight—a child. This is a difficult time. It comes as a shock for a lot of people. Cindy and I have had a lot of time to prepare for this. We knew that the time on this earth together would not be long. I'll take my little kids and raise them the way their mommy wanted them to be raised."

Cindy was buried with her feet pointing east, in the Mormon custom, to prepare her to rise to face Jesus in the second resurrection. At her head, a gravestone of speckled granite read, "Cindy Lynn Ray, June 17, 1964 – July 23, 1987. Our Mommy." On the back of the stone, with a picture of the Mormon Temple, was this Bible verse: "Greater love hath no one, than to lay down their life for a friend."

Fifteen

Cindy Ray was buried on the day that Albuquerque's district attorney officially announced he was seeking the death penalty for her killer, Darci Pierce. The crime still was the biggest story in Albuquerque. District Attorney Steven Schiff announced in time for the evening newscasts that the case would go before a grand jury on August 6. He said he would seek indictments for first-degree murder, kidnapping and child abuse. Evidence would be submitted to show that murder was a motive during Cindy Ray's abduction, which under New Mexico law was punishable by death.

At a news conference with Schiff, Police Lieutenant Roger Anderson said that Darci had used a replica handgun to force Cindy to drive with her. And Dr. Ross Zumwalt, who did the autopsy, told reporters that Cindy was alive but unconscious while her baby was being removed. Schiff then opened for questions.

"Steve, have you been able to determine what sort of instrument was used to remove the baby?" Schiff tossed it to Zumwalt.

"The object that was used to open the abdomen was an object that was fairly blunt. It was not as

152

sharp as a knife and caused tearing of the tissues of the abdomen and the uterus, as well as cutting it."

"Was it a key?"

"It could have been."

"Did Darci Pierce have prior training or understanding?"

"Well, I don't know who did this. The person who incised the abdomen did so in a horizontal fashion just above the pubic area, a very similar location in which many cesarean sections are done."

"Doctor, does that surprise you, in any way, that this blunt instrument could have been used, first of all, and second, that it did not apparently injure the child?"

"Yes and yes."

Lieutenant Anderson said that police had learned of one prior pregnancy by Darci Pierce that was aborted in the sixth month.

"How about all the false pregnancies?"

"We're also of the understanding that she may have had one other false pregnancy where she played the role of being pregnant for a number of months and then claimed that the baby was stillborn."

"Lieutenant, what about the kidnapping itself. I understand there was something about some scratching on the side of the car door?"

"The scratching on the car has been reported as a signal for help. Our criminalistics people have further examined that scratching and determined that it is probably the work of vandals some time considerably prior to the actual attack. The word that is scratched in there, that appears to be 'help' is actually 'head' and it's part of a filthy expletive, quite

153

frankly." Anderson said there was no indication that Darci knew Cindy prior to the murder, but Schiff wouldn't allow him to say whether Darci stalked her. He said the replica gun was found in the car and that there was only one suspect in the murder.

"Do you have any idea as to how Mrs. Pierce fooled her husband that she was pregnant the last several months?"

"Our understanding is she began gaining enormous amounts of weight, to the extent that her abdomen area swelled to the extent that it appeared that she was pregnant. She fooled, obviously, a number of people." Schiff would not say whether Darci had confessed, although she had six days earlier. Neither would he respond to queries about Darci's previous trip to the Acura dealer. Anderson noted no previous psychiatric history and no medical background. Zumwalt reported the umbilical cord torn and the placenta left with the body. Cindy was strangulated, he said, "with some sort of garrote of fairly soft material."

"Were there any attempted aggressions on pregnant women prior to this?"

"Not that we're aware of, no."

The reporters asked about Darci's sanity, and kept returning to the details of the cesarean.

"Just one incision?"

"No, it was a combination of numerous passes with a fairly blunt object that tore layer by layer through the abdominal wall," said Zumwalt.

Looking for the right sound bite, they also asked Zumwalt leading questions.

"Doctor, would you say that the delivery of this

baby in the manner it was born, was miraculous?"

"Very unusual, perhaps miraculous, yes."

"Would you say it was an unusual experience?"

"I don't really know because I don't know of any-body who's ever tried it before."

"If Cindy had died from the strangulation would the baby had any chance of living?"

"Supposedly infants have been delivered from dead mothers within the first several minutes, perhaps up to ten minutes or so. In this particular case . . . there was evidence of bleeding within the abdominal cavity. That along with the fact that the infant was delivered alive and the appearance of some of the other organs in the body which looked pale, as if they had lost a lot of blood, led me to conclude, with reasonable medical certainty, that she was alive at the time of the incision."

"There wasn't any indication that Mrs. Ray had started labor?"

"No such indication by autopsy."

In her jail cell that evening, Darci Pierce watched the TV news on the funeral and the news conference and began shaking. She told a counselor she wanted to kill herself. "For a while I did not know if I was alive or dead. I was afraid I had already hurt myself." When she felt herself lose control, she asked a guard for help. She also said she was dealing with jail "by just not being here. I've done this all my life when faced with unpleasant situations. I just go away. I'm not really anywhere. When I get angry I see white, everything just goes white."

155

Darci continued under suicide supervision with nothing in her cell but her uniform and a blanket. She complained about no sheets. "If I'm going to kill myself I can use my uniform or anything else." She said she had tried to kill herself once before, at the age of twelve, by inhaling gas fumes. The next day, July 31, Darci reported feeling numb and immobile and afraid she had hurt herself. "Sometimes I'm afraid of losing control. I'm not sure I can control myself."

Darci's eating habits were being carefully watched, as well. During her first six days in jail she ate nothing, except for a cheese sandwich at the time of booking and a little water and milk in the morning. On August 1 she ate a little lunch. But as the days passed she appeared more and more anxious at her fate. She told a psychiatric aide that she had entered a "void" state of mind to cope with it, and that she had done so since she was a small child. She said the void occurred often and she couldn't remember two days of the previous week. It was difficult for her to describe her voids, except that it was not daydreaming. And the aide noted that when Darci told of the void state, she was articulate, intelligent and insightful. In the first week of August she still was not eating. "I'm living for my husband only," she said.

On August 6, Darci was found with a pen in her room, writing, and it was taken from her. That was the day a grand jury formally indicted her for first-degree murder, kidnapping with great bodily harm, and child abuse. A bench warrant was formally issued for her arrest. Darci told a guard she hoped to get out on a lower bond, but it never materialized.

On August 11, Darci began the first of many psychological examinations. Susan Brayfield-Cave, a wild-haired, attractive, clinical psychologist from Santa Fe was hired by the defense to see Darci for twelve hours over four visits. Darci was, at first, cautious and a little bit paranoid about her safety, the psychologist reported. "She generally had a pleasant, soft-spoken demeanor, cheerful, outgoing." But that changed as the evaluation progressed. When talking about babies or about the pregnancy she had lost, Darci cried. When she talked about the crime, she was halting and stared into space, speaking almost monotone, with one-syllable, one-word answers. She had to be prodded to talk.

"It was remarkable, the change in her demeanor," said Brayfield-Cave. "Sometimes she could be cute and friendly and outgoing and other times she could be very withdrawn." The psychologist administered four tests: a Wechsler IQ test, which measures thinking style; a Rorschach ink blot; an incomplete sentence test; and a Minnesota Multiphasic Personality Inventory. Basically they showed Darci to be very intelligent, even superior. Yet she gave inappropriate answers at times, showing signs of illogical thinking, and impulsiveness. For example, when asked to explain the proverb, "Shallow brooks are noisy," she said, "The deeper something is, the more intent, as in a person who thinks a lot, compared to a person who runs off at the mouth." Asked to explain "One swallow doesn't make a summer," Darci said, "Just because you see the first signs of something, it doesn't mean it's actually there." The psychologist couldn't help think of Darci's false pregnancies.

Darci tested well on vocabulary, except for emotional words like compassion, remorse, fortitude and delusion—another little glitch in her head. Darci knew what appropriate behavior was but there was a disparity between that and what she did, the psychologist concluded. On a schizophrenia scale she scored highest, an indication of a person who tends to overdramatize and exaggerate problems but also someone who had experienced a large number of bizarre incidents. She also scored high on paranoias, being suspicious of other people and their motives and she was very angry, feeling that she was treated unfairly within her family and possibly by society. The standard ink blot showed another peculiarity. Intelligent people usually give a high number of responses and Darci gave very few, indicating a lot of anger and defiance. She had an active fantasy life and was capable of empathy for other people. But relations had been conflicted, she had been very deeply hurt in some of her more meaningful and important interpersonal relationships.

Overall, the tests showed Dr. Brayfield-Cave that Darci was very emotionally responsive, with lots of intense feelings but not a lot of conscious control. Her emotions overwhelmed her, and there were signs that her emotional development may have been stalled at a young age. Most of the time she was in good contact with reality, although there was very deep depression and a suggestion that under stress irrationality showed up. Emotionally, Darci liked children and did not like to see a child cry. She was pained when someone took advantage of someone else, and she had remorse, in particular, wishing that

158

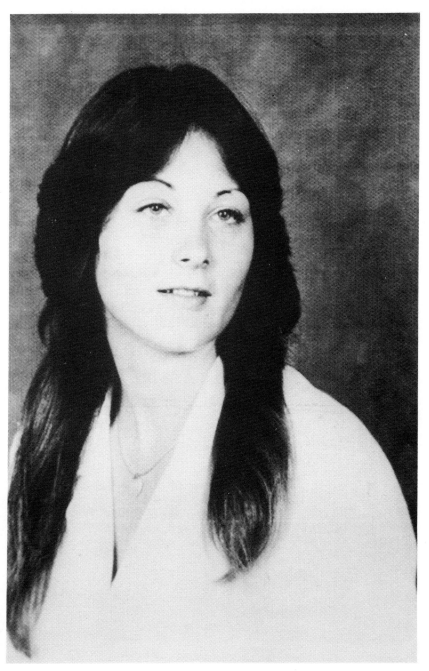

Cindy Lynn Ray

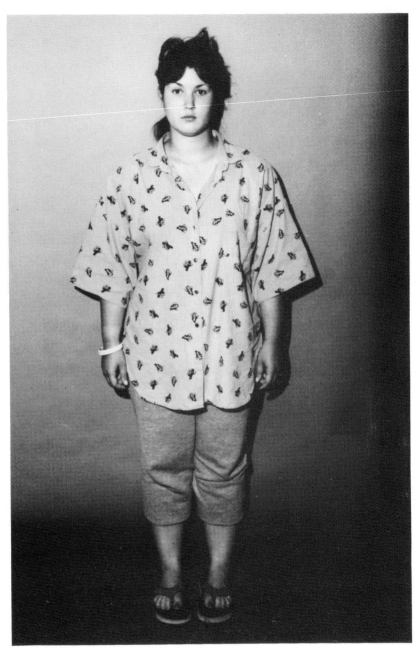

Darci Kayleen Pierce

USAF Ambulatory Health Center housed the ob-gyn clinic where Cindy Ray was abducted by Darci Pierce on July 23, 1987.
(*Courtesy of Michael Gallegos*)

Darci Pierce drove Cindy Ray to the murder scene in the Albuquerque hills in her white Volkswagen bug.

Darci Pierce used Cindy Ray's own car keys to perform a crude caesarian section on her then left her to die.

Darci led police to this deserted spot in the hills where they found
Cindy Ray's body.

Detective Tom Craig was one of the investigating officers at the scene of the murder. (*Courtesy of Michael Schwarz*)

Rob Mohr was the car sales manager at the Acura dealership where Darci drove after she committed the murder to ask for help.
(*Courtesy of Michael Schwarz*)

Car salesman John Drexler drove with Darci Pierce in the ambulance to the hospital.
(*Courtesy of Michael Schwarz*)

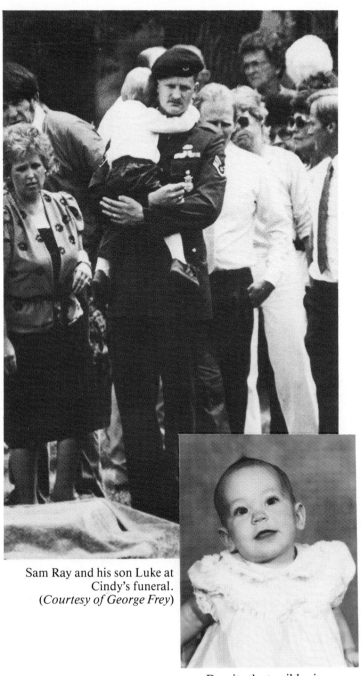

Sam Ray and his son Luke at Cindy's funeral. (*Courtesy of George Frey*)

Despite the terrible circumstances of her birth, Amelia Monik Ray miraculously survived.

Darci Pierce, right, is led into court by her attorney, Assistant Public Defender Tom Jameson. (*Courtesy of Michael Schwarz*)

her own mother had aborted her, that she had not been born and adopted by the Rickers. She told Brayfield-Cave that when she was a child she was never really a child and didn't have a childhood. And she had failed at the most basic thing a woman could do—having a baby.

The psychologist's report gave the defense team just a glimpse into Darci's mind, one that needed fleshing out with details of her life. In time, the report proved a remarkably accurate outline. Darci was sick and her life was strewn with symptoms. Her defenders were only beginning to see the strangeness within.

On the evening of August 12, Darci received the indictment papers, and the next morning her mood and behavior changed drastically. She became depressed, hopeless and did not want to talk to anyone, including Ray. "It doesn't matter. What's the use?" she kept saying. She refused medication and refused to see her attorneys. She called her previous good mood a facade she could no longer keep up. "I've felt this all my life—out of control."

At 6:00 P.M. on August 12, Darci became motionless, lying on her side on the bed with her eyes open, the pupils wide. She remained that way for three hours. At one point, tears ran for thirty seconds, without a blink. When a psychiatrist saw Darci she was lying on her right side, covered with a blanket, "in a state of catatonic stupor." The next day Darci began looking in her room for something to hurt herself with. She found a crack in the toilet bowl and began scratching herself. She was moved to another room. When a therapist showed up later, he found

159

her sitting on the floor, joking and smiling. "Nothing matters anymore," she said. Jailers again put her on a twenty-four-hour continuous sight observation. An officer was ordered to sit outside her door and watch her constantly. Noted therapist Chavez: "Resident appears quite unstable and unpredictable."

As Darci played out one small drama in her cell, a bigger one was being written in Portland, Oregon. By August, the roses in the public gardens had ripened and the fragrance of fallen petals was gone, drowned by the stronger smell of the rivers. It was dry for a change, except for early morning mist that covered the Willamette. The river divided the city into natural halves, and a line along Burnside Street, which ran east and west, cut it again into quarters. Southwest was the hilly side, where mansions clutched the rocks. The northeast, across the river, was industrial: the mills, the docks, the mixed-race neighborhoods. Here the products of Oregon came to port, grain and lumber. The northwest was a mix, with drugs in Old Town and upscale homes nearby. The southeast seemed to go forever on fertile ground, a suburban exurban quarter. That was where Darci Pierce had come of age.

Within a few square miles her life had been played out, on a stage that no one appreciated until the murder. Through the summer and into the fall of 1987 a race took place between the opposing factions of her destiny, to find facts about her, clues as to why she killed Cindy Ray.

On the one side was the FBI, in the person of

160

agent James Maher, who began searching for people whose names came up in the early sketches made by the family. He was looking for proof that Darci wasn't crazy.

That was the problem for the defense, too. "It was a disturbing case," said Tom Jameson, who with Bill Chambreau journeyed to Portland to retrace Darci's life. "You had a nineteen-year-old woman who was attractive, intelligent, friendly, articulate, a really genuinely likeable person who I like very much, and I really think is a really wonderful person. The flip side was convinced that she was pregnant, her body transformed, she kidnapped a woman, strangled, killed her, performed the cesarean section with a key: the acts of a monster. An inhumane act. It's almost inconceivable that a human could do that to another human. It made you start thinking about animal behavior, if you could even imagine something like this.

"We went to her house, went to her schools, sat in her parents' living room, talked to her teachers, talked to her friends. It was sort of like trying to relive someone's life. That was our job, to go back and find out who she was. At that point we thought we were fighting for her life, that they were going to try to execute her. I got to know more about her than I know about anyone in my life. And it was more and more disturbing as you went along.

"You had the girl next door who you'd just be thrilled to talk to. People liked her. She was friendly. She did what all the other kids did. She baked cookies. She chased after boys. She had teachers who thought she was wonderful. She was a nicer-than-average person, a brighter-than-average person, a more-articulate-than-average person, a more-creative-than-average person.

"We met all the actors, participants in her life, none of whom could have ever predicted anything like this. Not an inkling. Not one person who said, 'boy, there was something really weird about Darci.' There wasn't anybody who even said 'there was something that made you shiver, or feel weird.' And that was very eerie. Nor were there signs, like, 'when she was twelve she used to mutilate cats and we walked into the basement once and she had six cats hanging from the pipes.' You almost wanted to hear that, and say, 'oh my God, that's great.' Then you could say, 'oh my God, this *is* a crazy person, this *is* an insane person.' "

In time, both the FBI and the defense team went by Darci's home, 4517 Southeast Seventy-ninth Avenue. Her house was green with a peaked roof and a long porch across the front, draped by a vine and many flowers. The house was surrounded by a chain link fence and accumulated toys, a small RV, a boat, a van.

By the time FBI agents called, Darci's lawyers had warned her parents and they found themselves reluctant with authority. Yes, she had been to South Africa, they said. They couldn't remember the city. No she had no specific medical background; she wanted to be an airline stewardess. "I'm sorry I can't give you any more," Mrs. Ricker finally told agent Maher. "But I'm sure you'll find out everything you want to know eventually."

She was right. Darci's life was laid bare for all to

see, to pick at for clues, to grind into assumptions, to fly to conclusions. The sad story really began before Darci Pierce was born.

Sixteen

Darci Pierce's mother was a teenager, a fifteen-year-old unwed student whose name she never knew, whose face she never touched. The teenage girl's father was a pots and pans salesman who sold his wares in homes.

In the fall of 1967, Sandra K. Ricker, a twenty-eight-year-old mother of two boys, and her husband, Kenneth B. Ricker, held a pots and pans party at their house in Toledo, Oregon, a little town outside of Portland. It was cheap entertainment and the Rickers didn't have much money. They lived paycheck to paycheck, grew a garden, and tried to vacation whenever they could get time away from the shop foreman.

Sandra Ricker had come to Toledo from Salem, the state capital, farther up the Willamette River, with a family that left her wanting. When she was six years old a friend of the family had sexually abused her. Years later, psychiatrists would argue that Sandra's abuse was a clue to Darci's life. When Sandra was eleven, she learned that her mother was having an affair with her father's best friend. When she was fourteen her mother left. "I was very angry because I loved my mother," she said much later,

164

when she began to remember the pain of her childhood. "I also felt very rejected that she would leave me." Two years later, at the age of sixteen she married Kenneth Ricker. A year more and she gave birth to her first child, a boy named Craig, a difficult birth. In another year Rick was born, and she almost died hemorrhaging. The Rickers wanted five kids but they stopped trying for fear of losing Sandra.

On the night of Craig's third birthday, he fell down a flight of stairs and banged his head hard, knocking teeth and part of his gums out, and he began to act a little funny. When he started kindergarten the teacher said he had epilepsy, which in those days made him retarded in the eyes of many, a slow learner at best. He required special education. Rick was a sickly boy, with ear infections. When he started school, the teachers called him retarded, too. The boys were eleven and ten when the pots and pans salesman came to call. It was a nice evening, that autumn night of 1967, and friends of the Rickers who attended decided to hold a party of their own. It was at that party that the pots and pans salesman got drunk and offered his grandchild for adoption. The hosts called the Rickers.

When Darci was just a baby, the Rickers moved to Portland and bought a house on Southeast Seventy-ninth Avenue, a neighborhood of small, clean homes, blue-collar families, and blue-collar blues. It was a neighborhood of Christian fundamentalism, of simple values and simple justice, right-wing and white, that hid behind lives of quiet, complex desperation. Sandra took the children to the Church of Christ on Duke Street. She went Sunday morning,

165

Sunday night, and Wednesday evening. Ken didn't go much. He didn't do much with the family because of his work on the graveyard shift of the sawmill, running a forklift. The exception was his two-week deer-hunting vacation each October. When he was home, it seemed, Ken was sleeping. Darci later described him as pussy-whipped and henpecked. He never disciplined the kids, never said no. That fell to Sandra, who slapped Darci on the face with her hand if she spoke back to her, and paddled her butt with a pancake turner. Her early family fantasies were headed by a man who was boss.

At the age of six, Darci began sexual relations with her cousin, Brad Vanderberg, the son of Sandra's sister, Donna. "I would be sleeping over and she'd start explaining different things, or doing different things that at the time I did not understand," Brad told a jury later. "I really didn't know what was going on, but at the same time, you know, I liked what was going on, and I didn't know if it was wrong, but I didn't know if it was right." The cousins never told anyone, and their intercourse continued until they were twelve years old.

In those same years, Darci began to tell lies. She would claim her brothers were picking on her when they were not. She told other kids her home was perfect. And she told everyone she got straight A's in school. Sometimes she made up stories to explain strange incidents, like broken toys she'd find in her room. She would get into trouble for things she couldn't remember doing.

Her stories got her into trouble at school. At their minister's suggestion, the Rickers enrolled nine-year-old Darci in the Montaville Christian School, one of many private fundamentalist academic institutions in Portland. Right away she had difficulty with reality, truth and honesty, said Tom Burgess, the principal. "She was a nice girl, but she had that habit, even at that young age." At Montaville students graded themselves and Darci generally scored around 90. But she couldn't resist the temptation to change answers while correcting her paper. The teachers caught her repeatedly. In her file at school were these notes to Burgess, written in Darci's childhood hand:

I don't think I should get a spanking because you didn't say disobedence [sic] would be a spanking, so I admit I have been playing around but did do some work. I only brout [sic] homework home twice and I think that's pretty good don't you. To tell the truth I really am going to start working. I bring homework every day, and after school straight to the books. I am going to really start trying so please forgive me for fooling around. I will try to do my best now okay.

Another letter read:

Dear Mr. Burgess: Thank you for your kindness and all. That you for helping me realize that wrong only makes things worse. Thank you for the rules in this school that we have to abide to and that give us the ability to do right. Your student in Christ. Darci.

This plaintive note appeared on a scrap of a school paper.

I now and always will have my work done and will not have any more trouble and will not have another spanking at school. So help me God please. From Darci Ricker. P.S. Put this in a record and keep till I die.

But after two years Darci's fourth and fifth grades, Burgess gave up on her. On April 11, 1978 he wrote to the Rickers:

I'm extremely sorry to have to let you know that our efforts to help Darci change her work habits and cheating habits have not brought about the desired results. We have talked with Darci about the problem, especially in the two areas of completing work and scoring honestly. In accord with the agreement that we made together with her, we will have to find it necessary to expel Darci from school for the remainder of the year. We are praying that this lesson will make Darci realize like nothing else has to this time, how important it is to do what she knows is right.

By this time, Darci was also promiscuous, first with boys and later with men of all ages. According to what she later revealed to psychiatrists, she was anxious to please and enjoyed being told she performed well. But her sense of it was that she was far more interested in the closeness of the sexual relationship than the eroticism. She wanted to be wanted.

Sixth grade could have been a turning point for Darci because she met the woman of her dreams, her teacher Sharon Gray, a tall, pretty, thin woman with long brown hair. Darci idolized Gray. For one thing, Gray was adopted; for another she drank tea, and Darci began a habit of having tea at school with her teacher. Ms. Gray thought Darci a special student, and gave her extra time. "Of the students that I have had, she was probably one of the most brilliant kids," she said later. But Darci also was a handful: moody, disruptive, loud, and so angry at times that she would stand up abruptly, yell and turn over her desk. She turned a desk over six or seven times a year, and Gray never knew why. Darci would throw books, and once broke the glass in the door. But Darci would never hurt anyone but herself. "A couple of times she was so upset that she would go in [a] corner and try scratching herself, scratching her arms," Gray said. The teacher found the best way to handle Darci in those moments was to reach out, touch her arm, and then hold her in an embrace. Although Darci was much stronger than her teacher, she would calm down.

Darci's moods would change abruptly, too. One minute she was smiling and the next she was staring out the window and frowning. Then, over would go a desk. She would also lie. After winter break Darci returned to school with a story that she had skied in Alaska. "She told me exactly how well she skied and how long she skied and the jumps that she took and the hotdogging, the splits and all that. She was teiling it to me like it was real," said Gray.

Gray, who later became head of the Portland Teachers Association and worked as a special education assistant to the governor of Oregon, said she could never figure out what caused Darci's behavior and mood shifts. "Some students might do certain things for attention-getting or because they're frustrated with the material, like a new concept . . . but with Darci I could never figure out the why." When Gray tried to get Darci's parents to help, they didn't respond. "As you work with the parents you start to get a feeling as to whether working with the parents is effective or not and in this case I stopped working—this doesn't sound very nice—I just felt that they were ineffectual in helping me deal with behaviors with her. I kept them informed. I would call them or I would write them notes, but I didn't try to set up plans with them. I just didn't feel like they had much control with her." Gray also wanted counseling for Darci but there was none in the school at the time.

To family friend Karen Head, the Ricker family was clearly dysfunctional when it came to Darci. "Her father was always asleep . . . which became a joke. When he was awake he wasn't much company. I never saw him take the kids anywhere. Her mother always wanted Darci to be in the limelight. When Darci had troubles and she would tell her mom, her mom really didn't believe her. I asked several times for them to get counseling throughout the year. They fell on deaf ears. They didn't want to hear that. I was usually told that I was getting the lies and it was my problem with Darci."

As Darci moved into junior high, her internal strife worsened. Her lying increased, absurdly so, and she was caught often. If she had a day off from school, she would tell her mother she was leaving for school and visit friends instead. She even lied to friends. On October 16, 1979, she wrote to a pen pal, "Do you like horses? Well if you do you're gonna die. I got twenty new horses the other day and they're all so beautiful. There's four pintos, five appaloosas, five thoroughbreds and five palominos. I really think they're all beautiful. Oh yeah, and one American Arabian (Stallion). Oh yeah, I might get put in the eighth grade instead of being a seventh. I might get to skip. Wouldn't that be neat! Well, gotta go now. Time for bed. P.S. Last Saturday was my birthday so I'm twelve now."

That kind of lying around her family led to a roll of the eyes, a wave and the comment, "Darci is just pretending again." Once while playing with her cousin Brad she collapsed on the basement floor, apparently unconscious. Brad ran for help, and got his mother all shook up. When his father arrived, he took one look at her and said, "Come on, Darci, get up, quit fooling around." And she did.

As a teenager, Darci had become somewhat of a tomboy, an athlete of some ability. She skied, she hunted with her father, she pitched in softball. She began an extensive run on orthopedists because of injuries: a sprained ankle, a thumb, a right wrist, a left middle finger, a right ankle, a left wrist.

Darci had few close friends, in part because of her lying, and also because of strange mood shifts. One who stuck it out over a long time was Rachael Mc-

Crainey, who met Darci in seventh grade. "We would be playing a game and all of a sudden she would just stop and decide to go do something else, something totally opposite of what we were doing." There was also a dark side that frightened McCrainey. They played "chicken" in traffic at night, lying in a four-lane street with no lights and moving only at the last minute. Rachael would move when the cars were a block away, but Darci wouldn't move. "I would end up stopping the car, bawling my head off, because she would just lay there and wouldn't budge." Darci would laugh and call Rachael a baby.

"Darci always wanted to be the princess in the big castle," said Rachael. She always wanted to have everything. And she lied if she didn't have everything. For their eighth grade graduation, for example, Darci claimed to have ordered an expensive gown from Paris. She talked about it in great detail. When she showed up at graduation wearing something quite ordinary, Rachael confronted her. "What about the dress from Paris?"

"I have no idea what you're talking about," Darci replied. She later told Rachael she was eloping, and that her biological mother was coming for her; neither story was true. She and a friend did run away from home one weekend, drawing money from an account to buy an airplane ticket for Salt Lake City because that was where the Osmonds lived. But she called home, scared, and her parents wired money for the return. Darci's mother was so upset she was bedridden over the incident, coming as it did atop other rejections by Darci. To her face, Darci called Sandra fat and reminded her that she was a high school dropout. When they argued, Ken Ricker always took Darci's side, and Sandra felt rejected by her husband. They even talked about divorce, and she considered suicide.

In 1977 a young minister named David Brink took over the Duke Street Church of Christ, where Sandra took Darci. She could out-talk her mother and put her down, he noted. In counseling sessions with Brink, "she could use very abusive language toward her mother. She disdained her mother sometimes, the way she talked to her, I cringed—'stupid woman,' that kind of attitude." Darci never showed any physical affection toward her mother, either.

As he watched Darci grow, Brink saw a girl performing life, watching others and imitating, but never really finding a sense of inner morality that would be her gyroscope. "Darci always wanted to be somebody. She was interested in high class. She was interested in expanding her mind and her world. But it was because she looked around her world and saw that was what you did to appear successful. There was no moral feeling. The whole thing was a game, with no purpose other than to end up in control at the end." It was, Brink later decided, the conscience-less behavior of a psychopath.

Yet there was always a side to Darci Pierce that wouldn't fit into that box. She never forgot her mother's birthday. When Craig, her brother, was in a car wreck, Darci stayed at his side in the hospital. When her grandmother went into a coma after open heart surgery Darci kept her mother company. In church, she helped with a bus ministry, picking up young people on Sunday mornings. In school, she and Rachael volunteered as hostesses, watching youngsters in grades one to four at lunch so their teacher could eat. They would play games with them when it rained, take them to class and read them stories. When Rachael's parents went through a divorce, Darci asked Rachael to go with her on vacation.

At the age of fourteen, Darci started high school at LaSalle, a Catholic school. She went there, she said, because she would have been killed in racial fights in public schools, so bad was her attitude about blacks. Her grade point average was 2.5, about a B. With new friends, she could tell new stories about her home life. She could claim to shop at Nordstrom's and live in a fancy house. That year she was selected to be a foreign exchange student with the International Rotary Club, an event that would take place in her junior year. It became another watershed in Darci's life, one of those that could have brought her to the light of normalcy, but instead plunged her deeper in the dark side.

At a Rotary picnic prior to going she met a quiet, thin young man from Seaside, a community on the Pacific Ocean one hundred miles west of Portland. His name was Ray Pierce and he was working in a hobby shop in Portland. He was a couple of years older but they liked each other and wrote during Darci's year away. While in South Africa, she lived with several host families—all white, with chauffeurs and maids and swimming pools, according to her letters back home. No one could separate the truth from the fiction in Darci's stories. A local doctor invited Darci to observe his orthopedic surgery, and

174

she claimed to have assisted. But she mainly watched, such things as carpal tunnel repair and the setting of a broken leg. She attended several schools there, taking on an accent, and received nothing but high marks:

"Darci was friendly, enthusiastic and willing to any task or favour that was assigned to her. She is popular among friends and teachers. Darci presented many interesting lectures to different classes and was in this manner an excellent ambassador for her country," wrote J.L. Coetzer, principal of the Hoerskool Rob Ferreira. Darci took biology, geography, Afrikaans, math and German. A second school principal, J.L. DuToit of Hoerskool Bergvlam, described Darci as "the most pleasant exchange student we have ever hosted at this school. Mature, friendly and great fun to have around." In South Africa, Darci lived her fantasy life and felt at home.

In her absence, at the Ricker home in Portland, Sandra and Ken began to talk again. "We really realized that our problems weren't so much with each other," Sandra said. Darci had come between them. Ken began to see that he had not been meeting his responsibilities.

While Darci was gone they took out a home improvement loan, to dig a new basement, panel the living room, lay new carpet, install a sliding glass door in the living room, and install a deck and pool. Upstairs, they remodeled the front bedroom as a sitting room for Darci, with new rugs and paneling. The Rickers were excited about their new look and wanted it done to surprise Darci on her return. Unfortunately she arrived early to surprise them, and

175

found the house in a mess. Having come from a mansion she was not impressed and said so. "She was so beyond our home that it hurt our feelings lots," said Sandra. In her new accent she told her mother how to act. "And so we weren't proper and that hurt me."

Instead of creating a bright path for Darci, the South African experience drove a bigger, insurmountable wedge between her and her parents. Returning as a senior, the animosity grew thick in the remodeled house. She had matured beyond her mother, and she wouldn't let up about her weight. "There's no room for fat people in my society," Darci said.

In January 1985 she moved out. "Her family basically said we can't deal with her anymore and we won't deal with her anymore," said Karen Head, who took Darci in as an alternative to living with Ray Pierce. The arrangement lasted five months. In the spring of her senior year, Darci and Ray asked her father if they could marry. He said no, an answer that shocked everyone. He had never told Darci no. When the young couple appealed to minister Brink, he declined without parental approval. "Rather than work on your wedding, work on your relationship with your mother," Brink told Darci. "You guys have fought for years. It's time to grow up. Bury the hatchet. Understand where your mother is coming from."

But the dysfunction continued. Darci was not invited to two family weddings that spring, her own brother Craig's, and that of her cousin, Michelle. Michelle didn't want Darci there to upset her special day. The trouble with Craig began when Darci found out his fiancée had given up a child for adoption. "You give cats and dogs away, you don't give babies away," she screamed to anyone who would listen. Darci crashed the wedding anyway, and Darci and her mother had a long talk, trying to patch up. Still, the wound did not heal. When it came time for Darci to graduate from high school her parents did not attend. They chose to send a diamond and opal necklace and Sandra stayed home and cried all day.

"I loved Darci very much. She had reasons that she didn't love me. It didn't matter. I always loved her, you know, and I had dreamt of my daughter's graduation, proms, marriages, just like any mother does for their daughter. And it hurt a lot not to go, but there was a lot of discussion between Ken and I, and we were really rejected. Ken was really devastated when Darci moved out and even he didn't want to go to the graduation. And I was very surprised that he wouldn't go. He just said no."

Seventeen

As August rolled into September, jailers watching Darci's every move began to wonder just how crazy she was. Notes began to show in the record: "Resident is 'playing games' with a plastic spoon—hiding it and forcing the correctional officer to search for it, or breaking it in two and hiding the pieces." It was behavior Darci acknowledged in talks with the therapists. She called the guards "watchdogs" who were becoming relaxed with their continuous observation of her. She liked to "keep them on their toes." She liked to test them and catch them in a mistake. She did it more for entertainment than out of hostility.

She reported hearing voices again, calling her name, but when the therapist tried to get her to talk about personal things, Darci locked up, saying she would "never take down the wall." She talked about suicide, too, but as a game. "If I tell you yes then I don't get my stuff. If I tell you no it may be a lie." She said she'd "do it on the graveyard shift as they do not watch her close enough." Evaluated specifically for suicide potential, Darci impressed a therapist as rational: "One cannot eliminate any chance of her suicide attempt under clear consciousness and fair

178

state of mental status as a manipulative gesture."

On September 5, at a pretrial conference, Darci's tentative trial date was set: Jan. 11, 1988. The attorneys began trading witness lists; through them the shape of their cases formed. The prosecution would argue that Darci was a manipulative, scheming criminal. The defense would plead not guilty by reason of insanity; their witnesses would show how she was unable to "form specific intent" as required by law. As a result of these moves and the initial findings of the FBI, cops and defense teams, the focus shifted to the workings of Darci's mind. She began receiving long visits by psychiatrists and psychologists hired first by the defense teams, and then by the prosecution.

Teresita McCarty, the UNM psychiatrist who first saw Darci holding the baby before her confession, visited Darci for seventeen hours. Through her contacts, Jean Goodwin, an expert on dissociative behavior and child abuse was hired to meet with Darci. Over the course of two months she spent twenty hours with Darci. Her testimony would become the key to her defense. Both attempted to understand Darci's pregnancy history, which turned out to be a tantalizing mystery in itself. The more they dug, the more bizarre it became, the greater the mix of reality and fantasy. Darci had told different stories for years. Piecing together that history was monumental psychiatric detective work.

The story began at the age of seventeen, with her visit to Portland's Adventist Medical Center emer-

179

gency room with abdominal pain in the spring of 1985, about the time she moved in with Ray Pierce. She thought she was pregnant, but a test proved negative. Gynecologist David Sargent found a cyst on her ovary, which he removed. Darci liked the soft-spoken doctor and returned to his office in April for a checkup. She was having a problem retaining urine in the bladder, which cleared up with treatment. At LaSalle high school, where she was a senior, though, she was depressed and anxious and a counselor recommended she sign up for counseling with Catholic Family Services, to help her cope with the operation and the estrangement with her parents.

On an intake form with Catholic Family Services on April 22, 1985, Darci listed as problems: "suicide and tumor pregnancy . . . I've just lost a baby and I'm not handling it very well." Darci somehow had translated the cyst into a pregnancy. In filling out more forms on April 24, Darci checked a number of problems. Under the category "physical or sexual abuse" she wrote "friend, age 12." She complained of no appetite, not sleeping well, poor school performance; she felt depressed, with emotions and feelings numb. She was unable to cope with day-to-day life, she had nightmares and thoughts of suicide, and was afraid to be on her own. The first social worker at Catholic Family Services to see Darci listed her own impressions: suicidal ideation, relationship problems, including boyfriend, school problems, miscarriage, surgery. She considered Darci's stress "severe" and recommended individual counseling. The fact that Darci had been treated only for a cyst never appeared in the record.

In June 1985, Darci visited Dr. Sargent again. She had been taking birth control pills prescribed by him, yet she had no period. He tested her for pregnancy, and it was negative. By this time she and Ray had set up housekeeping in a small tan and white modular duplex on a cul-de-sac not far from where Darci's folks lived. Ray was working at the hobby shop and had enlisted in the Air Force. Darci worked after school at a hamburger stand and the Hard Luck Cafe. They were pretty much alone, due to the trouble with her parents, and the distance to Ray's home in Seaside. Darci's dream of becoming an airline stewardess appeared dead. She focused instead on Ray, on keeping their apartment, and on getting pregnant.

Shortly after her graduation from high school she thought she was pregnant again. Her periods were erratic and her body was changing and a home test was positive. Dr. Sargent found her uterus expanded but did not test her. He was encouraging.

On July 2, after four sessions with Catholic Family Services, Darci ended her counseling. In the termination summary, counselor Jan Coleman wrote: "Darci became depressed after a miscarriage, which I think forced her to look at her relationship by her adoptive mother which hasn't been good. When she got pregnant again depression lifted." The reason for the termination: "Getting married. Again pregnant."

On August 26 Darci began bleeding. Dr. Sargent started a series of serum human chronic gonadotropin (HCG) hormone tests, which measure the amount of hormone put out by the pregnancy to direct the early weeks of cell growth before the placenta becomes fully functioning. Normally, HCG levels rise and then fall as the placenta takes over. If they continue to rise there is trouble ahead, miscarriage or cancer. In Darci's case, that's what happened. The HCG went off the chart. An ultrasound showed a pattern much like a grape cluster, a molar pregnancy, a type of cancer.

On September 11, 1985 Dr. Sargent performed a dilatation and curettage, dilating the cervix and suctioning the growth from the uterus. When bleeding continued a second D&C was performed on September 17. From the hospital, Darci called her mother and they cried together on the phone, feeling closer than they had in years. Her mother knew how badly she wanted a baby, and how it would make her feel. Sandra Ricker brought Darci a Care Bear. "I had read somewhere when a person loses a child in the hospital it's good if they can go home with something in their arms and not empty-handed," Mrs. Ricker testified later.

Dr. Sargent felt Darci's reaction was normal—disappointment, but nothing unusual. He prescribed a heavy dosage of pain medication, which she took for a week. It left her feeling high. When she ran out of pills one day, Ray found her crying in great, wracking sobs, like a hurt child. This continued for days. He'd come home from work and find her lying on the bed, hugging her Care Bear and crying. Dr. Sargent advised Darci not to get pregnant for a year. Because of the possibility of cancer, he wanted to check the HCG levels for a year. If they dropped steadily to a nonpregnant level the chances were nil, but if they stayed high she could be treated. Choriocarcinoma was one of the most treatable cancers, with a nearly 100 percent cure-rate. The tests began weekly right after the D&C. Darci was seventeen and there was no reason for her not to expect children in the future.

In October 1985, Darci began working at G.I. Joes, an overgrown, upscale Army-Navy chain that sold outdoor wear and equipment. The store was in the Eastport Plaza, about halfway between Ray and Darci's apartment and Darci's folks, on busy Eighty-ninth Street S.E. The manager, Dan Locke, hired Darci to work twenty-eight to forty hours a week in the ski shop. She was a good worker, well-liked, and she became friends with a couple of fellow clerks, revealing to them she had just suffered a "miscarriage." Pregnancy was a major topic at the store because of all the women having babies.

A month after starting there, on November 19, 1985, Darci's sister-in-law, Mary Ann, who had married Craig, was delivered of a baby boy, Joshua Leroy. They were living next door to Ray and Darci and Darci held a birthday party for Craig (his birthday was November 21). "We were sitting there eating dinner and we were talking about the baby and Darci said I could leave the baby over there for the night and that she could breast-feed it," recalled a startled and upset Mary Ann. "Wouldn't it be neat if we both could breast-feed Joshua?" Darci said. Mary Ann's relationship with Darci had been strained anyway, since giving up an earlier baby for adoption. Mary Ann kept a picture of that child on her mantel, and Darci told her it didn't belong there.

Through the winter of 1985-1986, Darci worked at

G.I. Joes and kept the apartment neat and clean. Gradually the crying jags diminished. Ray thought she was over the molar pregnancy. She spent time with her new girlfriends at work, and in their homes. "She loved children and was very patient," said Tina Otis, who shared a locker at work. Darci sometimes watched Tina's son, Zachery, who was one-and-a-half. Darci told Tina about her own childhood, beginning with the adoption. Dorothy Lynn Spain, who worked in the sporting goods department, also became close to Darci. She had stepchildren, Connie who was nine, and Jessie, an eleven-year-old boy, and Darci often visited. The women had the same physician, David Sargent, and talked often of having children of their own. In February or early March of 1986, Dorothy Spain announced that she was pregnant and due in November.

That same month, Ken Ricker entered the hospital for an appendix operation, and when Darci came to visit she was wearing a loose-fitting dress. "Oh, good grief," thought her mother, "is she pregnant?" Darci said nothing about it. In March, Ken had a heart attack and Darci stayed with her mother for three days and nights. She and Ray wanted to marry as soon as her father left the hospital, but Sandra and Ken felt it was too soon. The wedding was postponed for a second time.

On April 23, Darci went back to Dr. Sargent, complaining of irregular and painful periods and pain during intercourse. He encouraged her to return to birth control pills and talked briefly about the possibility of infertility and the need for a workup if she continued to have a problem. On May 13 she

184

came in for another HCG test, which showed Darci was not pregnant.

But at G.I. Joes, Darci began to wear maternity clothes and claim that she was three or four months along and due in September. She said she had not told them sooner for fear of building expectations and losing the baby. It was a clear lie, and telling it placed Darci on a treadmill that she would never escape. Dan Locke thought it strange that Darci's pregnancy followed so closely on the heels of her friend Dorothy. But everyone accepted her word. Tina Otis even touched Darci's stomach sometime that summer, and it felt hard. Her breasts were larger and she was gaining weight. "If I lose this baby," Darci told her, "I'll go insane."

In Dr. Sargent's office, however, she was telling a different story. Because of some vaginal bleeding she returned August 28 and worried that she was having trouble ovulating each month. A pregnancy test was negative. Dr. Sargent gave her some forms to chart her morning temperature and spoke of the possibility of medication to induce ovulation. He may also have mentioned endometriosis. But Sargent didn't suspect that in Darci's case. If Darci thought she was sterile, she never brought it up. "She didn't act that desperately for a pregnancy. She didn't pursue it," said Sargent. "It didn't seem to concern her—and here all the time she was faking." The September 1986 HCG test was negative for pregnancy.

At work, meanwhile, Darci told coworkers that her due date had been pushed back. At home, she told Ray for the first time that she was pregnant, and due in the spring of 1987. Darci turned eighteen in October, caught now in two lies.

On November 3, Dorothy Spain gave birth to a daughter. Within days, Darci announced to her co-workers that her labor would be induced November 15 and that she was taking maternity leave, a benefit that continued to pay her for some weeks before and after delivery. She told Ray she was taking leave under doctor's orders and asked him to pick up her check.

On November 15, the supposed date of Darci's "inducement," Dorothy Spain called the Adventist Hospital and asked about Darci. But there was no record of her being admitted. Frantically she called Darci, but Ray said she was at her mother's house. Darci returned the call later that night and told Dorothy that the baby had died in her womb. They cried together over the phone. The next day, Darci called Tina Otis and told her the same story. Otis notified store manager Locke, who sent flowers on behalf of the staff. When the flowers arrived, Darci called Tina and chastised her for telling anyone. That evening, Darci drove to her mother's house, came in to the kitchen and asked her to sit down.

"Mom, I have to talk to you." She sat at the breakfast bar. Sandra sat at the dining room table. Darci began crying. "I've done a terrible thing. I told people at work that the baby was stillborn."

Now it was Sandra Ricker's turn to cry. "Darci, you and Ray will never be blessed. You're telling a lie on a baby."

The next day Sandra Ricker received a call from one of the women at G.I. Joes, a woman who had known Darci all her life. She was very upset and said

186

they were grieving at work and wanted to know if Sandra had seen her daughter. "I probably acted crazy," said Mrs. Ricker later, "because I wouldn't go along with the lie. I said no, I haven't seen her."

Ray wouldn't lie, either. He picked up her check but didn't talk to anyone about it. Darci had to get herself out of the mess herself, he said. She did it by cutting off contact with her friends at the store. When Tina Otis offered to come over, Darci grew cool. Over the next few weeks, Dorothy Spain talked to Darci on the phone, but saw her only once. She looked tired, but not much different physically. The dead baby, Darci told her, had been very small and had had only two valves in its heart.

Eighteen

Despite her odd behavior at G.I. Joes, Darci's family accepted her pregnancy but not her marital status. Early one evening in November, Sandra Ricker went to the little apartment where Darci and Ray lived and confronted them.

"I felt something had to be done. He was getting ready to go in the service. And they were doing nothing about getting married, and there was going to be a baby," she said later.

"You were going to get married so many times, what's holding you up now?" she asked the pair. "I want to see you get married before you go in the service. Take the responsibility. Face the responsibility." At one point she went over to Darci, put her hands on her tummy and said, "I love this baby."

The pressure was too much. Darci returned to David Brink, the minister. "We're ready to get married, and I am ready to start talking to my mother, to reconcile with her."

"That's great," Brink told her. "I'm glad you're finally waking up and smelling the coffee. Let's line up a time." Sandra and Ken joined Darci and Ray in a tense session with the minister. Brink noticed a remarkable change in Darci. "Instead of Miss In-Charge, she was just as sweet as she could be. I remember thinking I couldn't believe the change in Darci."

188

Darci told Brink she and Ray wanted to make a home for the baby. "My mom was right about a lot of things. Look at me now. I am going to be the ideal mother. This kid is going to have a good start in life." Brink described Darci as "sweet, teary-eyed and subdued. She was just a different person." Through all five premarital counseling sessions, she and Ray would sit and hold hands and talk of their plans. "She was the domesticated, finally-settled-down gal."

Only later, in retrospect, did Brink see that Darci was not sincere. "The change wasn't an inner force. It was from exterior forces. I had painted a picture for her in previous counseling sessions of what I would like to see her be before the wedding. When she came back she was that exact picture. That blew me away. I remember thinking, 'Wow, this is a miracle.' So many kids go bad and here's one that's finally doing great. I was really happy for them." The wedding was set a month before Ray left for basic training in the Air Force.

In Darci's family, grand preparations began for the wedding. Invitations were sent. Three showers were planned. Darci and her mother, close once again, went to a maternity store to buy a wedding dress, because her tummy wouldn't fit into a regular wedding dress. Sandra's sister, Donna Vanderberg, threw a shower at her house. Sandra made the cake, Donna did the flowers.

Darci and Ray got married in Brink's Church of Christ on December 13. Two days after the wedding, Darci went to see Dr. Sargent, complaining of a sore throat, a fever, nausea, and breast tenderness. She also told him she thought she was pregnant. They

189

talked about doing another pregnancy test, but Darci declined. Two days later, on December 17, Darci began a period.

Christmas brought an even greater outpouring of good family vibrations. Sandra's other sister flew out from the East with her family. It was after Christmas dinner that Darci lifted her blouse and said to her Aunt Donna, "Look, I'm getting so big." Later, Ray's mother held another shower in Seaside, where she received diapers and crocheted Afghan blankets.

When Ray left for basic training January 15, 1987, Darci moved in with her parents, and Sandra Ricker hoped their time together would heal their rift. But Darci began spending most of her free time with a pretty woman named Carol Raymond whom she had met through their husbands. Jerry Raymond had bought a radio-controlled car, and Ray knew where to race it in Eugene. Afterward the men stopped by the house and the women met and hit it off. Carol was a statuesque blonde, a self-assured medical receptionist with two children, ages nine and six. Her husband was a retail manager for Smith's Home Furnishings, a Portland chain. Carol thought Darci very bright and mature, and invited her to dinner. They shopped, watched TV and talked nearly every day, seeing each other two or three times each week. Darci visited at the Raymond house often, making extravagant meals for them. They grew very close, comparing notes on child rearing, men, babies, and sex. Darci confided in Carol rather than her mother, and that hurt Sandra Ricker. Even Jerry Raymond began to complain about the time the women were spending together.

A few miles from G.I. Joes, on Eighty-ninth, there

was a religious retreat called the Grotto, a fern and moss-covered wood, filled with tall trees that filtered the sun into long, narrow shafts. Set against a cliff, the Grotto was surrounded by cool paths and stations of the cross. Darci and Carol spent hours walking the paths, talking and growing close. Carol considered her new friend very spiritual.

Carol also was impressed with Darci's knowledge of child rearing and pregnancy. Darci told her she was five months pregnant. Over lunch, or during their evening calls, Darci would tell Carol of her visits to Dr. Sargent and his reports that the pregnancy was going well. Darci never told Carol that on February 23 a pregnancy test was negative.

Dr. Sargent, for his part, thought Darci was taking the bad news in stride, although he noted on her chart her weight gain, nearly fifty pounds. They talked again about starting temperature charts, to track her ovulation. He talked about prescribing chromaphene to induce ovulation, but so far there was no solid evidence that Darci was sterile or suffering from endometriosis.

Gradually, Darci grew almost dependant on Carol Raymond. She complained often that Ray was remote, his first love his radio-controlled cars and helicopters, and that he spent too much money on them. She wanted money for baby things, and Ray didn't seem interested in the baby, Carol said later. "That just broke her heart."

With Ray out of town Darci asked Carol to attend childbirth classes with her, but when they arrived they found they had missed two previous sessions. She was told she could make them up. The class dealt with medications and cesarean sections, which Darci thought repugnant. "I never want a C-section," she told Carol.

"I tried to reason with her that C-sections were just another way of bringing a healthy baby into the world and you really have no choice. It's usually an emergency situation and there's always that possibility. You have to be open to it."

Darci insisted, no cesarean for her. She wanted a natural childbirth, and wanted Carol there to help, rather than Ray. Every once in awhile she'd turn to Carol and say, "I'll be at your doorstep with the baby."

As the soft air of spring descended on Portland, Darci's relationship with Carol Raymond took a sweet turn and became a sexual liaison, too. Darci initiated the lovemaking. "She's a very flirtatious young lady. She was very seductive," said Raymond. The night it first happened, Darci called Ray in Texas and excitedly described it. Ray's response was never recorded. But by this time Carol Raymond felt that Darci was clinging to her excessively. When Ray's orders arrived for Kirtland Air Force Base, Carol secretly breathed a sigh of relief.

The transfer did not sit well with Sandra Ricker, who wanted Darci to have the baby at home and not travel so close to her due date. "I thought it was endangering a baby to drive down there," said Mrs. Ricker. "I'd never been there. It was like living in the middle of nowhere to me, a long ways. I was very concerned about them driving in a moving van, with Darci driving the Trans Am. It didn't make sense." But move they did, with Ken going along to help.

After they left, Sandra Ricker began to plot a surprise visit, at the time of birth, to help with the baby. She called Dr. Sargent's office to find out the due date precisely. The nurse told her that patient information was not given out, but that Darci was not being treated for pregnancy. In fact, on February 27, two months before, a pregnancy test was negative.

"I was shocked beyond belief," said Mrs. Ricker. "I didn't know what to think. Somebody is going crazy here and it must be me. I called the doctor's office again and asked them to double check the date. Could it have been the previous year, the year of the cyst? No, they assured her, the test was negative in February. Sandra Ricker called her daughter in her new duplex in Albuquerque.

"Mom, you know I'm pregnant," Darci laughed.

"Yes, I know you are." Sandra Ricker said later. "I had decided that the test they gave was the hormone count, and that was the test that came back negative."

Darci continued to pour her heart out to Carol Raymond, in letters, cards and as many telephone calls as she could afford. She wrote almost daily and called once or twice a week, painful letters of a lover missing a mate.

"I miss you a whole bunch and even cried a bit today. Sometimes (most of the time!) I can't get you off my mind. Everything that happens somehow reminds me of you and everything I'm seeing and experiencing I keep thinking I wish you were here for it, too."

Darci also wrote poems to express her feelings for Carol. "I only hope that you can cherish these half as much as I cherish you."

"From you, I learned,
a new kind of math.
You taught me that
one plus one
can make one.
Now, from you
I have also learned that
two minus two
equals zero."

Another, that psychiatrists puzzled over later:

"I had sealed my bargain
with fate.
resigned myself
to lonliness
and stripped and arranged
my life into
orderly,
functional compartments
each a self-contained unit
unconnected
to the others
in the same way
I rake the fall leaves into neat and tidy piles
then you came along and I stand by
helplessly, while an unexpected
gust of wind
scoops up the dead leaves
and swirls them about
in a multi-color whirlwind
leaving my life once again

194

in hopeless disarray.
You were not supposed
to happen
my friend."

It was clear from her letters to Carol that Darci was lonely in Albuquerque: "I have to stop myself from sitting most every moment of my day writing back to you . . . When Ray doesn't want to do anything but watch TV I feel like I'm wasting my life—that there is so much I could be doing and sharing with you instead." In Portland, Carol acknowledged Darci's feelings but kept her own letters brief accounts of family and work.

On May 14, Darci reported to Carol some contractions in the night. "They woke me up at 2:22. They were five minutes apart and getting stronger. I should probably think about packing a bag. Ray dozed off and would wake every once in a while to see if I was O.K. or if I was ready to leave yet and then doze off again. Not me! Boyo. I was wide awake. About 5:45 this A.M. they just stopped. Ray said yesterday that I would probably go into labor last night or today because he bought me a new sundress yesterday . . . it looks like a giant, oversized blue and white shirt. It buttons down the front."

Scattered through her letters were snide references to a woman named Tammi, with whom Ray had gone to boot camp. After Ray and Darci found their duplex, she said, "I received a bouquet of flowers from you know who, Tammi of course, welcoming me." Carol thought Darci was suspicious of Tammi and Ray. "She didn't trust this gal. She suspected that they had become lovers." On May 21, Darci revealed to Carol that she had opened a letter Ray had written to a girl next door in Portland.

"He's in love with her and has been for many years . . . Ray has always led me to believe they are/were nothing more than friends . . . I just don't need this. It used to be that I believed Ray would never go for another woman and suddenly I'm confronted with two—one emotionally and the other physically . . . Is he bored with me and looking for someone else? Is he just supplementing himself until the baby is born and does he honestly feel he can have his cake and eat it too! I think my biggest problem is that I need to have this baby and get back in shape. Ray is always reminding me what a knockout and turn-on I was. Maybe that's all it will take. I guess my marriage is worth trying something to save."

In late May Darci reported to Carol that an ultrasound pushed the due date back.

"Ray is so worried about how long it may be before he can screw me again after the baby is born that he takes every opportunity to do it now. He affectionately calls his lunch hours 'nooners' and the guys at the office are always kidding him about why he always comes back from lunch with a big smile on his face . . . you know me, insatiable, but sometimes I'm just not in the mood and he doesn't have the time to do what is needed so that I'm just willing."

196

Finally, she reported losing her mucus plug and with it the sex.

On June 19, Darci told Carol that her cervix was dilated to four centimeters. Two days later, Carol wrote her a note about big phone bills. To Darci, Carol was growing distant.

"Please, Carol, if there is something on your mind, please share it with me. I'm here for you, always. Except for looking out for myself, you are the most important thing in my life . . . call me collect. I mean it. I miss our closeness and total sharing so very much that I dream about us having lunch . . . you're my inspiration that keeps me going from day to day."

About this time, Darci wrote another letter, to her old friend Dorothy Spain in Portland. She and Ray were settling in, she reported, and the healing following the stillbirth had begun. She and Ray were talking about having a family, but it would be many years before they did so, Darci wrote.

On July 21, two days before the murder, Darci wrote a last letter to Carol Raymond, sensing perhaps that her whole life was slipping away. It had a different, almost philosophical tone to it:

"One of the greatest joys in my life is our friendship . . . I don't think either of us suspected, when we first met, that we would stand where we do today, sharing the close harmony of our abiding friendship. But we grew together

197

through the days, sharing laughter and tears, thoughts and silence—all the things that have become an unforgettable part of who we are. You have always encouraged me to share myself fully, my hopes, my dreams, my secret pains and sadness that I have come to understand that in the light of your concerned understanding of the same. No one knows where tomorrow will find us walking; if together or apart, I know that I've found in you the lifetime friend I have always asked for, and that the years passing will never change but only strengthen our enduring relationship. Darci."

That was the last Carol Raymond heard from Darci until the night of July 23 when she called from the hospital delivery room with the breathless news: "I had the baby." Carol was ecstatic. But Darci was acting funny, not wanting to be examined. Carol tried to convince her. "It's okay," Darci said calmly. "I'll see my doctor tomorrow morning and I'll have him look at me. I'll be home tomorrow. Call me then and we can talk."

198

Nineteen

On December 11, 1987, five months after the murder, Darci Pierce's defense team formally told the court that she intended to plead not guilty by reason of insanity. Under New Mexico law, that put the burden of proof on the prosecution to prove, beyond a reasonable doubt, that she was sane at the time of the crime. In essence that meant that the state had to prove that Darci knew what she was doing and that she knew that it was wrong.

The defense, on the other hand, needed to prove the existence of a long-standing mental disease that prevented Darci from knowing what she was doing, from understanding the consequences, or stopping herself. The New Mexico law is very specific about what kind of "disease" is allowed. The insanity defense meant that the trial would be a battle of psychiatrists.

Darci's personality was in the midst of a dissociation or had broken into parts.

Dissociation is a broad psychiatric category, covering behavior from self-hypnosis to multiple personalities—famous cases like "Sybil" and "Three Faces of Eve" come to mind. But in Darci's case, the personalities were not as clearly defined, McCarty said in her later testimony.

"Think of a little girl that dissociates. You know it but nobody else does. And this little girl's mother has just made a chocolate cake and says—typical mother fashion—'Don't you dare eat any of this, because I'm saving it for supper.' Mother leaves room, little girl changes, dissociates from part A to part B. Part B didn't hear what mother just told her, has no knowledge of that warning; part B sees a chocolate cake and says 'Great!' and eats a piece. Mother comes back into the room, child switches back to part A, and in a typical fashion mother would say, 'Did you eat a piece of this cake?' And little girl, who's part A now, says 'No,' quite truthfully because she is the part that did not eat the cake. But mother looks at little girl and she's got chocolate all around her mouth.

"Being in that room with Darci on the day after this crime happened was like being with that little girl with chocolate around her mouth, except in this case, [the] chocolate was the baby that she was holding. She was telling a story that all of us knew was not true, or very likely was not true, because she hadn't had this baby. And yet she was telling us a story that she believed, about going to Santa Fe and getting the baby from a surrogate mother. Her belief in the story was what led me first to think that she was dissociating. The next thing was that the story that she was telling was so vague, it was like a fairy story. 'How did you get to Santa Fe and how did you get back?' To her it was like, well, you follow the yellow brick road, you know. When they would press Darci on streets and things she said, 'I don't know' but in a way that showed it didn't bother her either. It didn't matter."

In September and October, Dr. McCarty visited Darci in the county jail five times, for a total of twenty hours, interviewing and testing her. The longer she was there, the greater her sense that Darci was suffering from a mental illness called "dissociative disorder" in which more than one personality exists in one body. As she looked at Darci's history — her lying, her promiscuity, her history of memory gaps and mood shifts — the more it appeared to be the work of changing personalities.

Darci lied because, like the little girl with chocolate, Darci would wake up in the middle of a conversation, or after some act. Unaware of what she had said or done, she picked up clues and made up a story, but she made mistakes that people around her knew to be lies. Darci was always considered a liar, and not a very good one at that. Her mood swings also pointed to dissociation. After taking police to Cindy Ray's body in near hysteria, she calmed down and chitchatted about South Africa. The same was true of her memory gaps around her sexual activities in sixth grade. Her recollection of intercourse at the age of eleven with a married man in a sauna gave one clue: "Well, I made eyes at him and then we were making love," Darci told McCarty.

"What did you say? What did he say to you?" McCarty asked.

"We didn't say anything. There were no words."

It was Darci's early sexual behavior — intercourse at the age of six with her cousin — that was McCarty's biggest clue to dissociation. Dissociation usually begins in childhood and almost always, in 90 percent of the cases, after some childhood abuse or severe emotional trauma. Sexual abuse is a primary cause. Darci's early sexual activity with her cousin would not be unusual following some kind of sexual abuse, even if buried in her memory. Darci must have learned about sex before the age of six.

John Bogren, Darci's lead defense attorney, didn't believe McCarty's analysis at first. A rough-stock Chicago Pole, Bogren was raised on the streets of a working-class neighborhood by a lawyer uncle. His father had died when he was three and his mother— "She wasn't all there. She was retarded, I guess." He was drafted from law school and became an infantry scout dog handler in Vietnam, walking point. "I got a little goofy out of that but managed to survive. I never dreamed of being a criminal defense lawyer." His uncle wanted him to take over his general practice, but Bogren walked into a public defender's office one day and never left. Seventeen years of defending the scum of the earth. "I've had all the thrills of a lifetime, over and over. Just what you see on TV, Perry Mason, the Lone Ranger attitude. Nobody expects you to win. It's fun. It's the only thing better than sex. To get a guy off is a wonderful feeling."

Bogren was forty-one when Darci's case landed on his lap. He'd pretty much seen it all by then: forty death-penalty cases, murderers, rapists, child abusers. "The lowlifes are people who sexually abuse their children. That's the thing I don't have stomach for. You've got your ten percenters who are just assholes. I can understand why people kill. I've seen it in Vietnam. I've seen anger, frustration, drug abuse. I seen a guy put six hundred rounds in a dead body. I can understand emotion. But certain things I don't understand, like why someone would have sex with their daughter. I don't want to understand."

Bogren saw Darci right after her arraignment. "I didn't expect to see what I got. She wasn't manifesting any outward sign of psychosis. I've never seen Darci act psychotic. If I did it was subtle. I've seen her change, but that can be attributed to mood changes. When you're in jail, people do change after a while, especially people who have never been in jail. I never overtly saw her become somebody else."

So Bogren didn't believe multiple personalities when he first talked to McCarty. The psychiatrist's scenario seemed too unreal, and Darci was too real, too normal. "I deal with crazy people all the time. We've got schizophrenics and paranoid delusional disorders. I can understand that. You give them some medicine and they're okay. Or, they're not okay. Then they put them in hospitals. I defended a woman who ran her car onto a sidewalk and killed an entire family walking along. That's real easy to explain. It's biological. The woman was undermedicated. But it's hard to believe that somebody who looks so normal is so crazy."

Bogren's thinking began to change when Dr. McCarty invited Jean Goodwin to join the case. Goodwin, a psychiatrist from Wisconsin, specialized in child abuse and its aftereffects, particularly dissociation and multiple personalities. Goodwin and McCarty had been colleagues at the University of New Mexico, with Goodwin in charge of the psychiatric residences. The two doctors had authored several professional articles together, among them studies of children who were incest victims. Goodwin was specifically asked to answer the question of whether Darci Pierce was insane at the time of the crime. Dr. Goodwin heard McCarty's theory, she read the record, and then she saw Darci six times during October and November. Twice she hypnotized her. Her initial focus was the lost time, Darci's patchy memory of the murder. The second was her bizarre pregnancy symptoms, and the third was a feeling that no one could ever get anything straight about Darci Pierce, even basic things.

When Darci first saw Dr. Goodwin, she listed her religion as Catholic, when in fact, she had grown up in the Church of Christ. She told McCarty that she was part Indian because her biological mother was Indian, but she admitted "I don't know anything about my natural mother." She suffered the ovarian cyst but told a social worker it was a miscarriage. She told workers at G.I. Joes that her baby was stillborn while telling her husband she was newly pregnant. She told Carol Raymond she was dilating in preparation for birth but wrote to Dorothy Spain, "I'm not ready to get pregnant, I'm still grieving over my stillbirth. I think it will be a long time before I'm ready to have a baby." There also were extraordinary shifts in her behavior in the twenty-four hours after the crime, from childlike to cheerleader to hardened liar. And finally, there was the whole shocking case, in which no one could imagine her killing a woman and performing a cesarean. Yet there never was any question about her competency to stand trial. She felt she committed the crime and that death was a suitable punishment.

"I eventually figured out that what was happening with Darci had something to do with the fact that she would shift," said Goodwin, noting the same clues as McCarty. "I would get close to her and she and I would be on the same wavelength and all of a sudden she would shift and I would lose her. But it took me a long time to figure that out. I spent probably my first three sessions with her feeling very confused, and that's unusual for me . . . We would be talking about the difficult time she had in sixth grade . . . and suddenly it was like a door would close in my face and I couldn't go any further. That's how I first experienced this shifting identity states. Goodwin diagnosed an atypical dissociative disorder, atypical because she could never get close enough to flesh out the different personality states. She could not claim true multiple personalities, yet Darci had many symptoms of it. On a checklist she filled out for Goodwin, Darci checked: "Looking in the mirror and seeing somebody other than myself. Sensing that something terrible has happened but not remembering what it was. Feeling that time is not continuous. Feeling that a part of me is like a child. Feeling that there are many different parts of me."

Goodwin agreed with McCarty that early sexual abuse was likely with Darci. Her adoption also was a source of emotional pain. She was teased by her brothers, she never bonded with her adoptive mother and by the time she was in grade school she was fantasizing about changing families. Her grade-school sex, her fears—her panic in the shower, the knife under the pillow, the nightmares, pot smoking, pain on intercourse—all were indicators to Goodwin of early, unremembered sexual abuse.

What happens to such children, Goodwin later testified, is that they compartmentalize their memories and emotions and relationships, separate from the individual or the "home body." Just as a rabbit puts itself into a trance when attacked by a fox, children who are traumatized use a form of self-hypnosis to protect themselves from mental pain. "And it gets to be a habit, so they're going in and out of the trance all the time. And that's why things get so separated, disconnected, torn apart, where they have different states of consciousness going on at the same time and different beliefs, different behaviors and different emotions."

Darci's childhood, she said, was full of clues to the disease. For example, when she found a piece of her unicorn collection broken, or one of her music boxes broken, she did not know why. "I build a wall around memory," she told Dr. Goodwin. "It comes to me in pieces. I can only fill in the in-between. I don't live with me very often. I don't know who I am, so I just act like people expect me to act." On the crime day she talked about biting the umbilical cord. "It's not something I can see, but it's something I know," she told Goodwin. "I don't understand why I have such snatches." When she tried to remember the actual murder, her memory was "dark flashes with no pictures but a doomed feeling." When she arrived at the Acura dealer and lied, it was to fill the gaps. "I just can't show up somewhere and not have a story." When the police challenged her version, she tried another story. "All I could remember was to think of black market babies."

In her jail interviews with Darci, Dr. Goodwin began to see two sides to her personalities: One, a smiling, compliant, naive, teenager who related well and was interested in cars, marriage and babies, and two, a hard-faced, manipulative convict who was guarded and interested in physical fights, sexual assaults, getting revenge and not showing emotion. A third part did the violence, what the rest of her experienced as a flash of light. The shifts between the states were subtle. For example, in one state she believed herself pregnant and in the other described how she faked it. In neither part were there normal feelings, anger or grief; those feelings came out on rare occasions, as they did after the molar pregnancy when she wept for hours.

Dr. Goodwin came up short of being able to find true multiple personalities of Darci Pierce. "It's not anything as dramatic as suddenly she's a furious monster going to kill someone, and the minute before she was a friendly, open teenager. It is a popular misconception that different personalities are black and white; they often cooperate, but to qualify for such the diagnosis of multiple personalities each part must have its own memory, behaviors and social relationships, and the patient needs at least two complete personalities under diagnostic guidelines.

But according to both McCarty and Goodwin, Darci's personalities changed under stress, and in the months preceding Cindy Ray's death, several parts of Darci "came out."

The first state—McCarty called it A—truly believed that she was pregnant and expected a baby soon. She gained weight, her breasts enlarged and her tummy grew round and hard. She missed periods and got sick in the morning. "Mrs. Pierce had wanted to be pregnant for so long, and in the face of

207

the real body changes she prepared for the delivery of a baby. She wore maternity clothes. She read baby magazines. She had a complete nursery furnished. She could talk to Mrs. Ray as one pregnant woman to another," McCarty testified. It probably also was the personality that told Catholic Family Services of her "miscarriage."

A second personality—McCarty's part B—knew that she was not pregnant but was aware of Part A's belief and manipulated and lied to protect the story. It probably told the stillbirth story at G.I. Joes. It moved its abdomen muscles to simulate a baby. It believed that Ray had married her because he thought she was pregnant, and needed to maintain the fantasy. As the pressure mounted to deliver a baby, this part considered stealing a baby from a supermarket. It also was the part that refused the pelvic exam at the hospital.

A third part—part C—was a surrogate mother herself, McCarty reasoned. She was so completely dissociated from Darci as to seem a separate person, the one who would give her a baby. It may have come from her adoption. She would give her child to a competent mother—Darci. This part was the fictitious Sherry Martin that Mrs. Pierce described as being her own age and looks. This part told the hospital admitting clerk about the coming baby, and it asked Mrs. Ray to give up her baby because she was willing to do so.

A fourth part—part D—thought she was sterile and had endometriosis with no hope of ever having a baby. It was sad and upset and thought missing periods were symptoms of sterility. It may have been the one who remembered early sexual activity with no emotion, and may have been the one who finally pieced together enough information to admit, finally, that the baby was not Darci's and that something had happened to Cindy Ray. McCarty divined two angry parts to Darci: a fifth part—part E—that broke the window in sixth grade and who killed Cindy Ray. A sixth part—part F—was angry with Sandra, her mother and fantasized about pointing a gun at her.

In her diagnosis of Darci, Dr. McCarty recreated the murder of Cindy Ray using the six parts she found. The description, revealed in both her written evaluation and trial testimony, was like a movie unfolding, a bizarre tableau of shifting faces, deep losses and murderous intentions. Here's how it went:

As June turned to July 1987 Darci Pierce was under extreme stress. At least part of her—Part A—was expecting a baby while part B knew she was not. B feared losing Ray and needed a baby to save the marriage. Family pressure built as the baby came overdue. On July 23 Darci was wandering aimlessly but ended up at the base hospital where pregnant women might be. When she saw Cindy Ray, part C, the surrogate mother, wanted to ask for the baby. "Her own history was that she had been given away relatively nonchalantly and so it was not outside of her belief system that someone who was pregnant might just be looking for somebody to give the baby to," said Goodwin. She had ideas about getting somebody to give her a baby for a long time—her brother Craig's child, for example. She even told Carol Raymond a fantasy about hiring somebody to run over her sister-in-law so the baby could be hers. After stopping Cindy in the parking lot, part A could suggest a talk over tea, but when she saw her husband's car at home, part B did the U-turn and headed out of town.

Once in the mountains, stopped beneath a tree, many changes took place in Darci's personalities, judging from memory gaps, said McCarty. When Theron Hartshorn showed up with his pickup trying to get by, Darci handled it as she always handled memory gaps—she made up a story. But in the lightning storm something triggered the violent part of Darci, part E, which hit and strangled Cindy Ray. "It's possible that yet another part dragged the body away and yet another part, knowing only that there was a comatose and supposedly dead pregnant woman there, desperately tried to do a cesarean section to save the baby," said Goodwin. Strangling required an aggressive, violent act, but performing the cesarean required calm, cool control.

Suddenly part A, the one who thought she was pregnant, found a baby in her arms and took off for the hospital, believing herself to be the mother. When asked to be examined, part B, the coverup master, emerged and prevented an exam. As the evening went on there were several changes. Part A could enjoy the baby, and part B made up the surrogate story. Finally, in the morning, the sterile part D, sent a baby that she knew wasn't hers back to the newborn nursery. She then started connecting the images and shadows that were coming to her with the information from police. She led police to the scene, becoming more and more distraught as she realized she had killed Mrs. Ray. Hysterical at that point, Darci dissociated again and became calm after leaving the scene.

The bottom line, said McCarty, was that Darci was suffering a mental disease on July 23, a disease of long standing, which took from her control of her actions. She did not premeditate the murder of Cindy Ray, and while she considered asking for her baby there was no indication that she planned to physically take the baby. Significantly, she carried no knife to do so.

In November 1987, Dr. Goodwin put Darci under hypnosis in the public defender's office with attorney Tom Jameson and two jailers present. Goodwin asked questions and Darci signaled answers with fingers, yes and no. Darci let Goodwin know about her personalities and several came out, including a young child. Then she talked about the "dark one."

"Is the dark one violent?" Goodwin asked her. "Does the dark one have violent thoughts?"

Darci said the dark one was a thirty-five-year-old woman who was not violent, and did not murder, but Darci would not let the dark one out to talk to Goodwin.

Watching the hypnosis video, the defense team froze. They could not use it in court because it could be attacked as hocus pocus.

Twenty

The man in charge of the case against Darci Pierce was Harry Zimmerman, a short, wiry, combative prosecutor given to wearing cowboy boots with his three-piece suits. The Darci Pierce case was high profile, and Harry Zimmerman loved being on stage. On weekends he played parts in a local theater. During the week he played the DA, rough and tough, the people's man.

Zimmerman put himself in charge of the experts, the psychiatrists. His colleague, Michael Cox, handled the rest, including cop reports. That was the easy part to prove against Darci. Zimmerman's job was more daunting, proving that this obviously crazy woman was not insane in the legal sense. She could be suffering from a mental illness without being insane. He needed to strip from the evidence proof that Darci knew what she was doing and understood the consequences, and that whatever was wrong with her head was not a mental disease, per se, but perhaps some personality disorder that led her to murder. In the course of his workup for the trial, Harry Zimmerman practically slept with texts on mental illness. With the world looking on, he wanted to win.

"This isn't the kind of case where you had a woman who was hallucinating. She knew who everybody was," said Cox. "A true insanity case you've got some guy who kills someone because he thinks he's the devil. Darci knew who the individuals were, their names, who she really was. So it was just a question of proving that the mental illness hadn't forced her to do these things, that she'd made a conscious decision. That she wasn't propelled by the mental illness but by emotions that people can't understand." In addition, because the case was a capital offense, the state had to show that Darci deliberated the murder and weighed the pros and cons.

Zimmerman and Cox thought they had a good case. There was evidence that Darci tried to cover up the crime, and there weren't that many facts in Darci's history to show that she had been crazy all her life. She had, in fact, been normal to most people, most of her life. "I think there are people who are just bad people, evil people. I think she's one of them," said Cox. "I don't know why. I don't think anybody does. I don't think the experts know. But they're out there, and every once in a while they do something like this. How many people have grown up just like that and turned out wonderful? There was just something wrong. She was just a wrong person, a bad person, probably from birth."

To prove their case, Zimmerman hired a psychologist and psychiatrist to examine Darci and her record, and to draw a conclusion different than that of the defense. The first was Julie Ann Lockwood, an Albuquerque psychologist who specialized in the

213

criminal mind. After three visits with Darci, totaling nine hours, Lockwood concluded, "Ms. Pierce is an intelligent but narcissistic young woman who is largely focused upon herself." Lockwood said there was no evidence of psychosis — loss of reality. Darci could see the world accurately, but her perceptions and responses were influenced by disordered thinking. She dealt with stress by withdrawing, disengaging and denial. She used fantasy, denial and dissociation as defense mechanism to deal with internal stress. She was a "person who lives out life as much as she can [in] the fantasy that she constructs within her head, because . . . her life has been so barren or empty, or, in many respects, intolerable."

Darci was preoccupied most of her life with her adoption, her revulsion for her mother and her desire to be a mother. "Since living with Raymond Pierce, these preoccupations appear to have become virtual obsessions," said Lockwood. Darci tied her self-worth to producing a child and said that without one, her life would be worth nothing. Having a baby, she thought, was a basic womanly act, and she wanted to "show her two mothers that she could be a better mother than they." Whatever else happened, Darci told Lockwood, having that baby in her arms at the hospital "was the most beautiful experience" she had ever had. Despite what had happened she "would not change having taken the baby to the hospital. She was mine and that was all that mattered."

Lockwood suggested hiring psychiatrist Phillip Resnick from Cleveland, Ohio. He taught at Case Western Reserve Medical School and directed the court psychiatry clinic. Lockwood called him and asked if he was willing to evaluate the case. After agreeing, Resnick collected nearly every scrap of paper and audio tape on the case, and on January 24, 1988 spent nine and a half hours with Darci.

Dr. Resnick said he found Darci bright, charming, and able to joke, be courteous, and thoughtful. She showed no signs of delusions. And although she had reported hearing men's voices, she had never told anyone about them before the murder. It was clear, right from the start of his interview, that Resnick was looking for evidence in Darci's life of antisocial conduct or personality, a character likely to engage in criminal acts without feeling particular remorse. Resnick found lots of evidence to support that.

"She admitted to me that she had done a great deal of lying ever since she was a little girl, that she exaggerated things; wanted to present herself as perfect. Even though her average was B or below she would tell people she had an A average to try to look perfect. She also told me that she was expelled from school. I thought it was interesting that in that file was a letter by Mrs. Pierce, in which she was ten years old at the time, and she said, 'I'll stop lying because I know the difference between doing right and doing wrong.' Kind of a prophetic letter," Resnick said.

"I found out that she ran away from home in the seventh grade. She also engaged in reckless behavior, speeding automobiles, repeatedly. She reported a number of physical fights she got into. She was suspended from school on two or three occasions and hit a girl with a chair. She was openly defiant to her mother and her mother told her that she was selfish and self-centered. She committed some vandalism, breaking of windows and she was not able to sustain a monogamous relationship. Then she related to me some measurable fantasies about killing her mother that she had from the fifth grade through the ninth grade. Here she would go up to her room, take her .22 rifle, sometimes she would have it unloaded, and she would press the trigger and have a fantasy of her mother entering the room while she shot her. She also had a hunting knife and thought with pleasure about what it would be like to stab her mother. An additional fantasy which is relevant . . . she talked of trying to arrange to have her ex-sister-in-law run over by a car so that she could get custody of her nephew, Christopher."

Resnick considered Darci's medical experience significant. She had wanted to be a paramedic, she watched orthopedic surgery, she read the *Reader's Digest Family Guide* on pregnancy, and she hunted with her father, helping dress a deer.

After moving to Albuquerque, the pressure mounted on Darci to have a baby, and she admitted feeling desperate in July. By July 23 she knew clearly that she did not have a baby coming of her own, he said. That's when she thought about stealing a baby. Resnick asked Darci why, when she made lunch for Ray on July 23, "didn't you just tell your husband that you weren't pregnant?"

"Well, I didn't want him to catch me in a lie," she said. "I was afraid I would lose him."

When she parked her car next to Cindy Ray's at the base clinic, it was a long shot, she admitted to

Resnick, to ask Cindy for her baby. "Mrs. Pierce, why didn't you go into the obstetric clinic and ask her?" Resnick asked.

"I wanted to do it in a private place," Darci told him, an indication to Resnick that she wanted no witnesses. Asked why she put the gun in her lap after Cindy got in the car, Darci said, "I just didn't want Mrs. Ray to leave"—a clear indication that she was holding Mrs. Ray against her will.

After hitting Cindy Ray in the mountains, Darci "carried out a very skilled procedure in a way . . . using just the right type of cut as an obstetrician would use in the most modern method . . . and she was successful in getting out a live infant. So . . . although she doesn't remember it, she must have been quite clear-headed and goal directed in how she carried this out."

Resnick downplayed the significance of "memory gaps" in Darci's life. Ray Pierce never reported anything worse than misunderstandings about going to dinner. And Darci's mother only said she seemed preoccupied sometimes after the marriage. In the county jail, Darci admitted that when faced with unpleasant situations she "goes away." Resnick thought that comment significant: what the defense called dissociative reactions "where she is a victim of them, may simply be really a description of what Darci Pierce consciously does." She also admitted to flashbacks to the murder, but wouldn't tell Resnick or anybody else other details on orders of her lawyer. "It's my opinion that she had additional memories that she was just unwilling to share because they were more incriminating of her than they would be helpful," Resnick testified.

Lockwood's analysis of Darci's memory gaps also differed from that of the defense team. She called them "dissociative experiences" that helped her cope by detaching herself from the pain of the event. They were not so different from memory losses that occur in other crimes, or in a car accident, she said. In all the cases in which Darci lost memory Darci had done something troublesome and violent.

Resnick found a number of incriminating pieces of evidence against Darci: at the murder scene, Darci tried to hide her act from homeowner Hartshorn. She said she wanted to be alone, rather than "Look, this woman is hurt, I need help." She did not want to be discovered carrying out a C-section. She also dragged the body behind the clump of trees, indicating an attempt to avoid detection. The test drive to the Acura dealer also indicated that Darci was planning the crime and wanted to case the area. When she led police to the body she screamed to Elisabeth Koehler: "I killed her. I'm a disgusting person," showing she was aware of the killing and of its wrongfulness. And to the theory of a long-standing illness, Resnick said Darci had been considered emotionally stable throughout her life, with only a couple of exceptions.

Darci's confession also revealed that she told Ray she was pregnant when she knew she wasn't. "So the whole plan of pretending consciously to be pregnant and then coming up with a newborn baby makes sense." She also admitted in the interview that she came to the hospital "to complete the scenario."

Summing up, Dr. Resnick argued that Darci suffered not from a mental disease but several personality disorders: antisocial, borderline, and narcissistic. She had suffered amnesia about the actual murder, but she had consciously lied, or "malingered" about her pregnancy. Malingering allowed her to gain acceptance among her workers at G.I. Joes, it allowed her to marry, to stay home, eat a lot and look fat, Resnick said. "By pretending to be pregnant and then coming up with a child would allow her to have this kind of fantasied family." It's possible that Darci even fooled herself with the pregnancy symptoms, but she knew she was not pregnant and knew she moved her muscles to fake it. Further, he reasoned, the killing of Cindy Ray had nothing to do with the false pregnancy because she knew at the time she was not pregnant and wanted a baby.

"The idea of cutting a baby out of a live woman sounds like such a brutal, inexplicable act that there's a temptation for the community to say, 'someone has to be crazy to do something like this,' " he said. But the crime could be understood in the context of Darci's whole life and her antisocial conduct. Such a person does not have the usual moral constraint to stop her. In other words, Darci Pierce wanted a baby, so she took a baby. "Ordinarily, if anyone else in this room wanted a baby they wouldn't take a baby by cutting it from another woman because of the capacity to empathize with the woman and the moral constraint that would stop someone. But if you couple a desire for a baby with the antisocial conduct and history, then it allows an understanding of the crime without having to look for a peculiar kind of crazy diagnosis"—such as multiple personalities.

Resnick's report for the prosecution read like a rapid-fire textbook of Darci's case as it related to New Mexico law. The test for insanity, he said, is that the defendant must either not know what they're doing or the consequences of it, or not know the wrongfulness of it or be unable to refrain from doing it. The law specifically precluded personality disorders from an insanity finding.

In comparing Darci Pierce to those tests, Resnick distilled from her history this evidence: her reality was not distorted and she was not out of her head. She even showed a gun to Mrs. Ray. Ultimately she accomplished what she set out to do, deliver a healthy, live newborn. Resnick said Darci also knew what she was doing, first by waiting for Cindy Ray in the parking lot, and then later denying any involvement in her disappearance. She knew it was wrong to kill: she considered turning back, she took Cindy to an isolated spot, she turned Hartshorn away, she told the Acura dealer she had delivered the baby herself, and she lied repeatedly at the hospital. Resnick also noted that while a cesarean is a bloody procedure there was not much of Cindy Ray's blood on Darci Pierce, indicating that she washed it off, either in a nearby stream or in a gas station bathroom.

Darci Pierce could have prevented herself from kidnapping and killing, he said. She heard no voice telling her to kill, she had an alternative of telling her family the truth, and she could have stolen a baby rather than murder for one; she actually thought about stealing a baby on both July 17 and

220

July 23, the dates of her "inducements." But she didn't act on that impulse, showing she could control illegal conduct even though she wanted a baby. The same was true of wanting her sister-in-law dead. She also showed extraordinary patience in waiting two hours for Cindy Ray. In a frenzy she would have gone into the clinic with the gun, so a mental disease was not compelling her. She also changed plans when she saw her husband's car at home, a controlled act.

Resnick agreed that Darci may have dissociated at the time of the cesarean and lost memory, but he argued that the dissociation or amnesia did not cause her to commit the act. That came from a logical, clear-headed plan. People often dissociated during stress, like the death of a loved one, to block pain, Lockwood noted, but the disease dissociative disorder is extremely rare, and patients are usually very distressed by the personality shifts and the loss of time. Darci shifted and remained cool. When she shifted from screaming at the murder scene to calmly talking about South Africa, it was not a personality shift but a way to disengage verbally, said Lockwood. "It seemed out of context, but if you look at her coping style, it all really fits."

Lockwood argued that Darci Pierce did not suffer from a diagnosable mental disease of long standing. She was a disturbed person with "mixed personality disorder," which involved lying and fantasy. "Having a baby was a preoccupation not so different from an obsession for money or power," the psychologist argued. The payoff was important to her sense of self. When combined with her pattern of lying, simulating and acting out her wishes, she had two choices, to give up the make-believe pregnancy or do something different.

Dr. Lockwood said she could not say precisely what Darci's mental state was when she struck Cindy. "It is possible that her obsession with producing a baby had become all-encompassing" and that, while she knew that taking the baby would harm Cindy, it had become "a matter either of irrelevance or indifference." Neither could Lockwood determine whether Darci's obsession created an irresistible impulse to take the baby or just an unresisted desire. "It is possible that her obsession with obtaining the baby that day so narrowed her judgement that she was incapable, at that moment, of assessing the reasons against such a choice; it is possible that she simply chose to ignore or reject such reasons."

As for premeditation, Resnick noted that Darci made her 5:00 P.M. deadline with thirty minutes to spare, that she checked out the Acura dealer the day before the murder and she befriended a salesman ahead of time. She even had one of the salesmen accompany her to the hospital. She had read a book on cesarean sections, she had filled her gas tank before waiting for Cindy. Darci Pierce had considered stealing a baby, a serious crime, suggesting a callous indifference to how a mother would feel if her newborn were taken. It was not such a big step from stealing a newborn to stealing a newborn in a uterus, he said.

The single piece of evidence that argued against premeditation, he noted, was that she didn't take a knife with her, and one could expect that, given her

222

intelligence. So the decision to actually cut the baby out may have been spontaneous. As a result, he said, he could not say with reasonable medical certainty that she did or did not fully weigh the advantages and disadvantages of the killing in advance.

Resnick delivered his evaluation on February 10, 1988. On February 16, the Albuquerque district attorney's office notified the court that it was dropping the capital offense. The case would not be a death penalty case after all.

It still remained for Resnick and Lockwood to provide a rational explanation for the crime, a crazy act by a crazy person. If Darci wasn't crazy—insane—how did it happen? In the conclusion of Resnick's evaluation, he provided this scenario:

Darci Pierce wanted a baby so that she could be a mother in a way that her mother wasn't. It would make her feel whole and fill an emptiness. When she was told she might have endometriosis, she concluded that she was sterile, causing her to feel as if she would never be a complete woman. She pretended to be pregnant and lied to coworkers at G.I. Joes about a stillborn, then she lied to get married. So she had practice faking a pregnancy, lying about it, and finding a last-minute explanation for not having a baby. Darci stalled and lied to put off the "second" birth while relatives filled her nursery with gifts. She was getting desperate in July. She feared she would lose her husband who she believed to be interested in two other women. And she would lose face with friends, especially Carol Raymond, who became pregnant herself in July.

Darci made up an induction date of July 16 and

223

then managed to put it off by getting the hospital clerk to lie. When she announced the new date, July 23 at 5:00 P.M., she had run out of time. "I had to figure out something before 5:00 P.M. didn't I?" Darci said in her confession. It was very important to her that Ray think the baby was his and she had strong feelings about adoption. Even after changing her original story at the hospital she didn't want Ray to know where the baby came from. So she was precluded from ordinary child stealing. She needed a newborn with vernix. It was a carefully staged, very successfully executed plan—with a single flaw. She did not anticipate the pelvic exam after a roadside delivery. She tried her best to avoid it, but eventually had to change her story at the hospital.

Most people wouldn't know how to do a cesarean, but Darci had experience dressing deer, and she was not squeamish about blood. And her background suited her to carry out an extremely brutal, inexplicable act. She could lie well. She was clever. She was self-centered and felt entitled to things that she wanted. She had a history of violent, antisocial acts. She had fantasized killing her sister-in-law, so the thought of killing a mother for her child had occurred before. Due to her antisocial personality Darci lacked the moral constraints that would stop others from pursuing a lethal act to meet her needs. Darci Pierce performed the ultimate theft, the theft of a fetus from a woman.

Twenty-one

The stage was now set, the scenarios locked in place. The legal showdown could begin. The jury would decide.

Professional courtesy aside, there was a certain disdain between the opposing lawyers for the tacks they were taking. Each knew what the other knew. The police file, the witness interviews, the psychiatric verbiage were piled several feet high in both offices, the shopworn public defender's office and the Bernalillo County District Attorney's office. There were no secrets among the lawyers, only a hardening of arguments. Armed with their psychological profiles, the two sides represented a classic confrontation over the mind of a criminal.

"If you look real closely at her history you see that sociopath," Michael Cox said. "She's always been willing to lie for what she needed." There was no sympathy from the prosecutor, so heinous was the crime. And it wasn't a rage killing; sometimes people accepted those. Everybody gets mad, said Cox. "This was so calculated, almost clinical. It's tough for the average person to sympathize."

Cox said he never bought the multiple personalities theory. "I think that's very trendy. As far as I can tell it's incredibly rare. And it's not all that hard to show when it actually occurs. She just didn't seem to have the background for it. It never seemed to appear. No one really said 'I saw a different personality'—even she didn't. Normally when they have it, they are available and people can distinguish them to a certain extent. But they couldn't even agree on how many personalities there were, who they were, what they did. It's a very seductive defense because you create another persona to carry the guilt. I don't even think Darci Pierce would buy that, if you asked her. She just gradually pushed herself into a corner, tighter and tighter, more and more difficult. And she finally got to the point where the only option was the unthinkable. But for her it wasn't very hard to think about at all. When it looked like she couldn't have her own children that made sense, but once it turned out she could then it didn't make any sense at all. It was a matter of timing. She couldn't have one when she needed one.

"The whole frolic doesn't make any sense if you buy into the [argument that a] desperate need for a child drove her to do this. It wasn't the mothering need so much as the manipulation you could get out of being pregnant, being a mother. If you really, desperately want a child you don't need to go through this incredible charade that she went through. She might steal a child, which is what most mothers do who desperately want to be mothers. They have a true mental illness that drives them to steal a child out of a nursery or grocery store. But to murder somebody first—that's special. And that takes something besides mothering love. She had

226

done it before, and got lots of attention. She went back to it.

"I think there's no doubt she was crazy. You don't do that unless you're crazy. I don't think she was legally insane. The legally insane are the kind of people who go and kill someone because they think they're killing the devil and saving us all. That's insane. People who do really bad things are not generally insane. Just because it's a bizarre thing doesn't mean you're so out of touch with reality that you don't know what you're doing. I think she knew exactly what she was doing. She had logical reasons to do what she did. It's just that nobody who had a real normal heart, like feelings, would do it. She didn't have those normal feelings that would stop her. I don't know why she lacked all that. Her upbringing didn't look that bad to me. I've seen a lot worse.

"Darci also didn't look like she fit the pattern of a woman abused as a child. Something must have happened to start her down the path, but I still don't know how that's going to get you to what she became. Most people I know who are sexually abused victims self-destruct. They don't turn into killers — especially female sexual abuse victims. Their lives are just kind of a mess. And hers didn't seem a mess. The defense tried to mine the family history to find some horrible things. I didn't see it. Her family tree, in terms of the way they dealt with it, was not all that strange."

Under New Mexico law, the jury could find Darci

227

guilty of murder, it could find her innocent by reason of insanity, or it could find her guilty but mentally ill, which put more of a burden on the defense team. After months of living with Darci's case, John Bogren and Tom Jameson were convinced that she was as much a victim as Cindy Ray, and an attempt was made to plea bargain the case, without success.

"She was strange as a kid. She was always strange," said Bogren. "Listen to that tape; you can hear it with the cops, when she's telling those outrageous lies, just her tone of voice. She's telling ridiculous lies without batting an eye. She's accused of murder, and she's off in some fantasy world. The description of the nurses, how she's clutching the baby and snaps, even when she's bringing the baby in—that's not a normal person. On a real level, I'd like to believe that the woman can do it, is mean and nasty and has the side of her that just doesn't give a fuck. But it's more than that. Nobody's that good of an actress. It was just bizarre, her actions.

"I spent a lot of time with her. She's a real nice, likeable person. She's funny, witty, mature—way advanced in years for her age—charming, cared about people. She related well to the people in jail with her. She was always concerned. She had this consuming thing about children, and women in jail who couldn't be with their kids. She really hated people that abused children."

Jameson also took issue with the deer-killing evidence, as if Darci had learned enough to do a C-section. "They wanted to come up with some human way to explain. I understand the impulse. I started thinking about the animal world, too. It's so removed from rational thought, what she did. I kept thinking, do animals do things like this to other animals? I understand their impulse. They wanted an explanation for how she could be capable of this. And since they wanted to portray her as a lying, conniving bitch who wanted a baby if it meant butchering a woman or not, then they had to say, 'hey, she butchered things before. To her it was just like butchering a deer,' which to me was completely ludicrous. They actually took one of the few, warm things she did with her father, where her father actually tried to include her and make her a part of something, and turned it around into somehow this was a lesson on murdering someone later in life. It was a ridiculous perversion."

Darci had recurring nightmares and recurring memory loss, Jameson said. The more she was probed and encouraged to acknowledge them, the more she remembered times in her life during which she couldn't remember anything. "They said she was a consummate liar. Yes, you're right, she was. When people are dissociative and they lose time, and they don't know what happened, they make up stories to cover for themselves. She was used to making up good stories. It was a life coping mechanism for her. Darci actually made it easy on the cops. Once whatever was going on stopped inside of her, she was very cooperative. She led them to the body and made a full statement. That's all the police could hope for. Sometimes bodies are never found. They didn't know what they were dealing with. They were puzzled by it. She solved the crime; she tied up the pieces."

Jameson said that in the end he made sense of

Darci's life and crime "in a bizarre way. It's not like link to link to link in a chain. But in a big picture it made sense: a child who was raped and abused early, who developed coping mechanisms to block out the pain of what happened to her when she was a little girl. And those coping mechanisms started getting out of control. She started losing control by blanking out. Her environment added to who she was, a dysfunctional family, her adoption, her abuse, it started spiraling and spiraling. She was the child she was going to have. She wanted to relive her life over again, by doing it right. She could be in control and she could relive the life she never had. She could heal the wound."

Twenty-two

Darci Pierce's trial began on March 14, 1988 in the courtroom of Judge Richard Traub, New Mexico District Court, Albuquerque. At 8:40 A.M. Harry Zimmerman and Michael Cox walked in carrying boxes on their shoulders, their court file in duplicate. Placing them on their table, which sat on the judge's right, they faced the jury box. With exaggerated motions, Zimmerman proceeded to put eye drops in his eyes. He wore a green-gray suit with a double vent and cowboy boots. He had just a slight paunch and a scrawny beard. He spoke in a direct way, like a small buzz saw biting into pine. Cox was tall and thin with a reddish, bushy beard and glasses that made him look something like an Anglo Castro. He had a soft voice with a push to it. They were accompanied by a tall, black investigator, who dressed like a man who knew style but could only afford K-Mart clothes.

A few minutes before 9:00 A.M., Darci Pierce arrived, wearing a pale blouse and a gray wool skirt. Her hair was long and brown with a wave to it. She was pretty, with pouting lips and a nice figure. She had lost more than twenty-five pounds since the murder seven months earlier. She was accompanied

231

by John Bogren in a gray suit with light stripes. Tom Jameson was tall, with graying hair, a graying moustache and glasses. He was thin and collegiate-looking with an understated manner of speaking and dressing that made him seem less important than he was. On the first day he wore a green khaki suit. Their backs to the audience, the jury box on their right, they were joined by Jackie Robins, a tall, plain woman with a bucktoothed grin. She was the chief public defender for the state—an administrative job in Santa Fe. She wore a long skirt, sensible shoes and spoke without emotion, in clipped, even tones.

The audience for the trial was composed mostly of women. They looked retired or out of work. A tall man with unkempt red hair and beard, a big belly, sneakers, and pants that were too short, who carried a backpack, began his daily vigil, too. The trial began at 9:10 A.M. as Judge Traub entered in his black robe. Traub was a big, gray-haired man with years of experience on the bench. He seemed always to anticipate lawyer objections and he spoke with gentle force. As the trial began he made decisions rapidly, with commonsense logic and simple language.

"Is the state ready to proceed?" Traub asked.

"Yes your honor," said Cox.

"The defendant?"

"Defense is ready," Bogren said.

"You may make your opening statement, Mr. Cox."

"Good morning, ladies and gentlemen," said Cox, facing the jury from a podium to their left. "On July 23, 1987, Cindy Ray left the ob/gyn clinic at

Kirtland. She was on her way to what's called the Champus meeting where she would learn everything she needed to know as an expectant mother about medical benefits and procedures. After that meeting she was due to meet her husband, Sam, and her son, Luke. But she would never see her son and never see her husband again, because in the parking lot of that clinic parked next to her was the defendant, Darci Pierce, and she was waiting for her.

"You've all heard and discussed some of what happened after she encountered her in the parking lot, and it's been described by some of you and many others as a bizarre act. As you hear from the evidence and all the witnesses, it was a bizarre act committed for rational reasons. What you will hear is a story of a con artist at work and of a deceit that had to be covered up, a deceit which led her into a position where she had to make a decision, a decision about getting a baby, and the only way that she could get a baby . . . was to take a newborn. The only catch was she had to kill someone to do it."

Cox told the jury that the only question to be resolved by them was whether Darci was insane. The difference in cases, he said, was that the defense psychiatrists relied on what Darci Pierce told them about the crime — and she was a "very, very believable liar." By contrast, prosecution experts were more skeptical and relied on the evidence. Tests showed she exaggerated everything, he said. She also told defense psychiatrists a "tale of woe of sexual and physical abuse and a horrible childhood." But Darci's "terrible problems" came from the leading question the defense asked her, like, "Have you ever heard

233

voices?" She would say "Yes," but Darci had not sought help for voices, and family and friends knew nothing about them.

"The defense psychologists will talk about fragments of personalities that did different things and fragments will eventually divide her personality into so many pieces that all responsibility and knowledge disappears. When you hear from the psychologist and psychiatrist for the state . . . they'll tell you that she's legally sane, intelligent, careful, ruthless, almost totally self-centered and extremely deceitful. What you will hear is the crime—the kidnapping, mutilation, murder of the woman and the taking of the child—was not the product of a diseased mind, but the product of a diseased, hardened soul, and that is the very essence of criminal responsibility, and will lead you to find her guilty of the charges."

Tom Jameson then took his turn at the podium, his voice cracking. "Ladies and gentlemen of the jury, this case is about insanity. It's about the insane acts of an insane mind. On July twenty-third of last year Darci Pierce appeared at a local car dealership. She appeared with a bloody dress and a newborn child. She appeared there with a wild story."

Jameson's emphasis was on Darci's "stories"—so wild that nobody would believe them. "Pay close attention to the lies. They're very important to this case. We will present evidence from medical doctors who have worked with Darci who will explain to you the importance of the lies and who will explain to you the insanity that exists within this woman's

234

head. They will explain to you that lies are evidence of her disorder. They will explain to you that lies are Darci's way of filling in the blanks of various points in her life. They will talk to you about the lies that have occurred all through her life and that these lies are also clues, little windows into the insanity that exists in her brain.

"The state will present evidence that Darci Pierce is a cold-blooded killer, a ruthless woman, a woman who would do anything, a vicious person, someone who is not insane. The nineteen years of Darci's life and the evidence you'll hear about it will not support that . . . all the witnesses we will present to you have known Darci throughout her life, a common thread exists, and that common thread is Darci's lies. You will hear about the momentum that was building up inside of Darci, the momentum that was bubbling inside of her brain, the momentum that ultimately led to her traveling to Kirtland Air Force Base on July twenty-third of last year on a hot, hot day and sitting in a small car in the hot sun thinking about a baby . . . As she sat there . . . her brain bubbled and churned until Cindy Ray came into the car to talk, to maybe share a cool drink."

With that, the state began its case, calling Samuel Ray to the stand. He was tall and thin, twenty-six, with sandy hair not much longer than it had been when he left the Air Force. He was wearing a yellow sweater. In the year since the murder, he'd been pounding shingles for his dad, he said. Harry Zimmerman pulled a small photograph, Exhibit 1, and

Sam identified it as his family, Cindy and Sam with his two kids. The photograph of Cindy and Sam had been taken in Germany, and the children, Luke and Amelia, superimposed onto it later.

"Is that a fair and accurate depiction of how your wife looked in July of 1987?" asked Zimmerman.

"Well, obviously she was rather pregnant in July. She had a permanent at the time of the picture. Her hair was a little curly and she didn't wear her glasses for the picture. Other than that, its obviously Cindy."

"And is that also a fair representation of what your little boy, Luke, looked like?"

"Yes, that's a picture from about the same period last summer. He's a blond-haired kid with blue eyes and he's just a cute little boy." Sam's voice was downturned, broken with frequent sighs that, at times, seemed staged. The photograph was passed through the jury box as he talked about his life with Cindy. "Cindy was shy. She wasn't loud. She stayed in her own little environment. Through her Tupperware she did have to go out and talk to people she had never met before but that was very difficult for her."

Sam traced Cindy's movements on the day she died, and told how tired she was. "Normally Cindy exercised extensively. She did the most difficult Jane Fonda tape at least three days a week." But on the morning of the murder she was tired. "She called about noon and I was very busy but I took a break and talked to her for a few minutes. She told me she had some difficulty with the Tupperware and she may have to go back up there and just shared the

236

things that were on her mind, but I think the main reason she called was just to tell me that she loved me."

Sam was handed a large crumpled sack from the clerk's desk, and began pulling items out: Cindy's shoes; her set of keys with her name tag and keys to the house, the bicycles, the padlock and the Blazer. He also identified her blue-tinted sunglasses and her purse. In the purse, Sam explained, had been the special undergarments. "When you go to the doctor you don't want to have to explain to the doctor what's going on. You don't want to be answering questions about things that personal and important to you, so she had taken hers off and put them in her purse, and was wearing regular undergarments at her appointment." Sam took a deep breath, closed his eyes and lowered his head. He wiped a tear and sniffed loudly.

Under cross-examination by Jackie Robins, Sam said that he and Cindy had moved to Albuquerque in January of 1987 and within a month Cindy was selling Tupperware, although she did not have her first party until March or April. She enjoyed selling and she was gaining confidence, he said.

"She had not had that kind of confidence before she started selling Tupperware, is that right?"

"This sounds a little too black and white. It was more of a process. Cindy was not afraid to talk to people that she knew . . . but when she went into public situations, when she went into a group of people, a crowded room, for instance, and sat down and waited for an appointment . . . she just kept to herself." Sam reviewed again taking Luke to the

237

Mormon babysitter, and Cindy's calls from the clinic. He also said they had driven their Blazer several times into the mountains and three times south on Highway 14, which led near the murder scene.

Sam Ray was followed by Raymond Pierce, a thin, wide-eyed young man with a tight, thin line for a mouth. He was wearing a light brown suit, with a light pink shirt and white tie. Though he entered from the back and walked past Darci's chair and sat directly before her, she kept her head down, her eyes averted from her husband.

Ray Pierce outlined his life with Darci, her medical history, and her desire for a baby, which surfaced particularly strongly during her stint at G.I. Joes. "I had heard her say more than once there were women taking maternity leave and she seemed to feel left out or needed to do the same." In September of 1986 Darci told Ray she was pregnant and due in April.

"Isn't it true that before she mentioned the pregnancy there was some talk of splitting up?" asked Cox.

"There was no talk of it. There may have been thoughts but there was no talk," Ray said. He answered questions matter-of-factly, with no emotion, as if describing a dull parade passing by. Lawyers for both sides thought Ray a bystander to the events that had swirled around him. Cox asked about the night of the murder and his return to the hospital, at 3:00 A.M., to be told the baby wasn't his. "What was your reaction to hearing that?"

"Needless to say, I was somewhat surprised," said Ray.

Cox then focused in, for the first time, on Darci's

238

alleged disease.

"Did you ever notice any significant memory loss on your wife's part?"

"Not significant, no."

"Did you ever notice any really serious kind of reality perception problems?"

"I don't think so."

"Did she ever complain to you of hearing voices?"

"Not that I recall."

"Or of losing days?"

"No."

"Or of hearing arguments in her head?"

"No."

"Or of being frightened by voices in her head, or anything of that type?"

"Not of voices."

"Did you ever notice any bizarre behavior on your wife's part at all?"

"Not bizarre, no."

Cox and Zimmerman then laid out their case in rapid fire order to the jury: Kelly Lyden, the admitting clerk, who nervously told of Darci's deception. David Sargent, Darci's doctor in Portland who outlined her true medical history. He had never told her she had endometriosis or was infertile. Jerry Fisher, the muttonchopped car salesman who sold the Mustang to the Pierces. He never thought Darci looked pregnant, but he had accepted her word for it. Rob Mohr, the Acura dealer who befriended Darci and ended up with a baby on his hands. Diane McDonald Gray, the medical technician who had turned away Darci from the base clinic because she lacked a positive pregnancy test. Angela Morgan, the woman who monitored Cindy Ray's baby at the clinic. She said she had seen Darci the day before walking the hall of the clinic. Elizabeth Herman, Cindy's Tupperware colleague, who cried when she recalled sitting next to Cindy, happily discussing their pending births. Sister Rosemary Homrich, who made the connection between Cindy Ray's missing baby and the baby Darci Pierce brought to the hospital. And Theron Hartshorn, the homeowner in the mountains, who found Darci Pierce at the murder scene while driving home. Zimmerman asked Hartshorn how Darci appeared.

"She was a little nervous."

"Did she appear irrational?"

"Not really."

"Did she appear out of control?"

"Not really."

"Did she appear out of touch with reality."

"That's hard for me to say. Not really, I wouldn't say."

Twenty-three

On the second day of trial, March 15, stirring testimony came from Elisabeth Koehler, the nurse who befriended Darci during the night at the hospital and eventually cracked the murder by placing the baby in her lap. Because there were only two women on Labor and Delivery that night, Koehler spent almost all her time with Darci and found things in common to talk about. They had both been to Africa, and Koehler had an adopted sister. Darci was awake and talking most of the night, she said, although she napped toward morning, just before the police arrived to question her. Koehler took out her IV and took her to the conference room in a wheelchair. "She again had answers for everything," said Koehler.

Because of a class in the conference room, Darci was moved to a smaller lounge, where the questions continued. "It was apparent that she felt more comfortable talking to me than to any of those men . . . As time went on it seemed more and more apparent that Darci had never been to Santa Fe and she really couldn't identify or didn't know the turnoffs in Santa Fe or the roads or streetlights, even distance between Albuquerque and Santa Fe. She said it took

241

her three hours to get there, things like that, so it was becoming apparent that possibly she hadn't gone to Santa Fe. So we were just discussing with her the possibility of maybe the surrogate mother could have been Cindy Ray. Was the midwife upset? Could possibly something have gone wrong with the birth and maybe the baby's mom wasn't okay?"

"Did you talk about concern about the baby?" Zimmerman asked.

"Yes, Darci always felt that it was her baby. She paid for it. She wanted it. She obviously appeared to be very attached to this baby, and at one point in the smaller room I asked her if she wanted me to go get the baby for her to see it. She had been asking all night. So I went and got the baby out of the nursery and brought it to the small conference room so Darci could see the baby and hold it."

"Did you talk about adoption some more?"

"I had mentioned to Darci that she was adopted when she was eleven days old and that I didn't think we could just keep the baby in the nursery forever, wondering who the mother was, and Darci couldn't take the baby home with her unless we knew who the mother was. So I did mention to her that I was afraid the same thing would happen to this baby that happened to Darci. We could keep the baby in the nursery for some period of time but certainly not a whole lifetime waiting for who its parents were, so it would probably go up for adoption if we couldn't find out."

"How did that conversation affect her?"

"She was upset and she was crying. I'm not for sure that she was crying but she seemed upset, and she did mention that it wasn't her baby and she probably would never be able to take the baby home, that it probably would never be hers." Koehler then took the baby back to the nursery and Darci broke down. "She basically admitted that she was afraid to continue to talk because she was afraid she would be handcuffed and taken to jail. She was afraid that maybe she had done something horribly wrong and that maybe the baby's mother was not okay and that maybe she did know who the baby's mother was . . . At that point she asked me to go get Steve Coppinger." When Coppinger emerged from his meeting with Darci, Darci said to Koehler, "Elisabeth, I killed her."

"I think she said that a few times, maybe even more than a few times. She was holding me and crying things like 'I killed her. I hope she's not dead. I've done something horrible.' " Koehler then described the ride to the body, and the wait in the car while police checked Cindy Ray's body. "She was holding me and crying, hugging me, holding my hands, very upset to the point of almost screaming that she had done something horribly wrong, that she killed her, that she hoped she wasn't dead. She had mentioned that her Krugerrand was there. I asked if she wanted me to ask the police to look for it and she didn't really respond to that, but she said her Krugerrand was there and that she wanted to get out of there and at one point she asked me to kill her."

"Do you recall the words she used?"

"She said, 'Eli, kill me, please kill me.' "

"Who is Eli?"

"Eli is what some of the people at work call me."

"All told, Ms. Koehler, throughout the course of

243

the evening, how much time did you spend with Darci Pierce?"

"I was probably with Darci Pierce from 11:30 at night until at least 11:30 in the morning, with the possible exception of a total of three hours that I wasn't in the room with her."

"And did you observe anything unusual about her behavior throughout the night?"

"Not really."

"Did you note any irrational behavior on the part of this defendant?"

"No."

"Did you note any extraordinary shifts in personalities?"

"No."

Dr. Susan Graham told the court of her suspicions of Darci's story from the moment she arrived at the hospital. "I didn't know exactly what the problem was, but there was something going on here that wasn't right." The umbilical cord was unclamped, and the baby's head was beautifully, fully round, with vernix and blood still on its face. Darci wanted the baby checked, but not herself and wanted to know about getting a birth certificate for the baby. Graham examined Darci and concluded that she had not given birth. She then wanted to admit Darci to the psychiatric wing. "I didn't think she had a gynecological problem. This was a person who had come in with two stories, with a baby, and even when she had agreed to be examined by us, was absolutely adamant that her husband not be told that this was not his baby. This is a circumstance I had never seen . . . Here was a woman who apparently had been able to convince her husband over a period of

months—a woman who had never been pregnant—
that she had given birth to his baby. I didn't know
where this belonged. The mental health center was
the only option I could think of at that time."

In his cross examination of Dr. Graham, John
Bogren homed in on Darci's seeming calm in the
midst of her lying storm. "She would give answers to
the police without much thought or reflection?"

"That is the way it appeared to me."

"What she was telling Dr. Slocumb [Graham's
boss], did that seem plausible to you?"

"No."

"Did she, in any way, become defensive when she
was confronted by Dr. Slocumb about the implausi-
bilities of the story?"

"No."

"Her affect seemed to change when she was holding the baby?"

"Her affect began to change when Elisabeth asked
her if she wanted the same thing to happen to this
baby as happened to her."

"And then there was a pause, is that correct?"

"That's correct."

"Did it appear to you that she was reflecting or
thinking about something?"

"Yes, that's definitely what it appeared."

"And this was the first time?"

"This was the first time that I had seen her do
what I would consider to be reflecting." After con-
fessing to Coppinger, Dr. Graham saw Darci crying.

"You did say that Darci did say, when she was
holding the baby, that this was the first time she felt
like a person?"

"Like a real person."

"Like a real person. Those were her words?"

"Yes."

On redirect questioning, Zimmerman asked Dr. Graham about protocol during the evening with Darci. She said they followed the normal routine, requiring an examination.

"Do you feel as though what you and Dr. Slocumb did throughout the evening was beyond what would normally be done under the circumstances?"

"A circumstance like this is so unusual that I can't answer that question. I mean, you're certainly not taught in medical school how you deal with this sort of occurrence and I hope that I never have to deal with this sort of occurrence again, ever again in my entire life. There is no protocol for this kind of a happening."

Dr. Graham was followed on the stand by John Slocumb, a professor in obstetrics/gynecology at the University of New Mexico school of medicine. He had watched Darci lie throughout the evening at the hospital, yet thought she was "acutely aware" of what was going on, with no loss of reality. His most riveting testimony involved the preciseness with which the cesarean was performed on Cindy Ray. Named after Julius Caesar, who supposedly was delivered that way, modern cesareans involved a small, low, horizontal cut through the muscle of the uterus. The muscles can be split rather than cut, and they heal better. That allows a woman to have a second or third child by C-section. He speculated that an untrained person would simply cut a vertical gash in the abdomen wall because it would be quicker.

In an operating room, a cesarean normally is done in five to seven minutes, he said. He estimated that

Cindy Ray's crude operation took 10 to 15 minutes, with the baby's survival at risk. In a cesarean the incision is by the baby's head, which must be pushed and pulled through the hole. Sometimes shoulders get caught. The usual procedure is to put one hand around the baby's head, and have someone else push on the fundus to push the baby out through the hole. In Cindy Ray's case, the size of the incision was the same—or smaller—than the ones doctors make.

Slocumb also testified that false pregnancies, when a woman feels she is pregnant, are quite common: 40 percent of women who thought they were in their first two months of pregnancy, were, in fact, not pregnant. It was rare—he had seen a dozen cases—to find a woman go to term with no baby. But some went to the point of labor. Their symptoms range from no periods, to bigger breasts and abdomens, morning sickness and fetal motion. He said that when women with pseudocyesis find they are not pregnant, they can't believe it, and eventually become devastated, as if the baby had died. Darci Pierce, he said, didn't act that way. "She had no emotion about the fact that this wasn't her baby, that she wasn't pregnant, and it was very obvious to me that she knew that this was not her baby and that she was not pregnant. Secondly, there wasn't a grief reaction about loss of baby. I did not see at any point throughout my contact with the patient any sign of grief about this pregnancy, or when the baby was taken from her."

The third day of trial covered the police reports: Tom Craig's detective work, Steve Coppinger's interview with Darci, the criminalistics and the autopsy. Craig, sporting a moustache, dressed in a gray sport

247

jacket with a white western shirt and blue tie, told of his unsuccessful attempt to pull a confession from Darci at the hospital. "When we would tell her we didn't believe what she was saying she would look straight in your face, straight in your eyes and continue with that lie. Or, she would come off and make up something new that would hopefully substantiate what she had been saying. She would look you straight in the face. She never blinked."

"Did that cause you any sort of reaction?" asked Zimmerman.

"It was spooky. My reaction was, my thought was, Helter Skelter. I was thinking of the book and the movie *Helter Skelter.*"

Craig identified photographs taken at the murder scene. "We found the body behind the stand of trees, between the stream and the stand of trees. The trees pretty much hid the body from view from the road. As Craig talked, Darci, wearing a creamy white skirt and blouse, sat quietly, eyes down, her hands folded in her lap. Her diamond and wedding rings were visible.

Under cross-examination Craig said that he had interviewed many homicide suspects but that Darci was different. She was more intelligent and articulate, and she didn't get defensive.

"You were wondering to yourself, 'Is she crazy or is she just lying to me?' Isn't that right," asked Jackie Robins.

"Those questions, yes, went through my mind."

"And that made the hair on your neck stand up, isn't that right?"

"It was the way she looked you right in the eye, yes, and lied to you."

William Reinig of the Albuquerque Police criminalistics lab then described the crime scene: the spot
where Cindy was found, the fetal monitor belt in the
tree, Cindy's sunglasses and the Krugerrand on the
ground. He described the contents of the Volkswagen, including the gun, and of Cindy's purse,
found in the grass. He also testified that no blood
was found on the steering wheel or gearshift of the
Volkswagen, and none of the blood found in the car
matched Cindy Ray's, despite the bloody procedure.
He said the stream running by the body had water in
it, in little pools.

Air Force agent Steve Coppinger testified about
Darci's strange change in composure after leaving
the crime scene and driving back to Albuquerque.
She noticed a Krugerrand ring on his hand and began talking about South Africa again.

"The whole way down the mountain and back to
the office, she was talking about South Africa,
wasn't she?" asked Robins.

"Yes, we stayed on that conversation."

"And she was calm and collected at that point?"

"Yes, she was very coherent and making herself
well-understood about her South African experiences." And when she got back to the air base, she
asked Ray to bring Coppinger a photo album of
South Africa.

The final state witness was Ross Zumwalt, the
medical examiner who would tell how Cindy died.
But before he began lawyers for both sides negoti-
ated concerning which photographs would be shown
to the jurors. Some were gruesome close-ups of the
wound in Cindy Ray's abdomen, with the umbilical
cord hanging out. There were close-ups of the

scratches that matched the Blazer key. Jackie Robins objected to the bloodiest of the pictures: "I think that the jurors are going to get kind of sick." Michael Cox argued for their introduction. "When I first heard about the case, I had pictured in my mind what I could see. That photograph, in my opinion, is considerably less gross than what I imagined. The main purpose of it is to show the incision . . . the care with which this was done." Judge Traub looked at the photographs and said, "Well, let me put it to you this way. The photograph is no joy to look at, but at the same time the case is no joy either . . . In view of the nature of the defense and what her mental attitude was, the state is entitled to put on their case. This one is very difficult to take, but I think it should probably be admitted."

Zumwalt then proceeded to describe the wounds on Cindy Ray, looking at each photograph through wire-rimmed glasses. He said the strangulation marks around her neck could have been caused by the fetal monitoring belt in her purse, the one found in the tree.

"Can you tell the jury how much strength is required to strangle someone into unconsciousness if such an item is used?" asked Cox.

"Well, it doesn't take a whole lot of strength to make someone unconscious."

"Would it be possible for a woman to exert that kind of pressure?"

"Yes."

"And you said it could occur within a few seconds?"

"That's correct." Zumwalt compared the scratches with the key and said the incision was made "by an instrument similar to a key."

"Doctor how is it possible to do that with a key?"

"Well, a key does have some rather sharp points and areas in it, particularly on the taut, stretched skin overlying a pregnant uterus. One could puncture through the skin with such an instrument. Once punctured through, the instrument could be drawn along and the skin could be sort of half cut and half torn. Once the skin was torn the underlying fat tissue and muscle tissue could be more easily torn and pulled apart with such an instrument." The Blazer key contained hair, fat tissue and muscle tissue in the points of the key, he said.

Zumwalt said he would expect a person performing a cesarean on Cindy to have a lot of blood on their hands and forearms. He also said it surprised him that the baby was healthy. "There were no injuries to the baby and the baby didn't have any evidence of having low oxygen. It surprised me that such a procedure could have been done without the normal, well-controlled hospital situation and have delivered a perfectly healthy baby."

Twenty-four

Darci Pierce's birth mother opened her daughter's defense, on March 21, the third day of trial, by slowly walking to the witness stand. She was a huge woman, in a blue and white dress, white sandals and glasses. She carried a white purse. Her chin was large and sagging. Her hair was graying, and she looked sad. She began with her name, age (49) and relationship to Darci.

"Were you ever sexually abused as a child?" Jackie Robins, chief state public defender asked.

"Yes, I was," she began, before Michael Cox jumped to his feet and objected. At the bench, out of hearing of the jury, Robins told Judge Traub "the reason we need to go into this is that we're trying to look at the family that Darci was raised in, in order to figure out how she became insane, which is our defense." Psychiatric witnesses would talk about the way Darci was treated by her mother and father, she said.

Traub allowed the line of questioning to continue.

"How old were you?"

"I believe I was around six."

"And what happened?"

252

"It was my, one of my family's friends, and he assaulted me."

"And did you always remember it?"

"No, I didn't."

"Have you only just begun to remember it?"

"Yes."

With that, Darci's lawyers set the tone for the defense. Without saying it overtly they let the jury know that Darci came into a family already wounded by abuse, which often is cyclical and repeated, generation to generation. Mrs. Ricker also told of her mother's affair with her father's best friend when she was eleven, and the anger and rejection she felt. Mrs. Ricker married at the age of sixteen. With her second child she almost died hemorrhaging, so she and her husband Ken adopted Darci Kayleen.

She said Darci matured physically faster than most girls, and it confused her. "She always wanted to be older than what she was because she looked older than what she was." Sandra Ricker's conflicts with Darci began in the seventh grade. "Darci did not like fat people, and I was always a fat person, an ugly nothing. I did not suit her. In her opinion I did not suit what she thought I should be as a mother." Darci was also a "daddy's girl," just as Craig, her son, was a "mama's boy." As a result, Sandra felt rejected by her husband because he would side with Darci. At one point the aggravation got so bad that she and Ken considered separation. Yet Darci often treated her well, she said. "She was probably the most caring person that I knew."

As Mrs. Ricker began to tell of Darci's childhood lies, she broke down and cried, and the judge called a recess. On her way out of the court, into a back room, Darci walked by the witness stand and

253

touched her mother's arm. After a drink and resupply of tissue, Mrs. Ricker said Darci led people to think she was mistreated at home. "I think because she had, again, a fat, ugly mother. I think she was really ashamed . . . She was always ashamed of our house . . . she led people to think that she lived in a better house."

Mrs. Ricker was blunt about Darci's adoption attitude, and about her cruelty when she returned from South Africa to a half-remodeled house. "She was so beyond our home that it hurt our feelings lots . . . we weren't proper and that hurt me." That rejection led to Darci moving out, and graduating from high school without her parents there.

Mrs. Ricker recounted the heart-wrenching story of Darci's false pregnancy, the stillbirth lie, and then the "new" pregnancy that led to the wedding at Christmas. She said she ignored the clues that Darci was faking. Then came the night of July 23.

"Did you get a phone call from Ray?" asked Jackie Robins.

"Yes."

"And what did he tell you?"

"That Darci had a baby girl."

"Did he tell you the name of the baby girl?"

"Yes."

"And how did you feel about it?"

"Well, we were just so happy because she wanted a girl real bad, and she named it, well, Amanda Michelle."

"Now, did you later find out that everything was different?"

"Yes," she said, dissolving in tears. As the court recessed she sat in the witness box sobbing. Darci walked by her again, her eyes down, her hands folded before her.

In his cross-examination, Michael Cox tried to paint a picture of a Ricker family that wasn't so abnormal.

"She was a little bit spoiled when she was growing up?"

"She was very loved, very spoiled," said Darci's mother.

"And so it kind of fell to you to be the one that did say no?"

"Yes."

"And sometimes children have to be told that, don't they?"

"Yes."

"So you became kind of the authority figure in the home?"

"Yes."

"And then she began to resent that didn't she?"

"I think so."

"On one occasion she told your minister that you had been beating her?"

"I think so."

"That was not true, was it?"

The defense then put on the family portrait, beginning with Ken Ricker, Darci's father, taciturn and colorless. Asked by Tom Jameson, "How did you come to adopt Darci?" He answered, "Because I wanted a daughter."

"And how did the adoption actually go?"

"It was a pots and pans salesman that was doing a show at our house and his daughter was pregnant and couldn't take care of it."

"When was Darci told about the adoption?"

"She was probably about six years old."

255

"What kind of child was Darci?"

"She was a very good child."

"Was Darci a moody child?"

"Not really."

"Were there any troubles with Darci as she was growing up?"

"Not particularly." Later he said she didn't get along well with his wife. He said he and Sandra disagreed on raising children. "I didn't think they should be spanked at times and she thought they should." He talked of their deer-hunting trips: "We had good times together." Hunting season was always around Darci's birthday, October 13.

"Would you be able to spend time with Darci on her birthday if she wasn't hunting with you?"

"No."

Ken Ricker knew Darci kept a knife and his rifle under her bed, and he would retrieve them, but she would take them back. "I guess she was scared."

"What did she tell you she was scared of?"

"Somebody breaking in the house."

"Had anybody ever broken in your house?"

"It's been broken in three different times . . . She always kept a knife under the pillow."

"Was she ever afraid to go outside?"

"Well, she wouldn't walk to the store by herself."

Ken said he wasn't wild about Darci seeing Ray Pierce "because he just wasn't the type of person I expected her to go with."

"And what kind of person did you expect?"

"Oh, somebody with a future."

Craig Ricker, Darci's older brother, testified next, calling her a "very happy little girl" but also describing how they bickered and how Darci came between his mother and father. "They were just having a hard time controlling her, she just wouldn't do what they asked." He told of his own son's birth, and how Darci shocked him by suggesting to his wife: "Wouldn't it be neat if you and I both could breast feed Joshua?" But Craig also said Darci helped them find a new apartment, and after a car accident, Darci went to the emergency room "and held my hand and just told me to hang in there. I was happy to see her." She also babysat Joshua and was good with him.

"Did your child appear to like her?" asked Jameson.

"Yes."

"And did you trust your child with Darci?"

"Yes, I did."

Craig's wife, Mary Ann, described Darci's resentment at her giving a child up for adoption, and her desire to nurse her next child. Then Donna Vanderberg, Sandra Ricker's sister, told the jury how she and her mother went to pick Darci up after her birth and adoption and the joy it brought to the family. She was close to Sandra, she said, talking three or four times a day on the phone. Their children grew up together, her Brad and Michelle and the Ricker three.

"Was there any trouble with Darci as a child?"

"To start with, she was basically a normal child, but as she got older, I think problems arose more and more . . ." Eventually the conflict with Darci depressed Sandra to the point of suicide, she said. Darci often asked about her adoption. "Sandra and Ken had given me the name of her biological mother in an envelope, which was placed in my safe deposit box. I never opened it. In case something happened to them and Darci would like to get ahold of her biological parents at age . . . twenty-one or so." She described Darci as a loner, who played alone but who envied the closeness of the Vanderberg family, and the kinds of vacations they took, such as the one to Disneyland in a motor home.

Donna Vanderberg also testified about a next door neighbor named Earl who upset Darci. "At one point she was quite upset because Earl—she would go over, back and forth and through to their home—had given her a kiss, not just a kiss . . . it was a very sexual kiss and it upset her very badly."

"How did she act towards this man named Earl after that?"

"Well, she didn't care to be around him." She described Earl as a close family friend, but Darci didn't want him to come to her wedding.

After Darci's South African trip, Donna suggested to Sandra that she and Darci go to counseling "because the problem isn't just Darci, it was everybody involved as a family."

Her son, Brad Vanderberg, Darci's cousin, later took the stand and shocked the courtroom with the news that he had slept with Darci from ages six to twelve. "It just kind of tapered off and then . . . we realized that this isn't right for cousins . . . and we just never talked about it or never did it again. It just kind of faded away."

Defense psychiatrist Jean Goodwin began a full day of testimony on March 22, around her diagnosis that Darci suffered from an undefined kind of multiple personality disorder. She argued that because of it, Darci was insane at the time of the murder, because different parts of her were in control at different times of the day. During the period of lost memory, Goodwin said, she was not in control of her actions and she could not prevent herself from killing. But Goodwin, a demure blonde whose soft voice was loaded with sibilants, and who was dressed in a green suit with a white blouse, could not clearly identify the personality states, nor could she find enough symptoms to meet the standard psychiatric diagnosis for a specific dissociative disorder. Goodwin said Darci also suffered from several personality disorders, which under New Mexico law do not count toward an insanity plea: somatization, in which Darci had multiple false pregnancies; factitious, in which Darci compulsively simulated pregnancy; borderline, characterized by impulsive behavior; and narcissistic, an exaggerated egocentricity and callousness with other people. She also found signs of conduct disorder, based on violence, substance abuse disorder and eating disorder.

On cross examination, Harry Zimmerman attacked Goodwin for having a special interest in, and perhaps bias toward, multiple personalities, the implication being that it clouded her diagnosis of Darci.

"There is no hard evidence that indicates sexual abuse before age six is there, Doctor?" he said.

"It depends on what you call hard," Goodwin said. "The symptom picture is one of the realms that I look at."

"You relied heavily on the sex abuse as an indicator of the dissociative disorder, didn't you?"

"Well, not that heavily . . . the precursors listed are sexual abuse and other emotional trauma."

"And the emotional trauma you referred to had to do significantly with this defendant's adoption, is that right?"

"Yes."

"And you talked about things like teasing from older brothers?"

"Yes."

"And you talked about things like this defendant's search for her natural mother?"

"Yes."

"These were all things that you interpret as emotional trauma that might be early indicators of dissociation?"

"Yes."

Zimmerman implied that Goodwin fed Darci leading questions about her diagnosis, and Darci filled in the blanks to fit Goodwin's preconceived notion. "You rely a lot on Darci Pierce's description in your diagnosis?" Zimmerman asked. Through a long hot afternoon and into the next day, Zimmerman made every attempt to trip up Goodwin and confuse the jury.

"Is it dissociative disorder alone that you believe makes this defendant insane under New Mexico law?" he asked.

"Well, see, it's more complicated than that, because I feel that, you know, as we proceed in the diagnostic process and begin to really combine the personality states that are present, when she loses time and can't remember, I feel that as we go through that and understand that—that will explain the factitious disorder and the somatization disorder as secondary to the dissociative disorder. So, in my view both the factitious disorder and the somatization disorder are part and parcel of her particular dissociative disorder."

"And you are guessing at this point, aren't you?"

"I will not be able to say that with more than fifty

percent certainty until I have contacted the personality states separately and documented what the sensations, memories, relationships, behaviors, feelings of each state are now and have been historically."

"Well," said Zimmerman, "who is sitting in the car waiting for Cindy Ray to come out of the clinic, was that [part] A or was that B?"

"That was mostly B and parts for which both A and B are amnesic," she said.

"These identity states—personality fragments that you talked about, Dr. Goodwin, you've never seen or talked to them, have you?"

"No."

"Just a hypothesis on your part, isn't it, Dr. Goodwin?"

"Which?"

"Different personality states?"

"I would say that at this point it's more than a hypothesis that there exist different personality states. It's hypothetical still to try to think through what they are but that this is a person who has memory gaps and during these memory gaps action occurs. I think that's more than just a hypothesis at this point."

John Bogren, in redirecting the testimony, asked Goodwin what it would take to find the personalities in Darci.

Treatment, she said. "I haven't had enough time and Darci hasn't had enough time. I generally expect that it takes about a year for a patient to accept this diagnosis and the meaning of the diagnosis, and what Darci told me was she just doesn't want to go back into her childhood, and she just instinctively knows that that's what the completion of the diagnosis process and treatment will involve."

261

Twenty-five

As the trial moved into its fifth day and second week, Darci Pierce's defense called a parade of acquaintances, so-called character witnesses. Sharon Gray, the sixth grade teacher and role model for Darci, who wanted counseling for her but never got it. Slim and tall, she winked at Darci during testimony. And Rachael McCrainey, the schoolyard chum, who remembered playing "chicken" in Portland traffic until Darci made her cry. Michael Cox, on cross-examination, asked her about the game, when Darci would stay in the path of the car.

"You always saved her at that point, didn't you?"

"Yeah."

"And the object of that game was, if you move, you lose, isn't it?"

"Right."

"And she always won?"

"Always."

"And that was important to Darci, wasn't it?"

"Yes."

"She always wanted to be better than other people?"

"Yes."

Tina Otis, the G.I. Joes clerk who shared a locker with Darci, testified about watching Darci go through her first false pregnancy. Dorothy Spain, another clerk, read the letter she received from Darci a month before the murder, saying she was starting to cope with the loss of the stillborn, but didn't want to get pregnant again. And Carol Raymond, whom Darci fell in love with before moving to Albuquerque.

Teresita McCarty, the psychiatrist who first saw Darci at the hospital with the baby, testified at length about her diagnosis of six personalities in Darci. She also said Darci had a mixed personality disorder, with borderline and narcissistic features. She based much of her diagnosis on blanks in Darci's memory, which Zimmerman tried to attack.

"It's true, is it not, that this defendant has quite a long history of lying for various reasons?" asked Zimmerman in cross examination. "You're not suggesting to this jury that the only lies she tells are to cover up gaps in her memory, are you?"

"The only way you know is you have to question her about each lie to find out what the origin is."

"This defendant lies for personal gain as well, doesn't she?"

"You'd have to give me some examples."

"Okay, she lies to be better accepted by people, didn't she?"

"Again, you'd have to give me another example."

"She has lied about achieving better grades in school than what she actually has, hasn't she?"

"Some people have reported that."

"And she lies, as well, about her expertise in playing the piano, doesn't she?"

"See, I don't know that those are lies; part of her could play the piano quite well, I don't know."

"It's difficult for you to tell if she is lying or not, isn't it?"

"You have to ask her and you have to work with patients who have this disorder a while to find out . . . because what's a lie for one part of her may not be a lie for another part of her."

The last defense witness was Darci's husband, Ray, who testified again how hard Darci took the loss of the molar pregnancy. He said he married Darci because he loved her and not because she was pregnant. He never questioned her pregnancy. "The woman was pregnant. Everything, her mannerisms. She would not take any kinds of drugs whatsoever, whether it be aspirin, something for the constipation, no drugs. She was taking prenatal vitamins. Her metabolism apparently increased, she was always hot, hot. She would walk around with a spray bottle and keep herself moist all the time. I was cool myself and it was cold. She looked pregnant. She was pregnant. She had an aversion to pizza and eggs, which is unusual for her. Just the mention of the words would make her nauseous. She was pregnant."

"What type of preparations did she make for the arrival of the baby?" John Bogren asked him.

"She took Lamaze classes, she bought a car seat. We bought a crib and changing table after we got here. We had baby clothes, a closet full of baby clothes. We have stuffed animals, diapers, bags of diapers that were given to us."

"Did she order a set of baby books?"

"She ordered a set of baby books. She's been getting *Parents* magazine from the day she told me she was pregnant."

"What kind of wife was she?"

"She was a real good wife. She kept an immaculate house. She keeps an immaculate cell. She's my best friend. We did everything together."

"Do you feel that Darci was open and honest with you in your relationship?"

"Yes, very definitely."

"Did she tell you about her prior sexual history?"

"Yes."

"Did she tell you about having sexual relationships with her cousin, Brad?"

"Yes."

"Did she tell you that she had a reputation in school?"

"Not in so many words, but yes."

"Did she tell you that she had an affair with Carol Raymond after your marriage?"

"Yes."

Under cross-examination by Cox, Ray said both he and Darci were anticipating having a baby in their home.

"And, in fact, for awhile she did have a baby at the hospital, at least in her arms?"

"Yes, I had a daughter for six hours."

The trial ended with the double-barrel blast of the state's shrinks, psychologist Julie Ann Lockwood and psychiatrist Phillip Resnick. Lockwood diagnosed Darci as having a mixed personality disorder with narcissistic, borderline and antisocial natures. She thought Darci was not insane, but a manipulator who knew what she was doing. Lockwood was particularly taken with Darci's lack of feelings about the victim, never calling her anything but the "victim." Under cross-examination by John Bogren, she said she could not know whether Darci, waiting in the parking lot of the clinic, intended to take the baby from Cindy Ray's stomach. "I have no basis on which to conclude that she articulated that to herself in any consideration or deliberate way. But what I can conclude is that she decided to wait for Mrs. Ray and to take Mrs. Ray with her in order to obtain the baby by persuasion."

"Is the fact that she did not have the instrumentality to perform the cesarean a factor that you've considered? That would indicate . . . it was not her intent when she first confronted Mrs. Ray?"

"That's one of the factors that argues against that intent. If you're going to persuade a pregnant woman who has not yet delivered an infant to give an unborn infant to you, and you need that unborn infant that day, then the question remains, how does one get this live child?"

"It's a little illogical, isn't it?"

"No question that it is, in terms of ordinary thinking, illogical. It is an uncommon act and so I think we tend to look at uncommon explanations and there may not be an uncommon explanation."

Dr. Resnick followed with his argument that Darci was sane, as well, but driven by an antisocial personality disorder, a borderline personality disorder and a narcissistic personality disorder. He concluded that she was consciously faking her pregnancy, but that she suffered real psychogenic amnesia at the moment of the cesarean section. Cox, of the prosecution team, considered Resnick's report the best forensic evaluation he'd ever seen. But Resnick took on the nickname "Dr. Death" by Bogren and the defense team. A tall, bureaucratic-looking man with short, dark hair, Resnick was asked by Zimmerman what he thought of the defense of dissociative disorder and shifting identity states.

"Let me begin by explaining something that doctors learn in medical school. They learn very common diseases like pneumonia and uncommon diseases like systemic lupus erythematosus. When they first go on the wards, there's a temptation for the new doctor to think about the strange and unusual. So something that clinical teachers often stress is when you hear hoofbeats, assume it's horses and not a zebra, the idea being that if someone has certain symptoms or laboratory tests and it can be explained by a common disease, don't assume that it's a zebra. I think in this case, the incidents of antisocial personality in the population vary between one and three. In other words, it's a fairly common phenomenon. Multiple personality disorder or those alternating personality states that Dr. Goodwin suggests Mrs. Pierce has, is an extremely unusual phenomenon. In fact, up until 1980, in the world literature there were less than two hundred cases reported. Extremely rare phenomenon. Dr. Goodwin happens to have a particular interest in multiple personality disorders. In my view, rather than see a horse as a horse, she was looking for a zebra."

In his cross-examination, Bogren led Resnick through an endless list of psychiatric criterion for his diagnosis based on the DSM3, the Diagnostic and Statistical Manual No. 3, the psychiatric bible for making diagnoses. Each diagnosis requires so many behaviors to be listed, and most of the cross-examination focused on whether certain behaviors in Darci's life—like violence—belonged in certain diagnostic lists. Bogren also noted that the diagnostic bible was updated as the practice of psychiatry changed.

"When did you go through medical school, Doctor?"

"1959 to 1963."

"And at that time, multiple personalities were zebras, is that correct?"

"That's right."

"And antisocial personalities were horses?"

"Well, you're referring to the analogy I used, but by comparison of relative frequency that would still be the case, yes."

"And under DSM3, under multiple personality disorders, it says, 'Prevalent recent reports suggests that this disorder is not nearly so rare as it has been commonly thought to be.' "

"That's correct."

"So, there appear to be a lot of horses that are now zebras, is that right? Let me rephrase it, there's more zebras now?"

"I would agree that in the last several years the diagnosis multiple personality is far more common that it was previously. It is still a rare phenomenon, not just as rare as it was once thought."

A final defense psychologist testified, to rebut Resnick's testimony, but by then the attorneys, the judge, the audience, and most certainly the jury, had heard enough. "My brain is fried," Bogren admitted to the judge. "I know your brain is fried, but so is mine, but so is everybody else's," the judge said.

After two weeks of testimony the jury was sent home for the weekend. The members would return on March 28 for final arguments and instructions. "Don't go home and decide the case tonight with your family and friends. Still keep an open mind," Traub told them.

Bogren, retiring to his office, said he "never felt so burned out. It freaked me out. The freakiest movie I've ever watched couldn't compare. I don't think I did a particularly good job in her case. Somewhere halfway through the trial I think I lost my mind. It was said by Goodwin that people who dissociate, if you hang around with them you start doing it too. I started getting freaky. Usually lawyers deal with concrete things, facts, true, not true, proven, not proven. Insanity and law don't mix. It's too subjective on one hand, and objective on the other. I never want to do another insanity defense just because of my fear, I guess. I don't know what I'm dealing with anymore."

In closing arguments Monday morning, Bogren told the jury that the key to the case was the key Darci Pierce used to cut the baby from Cindy Ray. "No one in their right mind could contemplate a cesarean section with a car key. The truth is Darci Pierce is insane, by any definition of the word. Why didn't she take a knife, or tool? Why didn't she conceal the body? Why did she take the baby to a hospital? Why did she tell stories nobody would believe?"

He recounted for the jury her sexual history, her habit of sleeping with a knife beneath her pillow, her fear of showers, and he summarized the psychiatric finding of multiple personality states. "You know this was a disease of long standing. This whole case is a contradiction. You know something's wrong here. It is a bizarre case. It deserves a bizarre explanation. Then, as if to confirm his own state of mind, he shouted, "There's a devil in this room."

Harry Zimmerman, by contrast, called Darci a cold-blooded killer. "The surgery was careful, precise, meticulous. Was she out of control? Was she impulsive? She did it to satisfy her obsession to have a child. It was the consummate actress trying to pull off the ultimate con job." With the last say before the jury deliberated, Zimmerman hammered at evidence that Darci planned the murder and covered her tracks. She dragged the body behind trees, she turned away a man who drove by, she washed her hands of Cindy Ray's blood. And in her own confession she admitted to other considerations, turning back or stealing a baby from a grocery store. "She knew what she was doing. There is no doubt that Darci Pierce was expecting a baby—in any way possible. What appears to be a bizarre act was done for a rational reason."

At 4:00 P.M. on March 28, the closing arguments having taken most of the day, the jury went home for the night. They returned on the twenty-ninth, the thirteenth day of the trial, to deliberate Darci's fate. It didn't take long. At 3:15 P.M. Judge Traub reconvened the court to hear the verdict. Because of New Mexico law with a possible finding "guilty but mentally ill" the jury never really had to sift carefully the psychiatric findings, which droned on in the final, warm days. They could say, with reasonable certainty, that Darci was crazy, but that she also had committed the crime. And that's what they chose to find. Guilty but mentally ill of murder in the first degree, guilty but mentally ill of kidnapping, guilty but mentally ill of child abuse. All verdicts were unanimous.

As she had throughout the trial, Darci heard the verdict with her head bowed and no outward emotion. Her mother, sitting behind her, cried quietly. As the jury filed out past Darci, several members looked at her face.

Prosecutor Zimmerman said he would ask for the maximum sentence of nearly fifty years "because she is a dangerous person, prone to antisocial behavior. She is no different than someone who robs a convenience store and kills a clerk. Her obsession was a

270

baby, not money."

Defense attorney Tom Jameson predicted that without proper care, Darci could kill herself. "How sad it is. The mother of the kid is dead. The husband has no wife. Now Darci just lost the rest of her life."

Bogren cried at the verdict and said Pierce would not get meaningful treatment for her illness in prison. Fear stalked the jury, he said. "She could be your daughter, your neighbor, the girl who babysat for you. I don't know how you get from a loving, caring person to a cold-blooded killer." His only success, he said, was convincing the state to drop the death penalty before the trial began. "After a verdict like this I go home and hug my kids, and hope that nothing like this ever happens to them."

Out on the street following the verdict, one juror hung around to be quoted by the news media. "This person must be mentally ill," said Tom Griego. "A person would not do this. In my fifty-eight years in Albuquerque, I have never seen or heard something like this." In an interview with the *Albuquerque Tribune*, Griego said, "I was mentally sick — it caused me to go berserk at twelve or thirteen. I had to go to a hospital for a year. That's why it was so easy for me to judge her case. I've seen people who were ten times worse than she was go into mental hospitals and be cured."

His comments were picked up immediately by the defense team, as the basis for an appeal. In a brief filed with the court, they said, it was "critical to seat twelve jurors who could fairly, impartially and objectively listen to psychological testimony." But during selection, when Griego had been asked if he had been treated by a psychologist or psychiatrist, he reported only a dizzy spell which was thought to

271

need a psychiatrist. But a doctor took care of it. He told the attorneys he had not been treated.

Following the newspaper account, Griego wrote the court, apologizing for not mentioning the depression he suffered at age eleven or twelve. "I was hospitalized on and off for about a year." On April 25, 1988, during a hearing on the defense motion for a new trial, Griego stated he had not been treated by a psychiatrist, after all, or hospitalized for a mental disorder. He had been hospitalized for depression fifty years before because of a speech problem. He also stated that Jesus healed him. He had told the newspaper reporter that he had a special insight into Darci's case, that he could see the devil in her and "since the first day" believed that she was not insane.

After hearing from Griego, Judge Traub ruled that no prejudice was shown and denied the motion for a new trial. In an appeal to the New Mexico Supreme court, the defense argued that because Griego had concealed the facts during jury deliberations, Darci Pierce was denied an impartial jury and was prejudiced. "It is apparent that Mr. Griego brought unorthodox views into the case and that he was not the type of juror the defense, had they been fully informed, would have wanted on the case."

On Thursday, April 28, 1988, Judge Traub sentenced twenty-year-old Darci Pierce to thirty years in prison. There would be no parole, no early release. She was sent to serve her time in the Grants, N.M. prison for women, seventy miles west of Albuquerque on Interstate 40. She was assigned to a medium security class and placed in a single cell of cinder block, in a pod of twenty-four cells.

Six months later in that cell, Darci Pierce turned twenty-one. It was the birthday on which her mother had promised to open her adoption file and give her the name of her natural mother.

Epilogue

Following the divorce that Darci Pierce filed, husband Ray Pierce remarried on September 2, 1989 and moved away from the duplex on Marquette Street. Laura, his wife, was a grade school teacher in Albuquerque. They honeymooned in Cozumel, Mexico. Ray had met her while helping a neighbor build sets for local plays. He still flew radio-controlled airplanes, but his dream of being an Air Force pilot had faded because of his age. His Air Force tour of duty was up in the spring of 1990. At Kirtland Air Force Base he was airman of the year for two years after the murder. His colonel complimented him for never taking his personal life into the office.

Sam Ray, Cindy's husband, is also remarried to a cute, blonde Mormon woman who was a school teacher. Luke began school. Amelia Ray, pretty as her mother, remained a delight and miracle to her family. She accompanied her father in a TV appearance on *Geraldo*.

"What would you say to those who are out there ministering to people that have problems, and counseling them?" Geraldo Rivera asked Sam.

"If you detect something's that wrong, don't keep

it back. Let people know so they can do something about it. Don't feel like you can handle it."

Darci's parents, Sandra and Ken Ricker, stayed in the green house in southeast Portland where Darci grew up. In the spring of 1990 a new van sat outside, and the lawn in front was beautifully landscaped with flowers and shrubs. Sandra Ricker lost weight and kept it off, reporting to friends that she was down to a size fourteen dress and her binges of gaining and losing sixty pounds had stopped. She came to the door in a housedress with a barking dog at her feet, one of Darci's two dogs from Albuquerque. The other had died. Mrs. Ricker opened the door a crack and kindly declined an interview, though she said there was "much to say. She's a lovely, beautiful girl that something went wrong and that's all I can say." She apologized for the accumulation of yard-sale stuff on the porch and shut the door.

David Sargent, Darci's physician, maintained his ob/gyn practice next to the Adventist Hospital where he had treated Darci. Her case, he said, had sensitized him to signs of distress in a patient. Changes, such as the weight gain he saw in Darci, now prompt questioning of his patients, beyond the medical problems at hand, to their lives and the pressures they live under. Since Darci's case he also had become a disciple of James Dobson, a California psychologist who founded "Focus on Family" and gained fame for his interview of Ted Bundy. Pornography was the root of child abuse, according to Dobson, who estimated that one in four girls were sexually abused in the U.S. "The outcome of Darci's story is bizarre but the situation is not that unusual, and that's scary," said Dr. Sargent. "We don't hear about most cases. It's the tip of the iceberg. It's really sad."

David Brink, the Church of Christ minister who married Darci and counseled her, said her case "really heightened my awareness of watching for danger signals, watching for signs of dysfunctioning in families that can produce this behavior. I've spent a lot of time researching it since. I'm a lot more sensitive now to the danger signal of sexual molestation. It is like getting hit by a car, emotionally. Knowing what I know now I would have probably probed when I began to see her sexually active early, when I saw the hatred with her mother. It is now one of the first questions I ask of people who come to me with heavy-duty problems, with high levels of anger. Have you been molested?"

In New Mexico, Steve Schiff, the DA who oversaw the prosecution administratively, became a congressman, representing Albuquerque in Washington. Prosecutor Michael Cox was promoted to deputy district attorney following the case. And Harry Zimmerman, who was offered a chance to play himself in a made-for-TV movie about Darci, should it be made, moved to San Diego in hopes of starting an acting career. He taught a course at law school and consulted on child abuse cases. He charged $160 an hour to discuss the Darci case.

Detective Tom Craig retired in July 1989. He began doing private detective work. He presented the Darci Pierce case to a special school on child stealing at the FBI academy in Quantico, Virginia. "Until I went to that workshop I thought that this was a pretty bizarre, pretty different kind of case. I found out that Ray Pierce isn't the only husband who's ever been deceived by his wife into thinking that she was pregnant. There were two or three other cases. These woman also needed to find a baby at the last minute. They went about it different ways. One lady went to a hospital and tracked a family down to their home and blew the mother and father away. We discussed ten or twelve cases and each agent thought his was the only one. It's not an isolated case."

Darci's case history also became part of class instruction at the University of Colorado Medical School. Dr. John Slocumb, the gynecological chief on duty at the time Darci arrived at the hospital, began using the case at his new post in Colorado, to focus on "things that don't fit. I try now to read between the lines, to look at things that don't make sense. Following the trauma in the hospital, Slocumb and the medical personnel in New Mexico underwent several psychological sessions to deal with the shock and grief. "I'm still shook by it," said Slocumb two years after. "It's painful."

Tom Jameson, who traced Darci's life for the defense, quit the public defender's office. "The case was disturbing, on a deep level. It was hard to decide what was more disturbing, the act or . . . that a nineteen-year-old is going to die in prison, not really getting much help and not really being able to live the kind of life we would all hope for. It's pathetic and sad. In many respects, I felt like, as much as she did something horrible, that in a sense she was a victim. There were victims everywhere in the case and it was really, really sad. It made me think a lot about what can be unleashed about child sexual abuse. I can't prove it but I'm convinced of it. This was someone who, at three or four or five or six, was abused by an adult, and it set off a chain of events that no one could have ever foreseen. When a child is abused, you know that nothing but pain and difficulty is going to come from it. Except this was like an atomic bomb of pain and difficulty. It also brought out the worst in society, the TV accounts, the tabloids. People were interested in her because she was an animal, not because of the real human tragedy, but the grotesque tragedy. It was very profoundly, saddening to me. It really shook me up. It made me think about being a lot less judgemental about people, 'cause you don't really know what's going on."

John Bogren stayed with the public defender's office, a changed man. "I guess I've seen it all now. It's time to do something else. Darci—we're talking about someone who is just as crazy now as she was then. And yet, on the surface, she is so normal. Knowing that she could snap anytime is sort of frightening. We're not talking about medicating her, we're talking about a time bomb waiting to explode. I don't doubt anything now, I guess that's how it changed me. Maybe the devil does exist. Maybe God does exist. Maybe there's going to be this ultimate battle over good and evil. I don't know. I'm not willing to doubt things the way I used to. It was clearly a supernatural experience."

On February 27, 1990, two years after her trial, Darci Pierce lost, by one vote, the appeal to the New Mexico Supreme court for a new trial. The court said juror Griego could still have sat as an impartial juror, although two dissenting judges disagreed, saying that Griego's attitude about mental illness and his willingness to make a premature judgement about Darci's guilt had biased him.

In her prison cell in Grants, Darci received the news with equanimity. She declined again to be interviewed. The college-level classes she had been attending were stopped and she began work in the prison gymnasium. She was receiving weekly counseling by a masters-degree counselor, but no psychotherapy. In the spring of 1990, Darci's parents visited, their semiannual trip.

William Chambreau, the social worker in the Public Defender's office, visits her once a month. At Christmas he brought her a set of watercolors, a gift from the defense team.